D0953358

The
Distance
Between Us

The Distance Between Us

MASHA HAMILTON

UNBRIDLED

BOOKS

This is a work of fiction. The names, characters, places and incidents
are either the product of the author's imagination or are used fictitiously,
and any resemblance to actual persons living or dead, business
establishments, events, or locales is entirely coincidental.

UNBRIDLED BOOKS
Denver, Colorado

Library of Congress Cataloging-in-Publication Data

Hamilton, Masha.
The distance between us / Masha Hamilton.
p. cm.
ISBN 1-932961-02-X
1. Women journalists—Fiction.   2. War correspondents—Fiction.
3. Loss (Psychology)—Fiction.   4. Middle East—Fiction.   I. Title.
PS3558.A44338 D+   2004021387

3   5   7   9   10   8   6   4   2

Book design by SH • CV

Second printing

FOR KEVIN CARTER
AND JOURNALISTS EVERYWHERE
WHO PUT THEIR BODIES AND THEIR SOULS
ON THE LINE TO COVER WAR

ACKNOWLEDGMENTS

To Dan Gilmore, Steve Hanson, Bernadette Steele and Nancy Wall for fiery discussions as the sun went down and for being fantastic midwives to this manuscript, and to Rebecca Lowen and Jennifer Stewart for always thoughtful reads.

To Fred Ramey, for treating Caddie as *real* from the very first (does anything warm a writer's heart more?) and for allowing her to live between these covers and for pushing me, with tact and wisdom, to be a truer writer.

To Marly Rusoff of amazing energy, for her belief in *The Distance Between Us* and her determination to get it published.

To Yaddo and all the people connected with it for the incredible, breathtaking gift of time and space.

To Heidi Levine, for two decades of friendship, for being *out there* every day, for sharing so much of it with me.

To Wendy Orange for being an unparalleled reader and cheerleader who always *knew* Caddie, and who would have hand-delivered this story to God if she could have found a way.

To Rupert and Arra Hamilton for unconditional support and the wisest of conversations, and to Matthew Hamilton, from my heart, for the gun stuff.

To David Orr, for believing even when I don't and seeing when I can't, and for always saying yes.

To Briana, Cheney and Daylon for making my life—and thus my writing—richer. And for giving it more attitude.

And to those met along the way, in the field and on the street, whose actions and words touched me and contributed to my understanding of war and love.

Thank you.

Anyone who has watched people crowding around the scene of an accident on the highway realizes that the lust of the eye is real. Anyone who has watched the faces of people at a fire knows it is real. Seeing sometimes absorbs us utterly; it is as though the human being becomes one great eye. The eye is lustful because it requires the novel, the unusual, the spectacular. It cannot satiate itself on the familiar, the routine, the everyday.

—J. GLENN GRAY, THE WARRIORS

One

THE WHOLE OF HEAVEN IS OFF-BALANCE as they rumble out of the city: clouds one moment, darting sunlight the next. A dust shroud swirling around the Land Rover prevents Caddie from seeing where they are going or where they've been. Far behind them, a mosque wails its hellfire summons to those who believe. It's noon, then, and men of conviction are submitting their foreheads to the ground in a graceful wave, while she barrels forward into the formless, blind middle of a day.

The Land Rover rattles like a crate of scrap metal. Her shoulders ache, she's inhaling cupfuls of powdered dirt and they have at least another ninety minutes to go. But those are only irritants. Her real worry is the driver, a complete unknown. Rob and the hotel concierge rounded him up when the regular chauffeur, the one Rob assured her was "the best in Beirut," didn't show. A driver is their lifeline in dusty, uncharted territory. This guy, well—she catches her breath as he swerves sharply and clips a roadside bush, aiming directly for half a dozen desert larks. The birds scatter and arc overhead, their fury sharp enough to be heard above the thrash of the engine.

"Christ," Caddie mumbles. In the rearview mirror, the driver gives her a squinty glare. Cobwebs form at the outer corners of his eyes, and dried grime thick enough to scrape off with a fingernail is caked behind his right ear. "Who the hell *is* he?" Caddie mutters to Marcus, next to her in the backseat. "Should we really be—?"

"Cautious Caddie," Marcus says. "He's okay. Rob wouldn't use him otherwise." He leans over Caddie to address Rob, who's on her left. "Right-o, Rob?"

"He's fine. Told you. Checked him out." Rob is focused on adjusting his tape recorder's input level. With his scruffy hair and taut energy, he looks like a street tough instead of a network radio reporter. Here, that aura serves him well.

"See?" Marcus says to Caddie. "Anyway, what's our choice? Sit on our bums all day?"

She smiles at him saying "bums" in his refined British accent. Something in him—his inflection maybe, or his humor, or his experience in the field—unknots her, and relieves her of the responsibility of having to control everything. Anyway, he's right. This story is too hot to pass: a Q-and-A with Musaf Yaladi, fiery-eyed, Princeton-educated thug-darling of the West, in his south Lebanon lair. The elusive Yaladi is a Lebanese crime king, dabbler in terrorism and chief distributor for weapons, bogus American one-hundred-dollar bills and the raw materials for heroin produced in the Bekaa Valley. With a couple punchy quotes from him, the piece will write itself. She'll be the only print reporter to have it. Page one for sure.

They'll be fine, just fine. Caddie would prefer fewer variables, but she's done her usual checking, narrowed the risks to a pinpoint. She's confirmed that they aren't traveling through disputed territory, that Yaladi knows they are coming, that he wants to do the interview. The only drawback is that she doesn't know this particular minefield very well. With Israel, the West Bank or Gaza, it would be different. She's worked that territory for more than four years now, she and Marcus, and those back roads are carved in her mind.

Marcus fingers the leather band on his left wrist, a gift from an Arab mother he once photographed and managed to connect with, he would say. Caddie would say charm. He stretches his arms, the muscled forearms tapering to delicate wrists, then widening to broad hands, and smiles sideways at her in a way that excludes Rob, the driver, all of Lebanon. She imagines licking lemonade from his lips, its bitter taste undercut with tangy sweetness. She rotates her shoulders to loosen them.

In the front passenger seat, Sven pats the video camera on his lap and chats to the driver in sunny, Swedish-accented Arabic. Long-limbed, he seems as comfortable as he would in his own living room. He's the most easygoing and polite of journalists, with an uncommon ability to nap anywhere on short notice. Caddie often runs into Rob and Sven on the same story. Privately she's nicknamed them Yin and Yang.

They pull up short before a barrier of razor wire and man-sized chunks of concrete spray-painted black with Arabic graffiti. A Yaladi roadblock. She didn't expect it this soon. The driver cuts the engine and the air grows defiantly still. The dust finally gives up and sinks.

A slouching man with a knife tucked into his belt separates himself from a concrete slab, sticks out a hand to collect their press cards, and then, self-important on squat legs, strides into a hut. A second roadside militiaman, baby face and pear belly, plants himself next to their Land Rover, machine gun cradled in his arms.

Caddie brushes the dust from her hair. She wishes again that she were more familiar with this route from Beirut to the south. They are probably twenty miles from the border with Israel, twenty miles from the Mediterranean Sea. The land is scraped and stingy, abandoned even by animals and insects, left to these imprudent men with their weapons.

"One-two-'twas brillig and the slithy toves . . ." Rob intones into his microphone.

"You're going to drain the battery before we get there," Sven says.

"Something's wrong with the goddamned pinch roller," Rob says. "If I don't get the interview on tape, I might as well have slept in, saved myself this cowboy ride."

Incessant worrying over the equipment, Caddie knows, is part of his routine. She has habits of her own. During interviews, she often makes up a ridiculous question or two that she would never actually ask, then imagines her subject's response. It's oddly soothing.

"You worry too much," Marcus says. "If the pitch is off, it's so slight no one will notice."

"Hey, bud, I don't worry enough," Rob says. "Otherwise I wouldn't be in the middle of fucking East Jesus letting some monkey point his gun at me."

Their guard has begun shifting gently from foot to foot, swinging his weapon as if in time to music. Watching him, Caddie almost hears her ballet teacher's shrill military voice: "One, two, on your toes, lift your head." She'd been, what? Eight, maybe nine years old, and remarkably clumsy, all clashing elbows and difficult knees. "Again, from the top. Let's plié . . ." She pictures this bulky militiaman, with his unexpected Santa Claus face, wearing a pink tutu. As he sways next to the hunks of ruined concrete, she is struck by a single, distinct wave she can identify only as elation.

How could she ever explain to someone back home what it is to cover a conflict? At least one like this that crisscrosses through the region, its front line changing daily, so that she can find herself unexpectedly *in it* at a moment's notice. Everyone with a television set observes the violence and horror. But, sitting on their couches, can they imagine the delight of unexpected absurdities? The rush of ecstasy, even, when the exotic intersects with the familiar? Or the way that seeing all this, up close, elevates a common life?

"I have an idea for dinner tonight," Marcus says near her ear.

"I'm filing tonight," Caddie says. "And you'd better be sending a couple pictures."

"That'll take half an hour. As for you, what? A couple quotes from the drug lord, a little local color from his hideout. You could almost write it now." Marcus shifts in his seat and pulls a crumpled receipt from his back pocket. "Here."

"I've got paper, thanks."

"How about your phone number, then?" he jokes, pseudo-husky, leaning in again to smell her cheek. She laughs, shoving him off. He winks, and the color of his eyes makes her think of olives resting in martinis.

Okay, so she's partial to his blond good looks, his humor, and his consummate skill with a camera. She likes that he's drawn to her face without makeup and her constantly disheveled short hair. But they aren't a *couple;* spare her that conventionality. They are colleagues. Plus lovers, when the mood strikes. Both of them journalists who find the story irresistible and plan to live in it a long time. Discussions about relationships soon bore her. Too much dependency invariably backfires, in her experience.

Usually she thinks Marcus agrees. There are, of course, those other times. Like in the hotel bar last night. She'd been talking about how she didn't want to sign another year-long lease on her apartment, and he'd said she'd become afraid to commit to anything, too hooked on the ephemeral news story to ever be satisfied with the solidity of real life. His tone was surprisingly wistful. She refused, though, to give him a serious response. They were in a bar, after all, with colleagues. *Screw you*, she'd countered, laughing. *News stories* are *real life*. And they were—a form of it, anyway, the way bottled perfume was a form of odor. *Besides, I'm just talking about a lease.* She could tell he wanted to say more, but he took another slug of beer, letting it drop.

The mustachioed militiaman who collected their cards strides out of the hut, shaking his head as though he's uncovered a plot. He motions. Their driver—what's his name? Hussein? Mohammed?—glances back without meeting anyone's eyes. Grains of sweat darken his temples and bead above his lips. He slides from the jeep, taking the keys with him, as if these journalists were inmates, plotting to drive off and leave him behind in the vacuous Lebanese landscape. *Christ.*

The gunman speaks to the driver in a dull slur that Caddie can't make out. Their guard is still swaying, his AK-47 balanced delicately in his arms and pointed in their direction. The crickets grow loud, unusual for midday.

The driver shuffles back and passes out press cards. Three.

"Excuse me," Marcus says. "Where's mine?"

The driver shrugs.

"Brilliant." Marcus swings out of the jeep, the two Nikons around his neck bouncing.

Their pear-belly guard stiffens, aiming his gun at Marcus's chest. Caddie reaches from the Land Rover to try to grab Marcus's arm, but he's too far away.

"Okay, okay." Marcus raises his hands. "I need my card back. Card. Back. *Comprenez?*"

The guard holds his gun steady.

"Tell him, Catherine." He's still grinning, still outwardly confident that this adventure is manageable, no more threatening than a Ferris wheel ride. But Caddie knows he drops her nickname only at serious moments,

"My colleague, please, must have his press identification," Caddie says in Arabic, addressing both militiamen, trying for a there-must-be-a-*small*-mistake smile. "Then we will depart, thank you."

The mustachioed militiaman speaks shotgun-fast to the driver—to Caddie it sounds like "these beans should be fried again in Syria"—and the driver listens without expression. Caddie's Arabic isn't bad, but now she wishes, deeply, for a better grasp of local colloquialisms.

Another man emerges from the hut. Shirtless, skinny and muscular, he appears younger than the others. His face is creased in irritation. His hair sticks up in tufts as though he's been unwillingly roused from bed. Carrying no weapon, he walks with shoulders high, hands alert, fingers slightly extended. Caddie's tongue suddenly tastes metallic.

"You still here?" The shirtless man speaks in English.

"I need my identification card." Marcus enunciates as if to a child. "What a *fashla*," he says to Caddie in an aside, using the Arabic for "mess-up."

The young tough squints. "What you want?" he asks in English, in a tone that convinces Caddie the best answer would be "nothing."

Marcus chuckles. "This guy speaks pretty good caveman."

Caddie speaks sharply, quietly. "Shit, Marcus. Shut. Up."

Yes, this sleepy-eyed militiaman is a fool, made silly by the handful of power he holds over a hut and two armed men. But Marcus, it's clear, has a case of Superman Disorder, the disease that worms its way into journalists, fooling them into believing they're so seasoned, their instincts so developed, that every risk is manageable. That even the clouds and the dirt will back off in their presence. That a little cockiness will simply give them Godspeed. She's avoided that pit of overconfidence. So has Marcus, until now. She shoots him a pointed look. He seems to need reminding that this is not a disciplined army. These are thugs led by a man who smuggles and kidnaps and kills. They let mood swings, and a very personal interpretation of Allah's will, dictate when and where they fire their guns.

"C'mon, Marcus. Let's get out of here," she says.

"I don't go without my card." Marcus takes a step forward and speaks in one long breath. "We're more than happy to scoot, you bloody bloke, but first, it would be brilliant if you could go peek under your pillow and see if you can find a little card, one with my face on it." He finishes with an ersatz smile.

The shirtless boy fighter surely can't understand much of Marcus's racetrack sentences or clipped accent. But he leans forward attentively as if examining vermin, then pushes closer to their Land Rover, bringing with him the scent of barbecued onions. He glances in Caddie's direction, then grips Sven's arm. "Go," he says in English, shoving Sven and motioning at their driver. "Go!" The word comes out guttural.

"Bit testy, aren't you?" Marcus remains jaunty, but he's finally edging back toward the jeep.

"Still, I think it's a good suggestion," Sven says, sounding strained.

The baby-faced guard, gratingly calm, lets off a shot into the dirt that produces a pregnant swell of dust. He levels his gun and jerks it to motion their driver forward. The driver shifts into gear. Caddie grabs Marcus's arm and tugs him back into the vehicle as the driver punches the gas pedal.

"My card," cries Marcus mock-meekly, raising his arms in an empty-handed gesture. Having lost, he's clearly decided to treat this as good fun. "Why *my* card?"

"Why *my* wife?" Rob speaks over the engine noise. "Life is arbitrary."

"Why do we always end up talking about your divorce?" Sven asks over his shoulder.

"Right," Rob says. "Who cares? Let's just get the interview. We've got to be almost there. When we get back, Marcus, you can tell the press office your card went through the wash."

"What wash?" says Marcus. "Who's holding out on me? Is anybody using anything besides the sink?"

He's too jovial, considering this nonsense could have caused them to be detained for hours—or worse. Caddie jabs him. "You won't even need the damn card in a couple days."

"Right you are. A whole month in New York." Marcus, oblivious to the edge in her tone, is annoyingly cheerful. "I'm overdue. So cheers-*ciao-salaam*," he says, running the words together.

She twists slightly away from him, reminded now however irritating she finds his reckless behavior, it doesn't bother her nearly as much as the fact that he has more or less spontaneously booked this flight to the U.S. He insisted he needed a break, had to get out, even yesterday was too late. She argued for days to get him to postpone it long enough to make this foray into Lebanon. Once they are done here, he's taking off. She only hopes that he doesn't miss any huge stories—major flare-ups of violence or government collapses. Nobody based in the Middle East takes photos as good as Marcus's.

Caddie glances behind them and her chest finally loosens: the roadblock is out of sight; surely the worst of the day is history. They pass a couple buildings still showing the kiss of battles—gapes and scars where walls should be. Then a patch of trees with leaves implausibly green against the fresh sky. Mt. Hermon rises in the distance, a landmark she knows, and the region becomes rocky again.

Their driver slows as they pass a woman in a long, loose dress and a headscarf who totes a toddler straddled on one shoulder, a basket on her head. She looks middle-aged, though she's probably in her twenties, eroded by having borne a child each year since age sixteen. Caddie has interviewed women like her. She lives in a one-room hut with a husband who shows more fondness for his gun than his family. Every day she scorches her fingertips making pita, and every night she rubs sore calves with callused hands. When she speaks, the wind carries away her words. When she needs help, she leans against a tree. She rarely knows surprise.

Their driver has courtesy enough, at least, to spare the woman the discomfort of being covered in dust. As they crawl past, she acknowledges them with the smallest of nods. Her toddler, frightened by the noisy vehicle and its load of strangers, lunges forward, blocking his mother's sight. She wipes his fingers from her eyes with her free hand in a gesture that seems to rebuke and soothe at once, and the intimacy of that movement sets off a longing within Caddie, irritating but not unfamiliar.

"Stop," Caddie calls out in Arabic. "Back up. Please."

The driver slows, shifting his face toward Sven for direction. He's been paid to cart them where they want to go and, *inshallah,* he'll do it. But Caddie knows what he's thinking: taking orders from a woman, no one told him about that. It appeals as much as walking barefoot on glass shards.

Caddie stares hard and Sven remains silent. The driver blows frustration out his mouth, then brakes and shifts to reverse, halting his vehicle alongside the mother.

"Caddie," Rob says. "What the—?"

Caddie turns her head away; she knows what he's going to say and doesn't want to hear it: that the criminal they will interview is as mercurial as he is dangerous and makes enemies with the ease that most people drink water. That there are warrants on his head in Syria, Israel and the United States and he's always on the move to avoid detection. That if they are late, even a little, he will not wait.

This won't cost them but a minute. Sven could move to the back and squeeze in next to them, leaving the front seat for the woman. Caddie herself will hold the child on her lap. A lift of a few miles might save this woman hours of walking.

She rises to make the offer.

But the mother's chin is raised in sharp rebuff, and Caddie recognizes—a moment too late—what she already knew. The woman would never climb into this car. She would be called a whore, and possibly beaten, if a brother or husband or even a neighbor saw her in a car loaded with foreign men, and with Caddie, who is not an ally, who is only an outsider, a stranger and transient. Who has no place pretending otherwise.

Even worse, she's just shed her journalistic detachment. The moment reeks of sentimentality, no greater sin among reporters.

With the Land Rover out of gear, the driver revs the engine. She feels Rob's stare.

The mother moves past, eyes averted. The toddler stares over his mother's shoulder, then ducks to hide himself. No one in the vehicle moves. No one speaks. Finally their driver turns to Caddie, his expression empty, his contempt strong enough to emit a sour scent.

She tightens her left hand into a fist, searching for a question she might ask this driver, one that could allow *her* to smirk. *What would you put on a vanity plate for this bullet-dodger?* 2-TUF-2-SPIT, she imagines him answering. That brings a smile that she hopes looks mysteriously smug to the driver, and to Rob.

Then she nods, a gesture intended to display confidence. She sits as the driver faces forward to lean into the gas pedal. The Land Rover jumps, leaving the woman in the trail of dust he had avoided the first time.

Rob speaks first. "Where the hell did *that* come from, Caddie?"

"This damned pressure-cooker," Marcus says. "Woman, you need a break too."

"As if we all don't," Sven says.

"Sunday brunch in the Village," Marcus goes on. "Mimosas and Eggs Benedict and a stack of frivolous glossy magazines. We'll go windsurfing off Long Island. You can browse all the bookshops on the Upper West Side. And buy fresh bagels every day."

For a moment, she does miss New York. She misses blending in, not having to concentrate on the language. And street signs—God, how she misses street signs right now on this dusty, no-name road.

Marcus smiles. "I see it in your eyes. Come out with me, away from this madness."

"The paper wants me here," she says.

"Tell them how dead it is; then they won't. Point out that everyone in your country is preoccupied by the election right now. About the Middle East, no one gives."

Caddie shakes her head. "It's never dead here, Marcus. And didn't you see all those farm-fed American boys in the Intercon bar last night? They didn't make the trip to get laid. Spooks, for sure."

"She's got a point," says Rob.

"CIA—so what?" Marcus grimaces in mock despair. "All that means is no photo ops for sure. C'mon, Caddie."

Caddie shakes her head. "If I need a break, I'll take a couple days off in Jerusalem."

"Why?" he says. "Why do you have to stay?" When she doesn't answer, he exhales in loud frustration. "Okay, then," he says. "But not me. That's the joy of being a freelancer." He puts his hands behind his head as though leaning back in an easy chair. "Poof. I'm gone."

The driver slows again to about five miles an hour. Except for scrawny gray bushes hugging the roadside, the area seems forsaken. "Enough delays," Rob calls, bouncing his right leg. "Let's get the show rolling."

"Don't worry." Sven half-turns in his seat. "We must be almost there. Isn't that right?" he asks the driver in loud Arabic. "We are there?"

Their driver doesn't answer—in fact, Caddie realizes she's never heard him speak. She has no idea what his voice sounds like, and that suddenly registers as odd.

Before she can ask another question and wait him out until he's forced to reply, she catches sight of a bush up ahead to the right, jerking in a way it shouldn't. The air hisses and loses pressure like a deflating balloon. "Hold it," Caddie says, but she doubts anyone hears because right then a passing shrub rises and makes an inexplicable *ping*. "Hey—" Marcus exclaims, and he half-stands, faces her and raises his hands as though to block her from the bush. Then he leans on her, shoving her down, and Caddie is dimly aware of a *crack* and grayish smoke as she hears Sven in the front yelling, "Gas, hit the gas you idiot, go, go, go for Christ's sake!" It occurs to her that their situation must be serious for cordial Sven to call someone an idiot, and Rob sinks to his knees on the floor of the jeep, pulling her toward him, saying, "Oh Jesus oh fuck oh Jesus," so she's sandwiched between the two of them, Rob and Marcus, and she's aware of a peppery scent, and then, at last, she feels the jeep plunge forward and she tastes the dust that has settled on the leather seats but she sees nothing since her head is near her knees and Marcus is slumped over, protecting her, and the air becomes too dense to breathe, as though she's underwater, and they seem to be turning because she falls to her left in slow motion and she realizes she should definitely be afraid right now, very afraid, yet she feels separate from it, in it but apart, like she's that dirt caked behind the driver's ear, and they spin to their right and Marcus, who is still covering her body with his own—God, he's heavy—half falls off and at that same moment she feels something sticky like tree sap on her cheek and she touches it and it's blood. "I guess I've been hit," she says, shifting her body toward Marcus, keeping her voice light because she's already been flighty today about the woman and her toddler so hysteria now is impermissible, and then she knows, she knows right away and without any doubt. The blood is his and he's gone.

SHE'S HEARD IT SAID that everyone's blood is the same color. An insistent moral position: we are all as one underneath. But it's not true—or perhaps it's that once spilled, the hue varies widely based on whether the day is humid, balmy, overcast. On whether the blood splatters on concrete, dirt, gravel, or grass.

She makes lists in her mind. Pastel rose and watery. Vivid as a police warning light. Eggplant-purple.

The blood that comes from Marcus's head is the color of raspberries, and sticky.

"I HAVE TO FILE," Caddie pleads. "It's a story. Even if anybody's . . . hurt. Especially then."

No, no, dear. The voice comes from a great distance as a lady with pewter hair and creamy uniform reaches for Caddie's arm, mops it with a cotton ball.

Caddie feels a sting. "What's in that syringe?" She puts her head back against the pillow, overcome by a desire to close her eyes. Then she tries to sit up, realizing at last that this is a nurse, and a nurse should know something. Caddie has to interview her. "Can you tell me the precise nature of the wounds—"

The nurse's head wobbles. *You can't get up yet. Please.*

"How—" Caddie breaks off for a second. "How exactly are you listing their conditions?"

Lie still, dear. Try to relax. The doctor will be here soon. The pewter-and-cream lady, still out of focus, removes the needle and swabs Caddie's arm again.

"I don't want to relax. I want to file."

She feels her arm being patted. *It's all over.*

The nurse's words echo. Overoveroverover.

. . .

THERE'S GRANDMA JOS, sleeves rolled above the bulbs of her elbows, chopping onions for chicken soup, her eyes oozing and her face rigid with loss.

Grandma Jos, kneeling to pray in the dusky church—one slow knee, then the other—her expression now flaccid with a resignation Caddie hates.

Grandma Jos, counting and recounting the cookie-jar money for that yellow dress with the lacy collar that Caddie can wear to the school dance, because Grandma Jos says she must look presentable now that she's "nearly of age." And though Caddie is embarrassed by the old-fashioned concept, and even more by frilly dresses, she loves this one because it's starchy in that new-clothes way that the church hand-me-downs never are, and without even the tiniest of stains.

Grandma Jos, coming down the street in time to see Caddie, already bandaged on one elbow, jumping her rusted bicycle over a makeshift wooden ramp. A growl—*Girl!*—softened quickly to her public voice. *Why does it always have to be dangerous to be fun?*

No. Grandma Jos is not here. Caddie is not a child. She has to pull herself from this fog.

SHE WAKES UP ALONE in a room devoid of color. Why do they do that in hospitals, as if bland and passionless were comforting? Her left upper arm is sore and taped up; she's tethered to an IV. She remembers a flight from Lebanon, vaguely. She gets up, pulling the contraption along with her, her hand rigid on the cold metal. Someone has left a newspaper on a table. The *Cyprus Mail*. So she's in Nicosia. She flips rapidly through the pages until she finds it: Award-winning British freelance photo-journalist, 41, killed in a . . . She skims to the bottom, where she sees her own name: Catherine Blair, 32 . . . In between her name and his, the words blur.

What makes her think, then, of that Walt Whitman poem she had to memorize and recite during a sixth grade assembly? *But O heart! heart! heart! O the bleeding drops of red.* What remote melodrama; no one would publish it today, and still school-children have to learn it. "Whitman," Caddie says aloud. She grips the newspaper and snickers.

Somehow, through none of her own doing, the laughter shifts into something else, something loud and unruly that makes her chest vibrate unnaturally. The nurse with the needle returns.

How did she let this happen? She's usually so careful, her caution more valuable than a flak jacket. So how could she let him down like this?

Kill those bastards.

"And you're sure that Sven and Rob, that my colleagues . . . ?"

They're fine. No injuries at all.

So where are they, then? Where the hell . . . because she needs to ask them why.

Isn't there anyone you want us to contact?

It was all set up. Yaladi *wanted* to be interviewed, damnit. There was no crossfire to get caught in, no shelling. A simple interview with a famous criminal.

Some relative somewhere? The nurse, insistent, squeezes Caddie's hand.

Relative? Not anyone living. Grandma Jos, the last to die, would be useless anyway. She'd show up straight from the airport with the Lazarus Department Store shopping bag she always carried, and she'd pull out a Bible and suggest they pray together. That would be the extent of it.

Caddie smooths the thin, bone-colored blanket that covers her legs. She makes her voice absolute. "No one."

The nurse disapproves. She stands motionless for a moment as though weighing her options. Eventually she sighs. *Maybe you'll think of someone later. For now, sleep.* She reaches to the cart and closes in.

THE DEEP PULSE OF NIGHT, its shadows a retreat, its tiny noises companions to breath. Night is a woman's hand spread wide to shield her, to protect her from shame. At night, it's all right if she finds herself musing without purpose, careening through memories, dallying longer among the dead than the living. It doesn't matter that pieces of herself have been scattered, that everything she does takes place some long distance away, that her emotions, once so tethered and well behaved, now threaten to cripple her.

The permissive night: she's begun to crave it.

Still, she won't give in to a dread of dawn; she won't be sunk by this sunlit heaviness. A flying leap, perfect form with arms outstretched and toes pointed, is what she'll try for.

They bury Marcus with a camera and one of those little boxes of raisins he always carried in his pocket. Does someone tell her that, or does she dream it? She isn't sure. She imagines, against her will, his hands draped over his stomach. Square hands, almost clumsy looking, with squat nails pressed to the ends of his fingers. But when he used them in a rush to insert film or change a lens or focus a shot, they were precise enough to mesmerize her. They became, then, the hands of a creator. When they touched her, she sometimes imagined herself to be one of his cameras. Though she and Marcus always avoided talking of the future, she knew that if she let herself, she could get addicted to those moments.

As a photographer, he was a master of angle and light and, most of all, passion. His photos of faces revealed secrets and captured essence, raw and unrelieved. He was known for the single shot that exposed a person's history. "Penetrating," one award committee said. "Too powerful to ignore."

She remembers being with him once in his converted darkroom. They were studying some photos he'd developed, full of expression and gesture, and suddenly he switched off the lights and slipped out, leaving her fumbling first for the wall, then the door.

Whatja do that for?

It's a life skill, Caddie. Always know how to find your way out of a darkroom. Or did he say dark room?

On the fourth morning, clear of drugs, she writes a letter to Marcus's parents in London. "A fine photographer and cheerful companion. He loved the story that he died for. Was committed to his work." A bit beside the point, but she can't say what she really means. That he was irreverent, and lemon-tasting, and intense and lighthearted at once, so often exactly what she needed. That already she misses the nights. That *miss* is not a strong enough verb. And that maybe she should have told him that.

"CATHERINE BLAIR?"

She raises her hand, palm out as though blocking light, and sees him through her fingers. A doctor this time. Milky white suit with shit-warmed-over grin. She shifts her body away. "Caddie," she says. "I go by Caddie."

"Well, Caddie. Good to see you sitting up and reading. You must be feeling well today."

Christ. This phony cheerfulness is more painful to witness than a child's tears.

"You were lucky with the arm. Everything checks out fine. Someone from your newspaper comes tomorrow, I'm told. We'll probably release you the next day."

"Right-o." One of Marcus's expressions.

"In the meantime—" He pulls up a chair as though someone had invited him to sit. "I'm here. We can discuss anything."

He emphasizes the last word. He thinks she'll find comfort, does he, in asking her questions aloud? As though to pronounce them one by one would remove the weight? *Okay, doc, tell me. Why, right after a shower, did he smell like citrus and taste like salt? How did he learn to cook spaghetti with such a flourish? Where did he get those lips, far more beautiful than mine, heartlips, lips that, in truth, belonged on a girl's face? And that way he had of looking at me sideways and making it feel more intimate than anyone else's straight-on stare and yet still full of freedom—how did he do that?*

The milk suit pats her arm, murmuring gently, urging her to speak her thoughts. "Go ahead." The painstakingly modulated voice shakes her free of reverie. "It's important to pay attention to your feelings."

Maybe, doc, but I don't need to share. Real journalists write in third person for a reason. Don't you know that, doc, don't you know anything? They disguise their opinions and never spill their guts, ever. Except maybe sometimes, maybe during the dense hours while children sleep, to a half-stranger in some poorly lit airport terminal in a Third World country after witnessing acts of unspeakable violence in towns with unpronounceable names. But not to neighbors or even lovers and certainly not to doctors. You can check my passport to see the countries I've visited, doc, but you'll never know where my head has been.

"Do you know how many people have been killed in this region in the last decade?" she says. "Have you heard of the slimeball we were going to interview? I knew the risks—we all did."

"Still—"

"We wanted to cover it. We were dying to." She meets his gaze straight on, silencing him for a beat.

"Yes, and that's—"

She holds up a hand to stop his words. She wishes she could ask him a question. She thinks while he waits, appalling eagerness in his eyes. *If your home were burning, which would you take first? Your pet, or your cash, or your photo albums?* She doesn't ask it aloud, of course. His answer, she imagines, would be to finally turn away. Who, after all, likes being dissected?

"I'm fine," she says, forcing out the word. "Fine."

His shoulders sag slightly at her dismissal. "Well. Let us know if you want to talk later."

THE FOREIGN EDITOR, Mike, paces in the waiting room. He no longer looks like the Mike she used to know, the one who transferred out of the posting in Jerusalem that Caddie filled. "Live tight and write loose" was his parting advice when he headed for Ben Gurion and a job in management with a couple days' worth of scratchiness on his cheeks and a rip in the right shoulder of his T-shirt. Now, straight off a flight from New York, his suit is starched enough to support his weight, and his hair seems polished. She crosses her legs, sits up straighter and pretends she's wearing boots, jeans and dangly earrings instead of a dingy hospital shift. Two others are in the room: a bent-nosed man and a coiffured woman with a run in her stocking. They're in street clothes, too.

"Living in an airport terminal, that's what this is," Caddie says, gesturing to take in the room. "One damned delay after another. And now you want more."

"It's a promotion, for God's sake." Mike leans on the windowsill. "You like New York."

New York. Where Marcus is supposed to be. Visiting photo galleries, eating late overpriced meals in closet-sized cafés. She cranes her neck to look out the window behind Mike. A leaf supported by an indiscernible breeze spins in circles. And they're way up on the third floor. What are the odds of something like that?

"I'm fine," she says at last to the window, sick of that word *fine*, but addicted to it, too. "I don't want to be transferred to New York. Least, not now."

"Caddie." Mike moves to a cushioned chair across from her, gives her a get-real look. "First of all, you're not okay. Who would be? But leave that for a second. This is about a career move. A job that'll be perfect for you. Roving correspondent based in New York. You don't have to get stuck behind a desk all the time like I have."

She shakes her head. "I'll have to wear smart clothes, get my hair styled. It's not me."

"It *is* you. Plenty of independence. And no one cares what you wear."

She gives him a comical glance. "Shit, Mike, look at you. They gave you a title and you're a whole different person.

Now maybe that's for the best, in *your* case." She grins, glad she can still tease.

Mike hesitates a beat. "Think it over for a couple weeks. And in the meantime, go to Vienna; cover a round of peace talks. They start next Wednesday."

So this is his counteroffer. It doesn't sway her. "Me writing *peace talks?* Get real, Mike. All analysis, no action? My copy will stink." She leans forward in her seat. "I want to go home."

"Jerusalem's not home, Caddie. It's an *assignment*. I used to cover it. Jon is covering it right now."

"Okay, an assignment. But it's where my stuff is. My books. My CDs. My underwear, for God's sake. Look, maybe I'll take your job, but not right now. I'm not going to run away just because I got shot at. You understand?"

He squeezes the arms of his chair with both hands. "I'm trying to work with you here, Caddie." He massages his forehead like it's bread dough. "If I talk them into letting you go back, there has to be no reporting."

"Yeah, yeah," she says.

"Your instincts are off; they've got to be. Besides, we already promised Jon at least six weeks."

"Six weeks?"

"Caddie."

"Okay. Sure." That can be negotiated later.

"And soon, very soon, we discuss this New York transfer again," Mike says. "But seriously."

"Right-o."

"In the meantime, you can listen to your music or snorkel

in the Red Sea or explore the holy sites. They owe you nine weeks' vacation anyway. Until Jon leaves, until we talk, stay off the job."

"Yeah."

"I mean it, Caddie. No fooling around. This isn't only from me. It's orders from on high."

"On High," she repeats, liking the weight the editor gives the phrase. Liking that she will be defying On High, the very thing that betrayed her.

Two

THEY ZOOM UP the narrow, winding embankment to Jerusalem, the road everyone takes fast and careless as if they're racing to shake the hand of God, as if they're so joyful to be in the land of Abraham that they're willing to die the moment they get there. The windows are down and Caddie strains forward. The air blasts her face, supports her shoulders and forces shut her eyes. The car leans and at that moment the memory of Marcus intrudes. She can't feel his full weight, only his hand, its fierce pressing at the small of her back, and his breath at her ear as though he were whispering.

"I don't *know* why," she says, pushing his image away. "For Christ's sake."

"What?" the taxi driver asks.

Caddie clears her throat. "Nothing."

The driver nods knowingly. A person muttering as she enters the Holy City is not uncommon; he takes it in stride. Caddie's colleagues will not so easily overlook it.

"Your first time?" the driver asks with misplaced confidence. She guesses from his accent that he is from eastern Europe, and two weeks ago she would have engaged him in conversation, asked where he was born and how he finds it here, what he likes and what he doesn't, how many children and grandchildren he has and what they do, because you never know where a good story might begin.

Now, though, she wants to eavesdrop on her own thoughts. She shakes her head. "Nope." Leans back and closes her eyes. The driver, giving up—what a shame, his passenger is lousy for conversation—turns up the radio and begins to hum along.

Caddie mentally lists the photojournalists she's known who died. Samuel Harris, a freelance television cameraman she had drinks with in a Vienna bar: hacked to death by a crazed mob in Jo'burg. Yuri, on assignment for Russian TV, who didn't talk much but was always smiling: reduced to crumbs by a roadside bomb in Lebanon. Reuters photographer Sandra Hutchison, who shared a breakfast with Caddie in Cairo: taken down by crossfire in Sierra Leone.

Caddie has refused to allow herself to picture these deaths. She walked away each time the topic came up in a group of reporters, hating the sentimentality in the voices of some of her colleagues, the undercurrent of greedy thrill in others. Part of a journalist's job is to stay detached, no matter how severe the tragedy or how close it lands. Reflect the story; don't absorb it, because if you allow yourself to feel the full force of sorrows and horrors, you will succumb to them—that much Caddie knows. The desperate moments will at best numb her, and at worst cripple her, and she will be unable to collect the quotes or the color, do her job. The repercussions of random destruction or deliberate hostility often lead to the most profound moments in people's lives. She has to be there fully to record that, and so, Caddie has learned to shut down a piece of herself. Disconnect, at least some.

Besides, getting drawn in was dangerous; everyone knew that, everyone who lasted. Kevin Carter—the name, to Caddie, was like a warning signal. Nothing, not even the Big One he won for his shot of a vulture lurking next to a cadaverous Sudanese child, could rescue him from the opaque morass he sank into once he lost his detachment, once the clear spot inside him went muddy. The horrors he'd witnessed were bad enough—including that near-dead child dragging herself along the ground, who brought to mind his own daughter. Then came the shrill criticism he faced for not helping the kid to the feeding center, for being caught up in the composition of a great photo, for sticking to the role of one who records—his job, after all.

A "Carter Moment" is how she's thought of it since. When a journalist teeters between getting the story and getting *into* the story. Compassion serves a limited purpose, as Carter proved. Three months after taking home that Pulitzer, he hooked up a garden hose to the exhaust pipe and gassed himself inside his red pickup.

Measured closeness and a dose of dulled feelings—that's what she has had to learn. That gets her the interview *and* keeps her safe.

Usually.

She opens her eyes and shrugs to rid herself of the doubts that stick to her like a burr. They're off the highway now, driving among the blond bricks of the city, following a finger of Jerusalem to its very palm. The driver drops her at the corner of her sinewy street and she walks the rest of the way, a few steps behind a nun. Three Hasidim hovering around a newsstand glance her way as she passes. A young Israeli in leather sandals spits out the shells of sunflower seeds as he hums a tune she recognizes, "At Khaki li Ve'echzor," about a fallen soldier. Someone's wash hangs from a rope strung between buildings, dark clothes coupling with pale sheets.

What a concoction, Jerusalem. It took Caddie no short while to come to terms with its heap of competing religious rituals: rabbis issuing eerie and obscure edicts about light switches and women's wigs; imams with their barely coded urgings to the street; priests swinging platters of incense and muttering in inconsequential Latin. All of it colliding and overlapping like an exaltation of crows within a city that often seems far too compressed.

She remembers striding off into Jerusalem alone that first day nearly five years ago, eager to absorb the territory she'd been newly assigned to cover. She tramped through the walled Old City, paused at an Arab café for a sesame-covered bread ring, and practiced her Arabic with the owner. She fumbled with the still unfamiliar shekels, then boarded a bus full of Israeli soldiers and eventually got lost in Mea She'arim.

By day's end, she sensed what lay over the city like a quilt: large rules with horrifying consequences. Rules way beyond the superficial restrictions of manners she'd known before. Absolute, binding, primitive rules that got their backbone from blood and stones and God. Rules that she didn't yet fully understand, but knew she had to follow.

THE FIRST THING SHE NOTICES as she steps into the building is that Mr. Gruizin has painted a thick scarlet stripe on her mailbox. Of course. He invariably heads downstairs with his paintbrush whenever one of his neighbors travels, whether on annual reserve duty, business trip, or vacation. He claims the stripe is a barrier to danger, intended to keep a wanderer safe. The paint on Caddie's mailbox feels rough and substantial beneath her fingertips. Does he consider his effort successful this time?

She unlocks her apartment door. Usually when she's been gone, she heads directly for her bedroom, dumping bags and jacket along the hallway. Usually she wants to inhale the leftover scent of *her* that lingers on the sheets, the towels. She's eager for the sight of the window across from her bed, its familiar view of the street below.

Now, though, she's brought to a halt by—*shit, by a bunch of inanimate objects.* Her desk against the wall, computer atop. She can see Marcus standing there kneading her shoulders, lacing his fingers through her hair, urging her to stop working. (Why *hadn't* she stopped working?) The coffee-table photography book of Paris he gave her last Christmas when they came back here after covering Bethlehem to sit side by side on the floor, opening presents, eating popcorn. The tall glass on the table next to the couch. He drank water from it—held in his right hand, touched to his lips—minutes before they left for the airport.

The air vibrates, becomes dense and watery.

Kill the bastards.

But how?

She looks at her own hands: these hands that twice wrung a chicken's neck. When Caddie was sixteen, Grandma Jos grew sick, so the chore of killing the chickens fell briefly to Caddie—before she gave up and bought them already killed and cleaned. Both times, she'd turned her head away and let her hands act on their own. And except for the initial revulsion, it was much easier than she'd expected. A chicken's neck is startlingly tenuous.

Now, though, her hands seem too small, too distant from her body to be of any real use.

Behind her, the front door opens. Ya'el has used her spare key. One arm is outstretched to embrace, the other wrapped around a can of Boker coffee. Ya'el's uncontrolled frizzy hair clashes with her off-the-rack blazer in earth tones, creased from a day working at the bank. "Oh my God, Caddie." Ya'el hugs her again and directs her toward the couch. "And Marcus. God." She smells of lipstick and black olives. "Which arm?" she demands in her husky voice.

Caddie lifts her left arm slightly and pulls away. "I'm all right."

Ya'el sits back. "I'm so glad you're finally home. I thought somebody would try to talk you into staying away for good."

"No way. Back to work. That's what I need."

Ya'el shakes her head. "Not back to work, not right away. But back here, yes. Where we understand, where we've been through it, too. This is your *home*. Now, tell me. Everything."

Caddie draws a large couch pillow toward her, covering her stomach.

"I know, Caddie," Ya'el says after a moment. "I thought I couldn't talk about it either. But it was a relief to talk with you. A *relief*, trust me,"

Ya'el puts her hand on Caddie's. Ya'el thinks she knows what Caddie feels. Her brother was kidnapped while on army duty along the Lebanese border, tortured and killed. Ya'el received a photograph of his bruised and mangled body in the mail from an unknown sender. For nearly two years she held futility like a knot in her gut. Then Caddie moved in, and the two women began talking. And maybe because Caddie was an outsider, attentive in a way that tended to draw people out, or maybe simply because the timing was right, Ya'el spilled it one evening. How furious she'd become. Afraid and sad. And, finally, how much better she felt after telling it all to Caddie.

Caddie never understood how releasing a flood of words could possibly be comfort enough. She couldn't understand why Ya'el didn't try harder to find out who sent that photograph, who murdered her brother. That submissiveness, a reminder of Grandma Jos, irritated her. But she never said so. She listened. A journalist's job.

Now Caddie clears her throat. "Tell me about the girls. And how's work?"

Ya'el stares a moment, then shakes her head. "I guess a sore must become a scab before it heals," she says.

The doorbell saves Caddie from having to reply. Ya'el opens the door to Mr. Gruizin, the mailbox painter, followed by Mrs. Weizman, carrying her rose-patterned soup tureen.

"Now, *bubeleh*, don't get up," Mrs. Weizman says.

Goulash. Mrs. Weizman's famous opinionated goulash— absolutely no to the green peppers but you can never add too much paprika—brought forth for each death, disaster, or even infection. So then. That means everyone in the building knows what happened. But Caddie should have figured that. Nothing is secret in this country for long; it's always been that way. Probably every Israeli over the age of ten knew when their enemy King Hussein toured Tel Aviv in bearded disguise, though no journalist reported it for more than a decade. For months, they all knew that Ethiopian Jews were being spirited into the country, even knew the government had dubbed it Operation Magic Carpet, though the censor had forbidden a word of it in the local or international media. When a military operation goes awry, the street knows hours before it's broadcast. So what's the surprise that news of the ambush has traveled from Ya'el on the fifth floor to Mr. Gruizin at ground level, back up to Mrs. Weizman on third?

Ya'el heads into Caddie's open kitchen with the soup. "I'll make coffee."

"How did you all know I was coming back today?" Caddie asks.

"We didn't," Mr. Gruizin says.

"*I* did," Mrs. Weizman says. Mr. Gruizin's eyebrows lunge into his forehead. "No, I did, Ya'akov. I *felt* it." She strokes Caddie's cheek with her papery fingers. "*Feh*, what a sorrow to see you so pale."

"What do you mean? She looks wonderful," argues Mr. Gruizin. "Am I right, Ya'el?" he calls.

Ya'el steps back into the living room. "She's coping." It comes out sounding like a lie, and Ya'el blushes and withdraws again.

Mrs. Weizman leans closer to Caddie. "How can you say so, with those washed-out cheeks?"

Caddie lowers her face but can't escape their stares. She starts to rise. "Ya'el, you need help?"

Mrs. Weizman reaches out a hand to stop her. "Sit, *bubeleh*."

"She looks better than should be expected, anyway," Mr. Gruizin says after a moment. "She's a strong girl. It's my red, you know. Did the trick. Kept her safe."

"Ya'akov!" Mrs. Weizman shakes her head. "I've never known such a superstitious man. Caddie isn't so superstitious. Are you, dear?"

Caddie manages what she thinks is a smile, but it fails to translate somehow, because Mrs. Weizman quickly takes Caddie's hands and squeezes them between her own, as though Caddie had broken down, instead of borne up.

"Oh, *bubeleh*," she says, her voice thick with intent to comfort. "Sometimes it's not the doctor but the rebbe who knows the cure. I remember once my palms started itching; they were itching for a week, all the time, night and day. I couldn't sleep, it was that bad. This cream or that cream, the doctors said, but nothing worked. Of course I thought of the old superstition, my grand-uncle used to say it all the time when I was a little girl, he would say, 'Nala, when your palms itch, you are going to come into some money.' But for a few shekels, I should keep waiting? I went to see Rebbe Kroyanker. '*Gevalt!*' I said. And he told me. He knew how to cure it."

Mr. Gruizin sighs. "We're ready already. What did the rabbi say?"

Ya'el, pouring them all coffee, gives Caddie a private grin. They've often laughed at how like an old married couple Mr. Gruizin and Mrs. Weizman are.

"*Nu*, this is the point," Mrs. Weizman says. "He told me I needed to make peace with my sister, we'd been arguing for months—about what, it's not important. And I thought, *feh!* A little squabble with my sister should cause this *tsouris?* The rebbe must be, forgive my disrespectful tongue, *meshugener*. But I was desperate. And what do you think? We made up. Three hours later my itching was gone."

"A miracle worker," says Mr. Gruizin.

"Yes, that's what I mean." Mrs. Weizman turns eagerly to Caddie. "So if you won't go to one of ours, you could see your . . ." she waves a hand, "whoever you go to see. Everyone can use a bit of God sometimes. Am I wrong, Ya'akov?"

Mr. Gruizin nods and begins to talk, but Caddie lets his words slide by unattended. She remembers the town church of her childhood, a smooth and generous pew, the congregation's voices soaring in hymn.

> *All praise to Him who came to saaave,*
> *Who conquer'd death and scorned the graaave*

She remembers the hard bread on her tongue, the heat of gathered bodies, and Grandma Jos leaning close, smelling of Ivory soap and talcum and mint tea. *A simple trust, Caddie, will lead us into the calm valley.*

Caddie never replied. She understood that Grandma Jos needed to imagine His arms around her to soften the hard angles of a life gone strangely amiss: her spouse—Caddie's grandfather—living twenty miles away with another family in a white house with yellow shutters, her daughter—Caddie's mother—sleeping somewhere in a corrupt city and bathing too infrequently, her granddaughter—Caddie herself—abandoned at her doorstep. To blame Him would have been foolhardy, because who would Grandma Jos have then? Grandma Jos thought she was teaching Caddie about religion, but what she was really teaching was what it meant to be alone.

Caddie knew even then, though, that a calm valley was not what *she* sought—it sounded, in fact, like torture. Nor, despite Grandma Jos's dire warnings, did she want redemption. Nor a savior, nor a tearful walk to the front to be welcomed into the community of believers. God, she already knew to be as icy as a winter dawn. He rarely paid attention, and was not to be trusted when He did. Grandma Jos used Him as an excuse for living with things as they were. Caddie had no use for Him at all.

"Caddie! Are you listening?" Ya'el touches her arm and Caddie looks into her friend's face and there it is again, Ya'el's effort to hide a worried expression.

Caddie can't still an involuntary shudder. "Sorry," she says. "Go ahead, say it again."

There is a moment of quiet, an exchange of glances, before Mr. Gruizin speaks. "You are worn from the flight. Of course, of course. Ladies, let's go."

"I'm all right." But Caddie's false words are lost in the bustle of everyone except her rising.

Mrs. Weizman's cheek, surprisingly supple, is against hers. "Your friend? He is between God's hands."

Ya'el speaks softly in Caddie's ear. "Tomorrow we'll talk."

Caddie forces a jaunty wave as though her homecoming were a delight, a celebration. She keeps waving until finally the door is pulled shut.

SLEEP DROWNS HER, QUICK AND WELCOME, but she wakes in the night to a sharp jab of panic. The five minutes replay. The driver slows. A bush moves. Marcus rises, then sinks. The Land

Rover turns. Marcus's lips: a scribbled line. His expression: surprised, then gone.

She lingers over those minutes as though they'd lasted hours, searches for clues as to how they could have *not happened*. Berates herself for going with a driver no one really knew. For making him pause for the woman with the child— perhaps without those wasted minutes, they would have sped past unprepared ambushers. And for being a woman. If she'd been a man, Marcus wouldn't have shielded her with his body.

She gets up to scrub the bathroom sink. She rubs the yellowing porcelain rhythmically, uselessly, as though it mattered. Not so long ago, Marcus brushed his teeth here. Not so long ago, he shot a roll of her coming out of the shower wrapped in a towel. Pseudoannoyed, she waved him away—"Cut it out!"—and they both laughed. Now she scours until her arm muscles ache. And keeps scouring.

Finally she moves restlessly to the couch near the open window. On the other side of the city, a siren weeps. Down the street, a car horn wails. Next door a man and a woman quarrel in Hebrew, the woman in trailing sentences shaded with meaning, the man with tiny bites:

"I don't care if he is your boss. You don't overlook something like that. That's pathetic. You have to—"

"Now I'm *pathetic?*"

"Look, what I'm saying is, you have to respond. It's a matter of how . . ."

How much it would cost to have one killed, just one?

It's a crazy idea. A nighttime thought, dark and fleeting. Caddie goes to the kitchen to warm some milk. There are two sorts of people, she sees. The innocent—Caddie used to be one—shut their eyes and sleep through the dark. Then there are the rest, knowingly guilty one way or another. Denied the nocturnal gift of oblivion and purification, they rise once and again to escape a vision or a memory, to yearn for dawn while fearing it, to quarrel or to plot. The texture of their daytimes, then, is distorted by the weakened quality of their sleep. Presidents, rebels, peacemakers and assassins: history itself has been radically altered by the toll of interrupted nights. There's a whole damn story there.

Eventually her chest loosens, her musings stutter and stop, her body slackens. The disagreement next door persists, its taut rhythm invading her dreams.

In the morning her legs are unsteady and her left arm twitches. The second cup of coffee stills her limbs.

She pulls on a long-sleeved shirt, tan pants and lace-up hiking boots. At a glance, she resembles a granola-munching tourist, a kibbutz lodger or visiting peacenik. Still wholesome, still healthy. Only the observant could pick up signs of her internal frays: she knows she's given to long pauses, and that bruise-like shadows underline her eyes, and that her skin has taken on a grayish cast she can't scrub off.

She shoves a change of clothing, a towel and two bed sheets into a sack, and makes sure she has a notebook and her press card. She won't be checking in with her office this morning.

She knows she'd be advised against heading alone for the religiously rigid Gaza Strip, focal point of anger and poverty and reprisals. And especially advised against pausing for a swim.

If you require a bloody sacrosanct dip into baptismal water, not there, not there. It's Marcus's voice. She doesn't imagine it; she hears it. *And when, by the way, did you get so devout?*

She turns away. She wants neither questions nor warnings, not from anyone. Gaza is a place that has borne violence and survived. It's where she'll go.

TAKING THE ROAD that traces the curve of the Mediterranean, she flashes her press card to pass the Erez checkpoint. The next stretch is littered with garbage, the buildings graffiti-soaked. Two boys on a donkey stare sullenly as she passes. The air, ripe with diesel oil and fish blood, deposits a slippery film on her cheeks. The beach stands empty, an outcast despite its tenderly beckoning waves.

On good days, days without gunfire, men in *jallabiya*s and women in embroidered linen skirts crowd themselves into the sea. When they emerge, wet and heavy, they disappear into separate tents to change. But the locals are home today, preparing for a funeral or a demonstration, on strike or maybe sinking into collective exhaustion. Gaza is not a tourist destination. This is where Samson was thrown into a dungeon and died. It's where, only months ago, Islamic militants burned down every liquor store, every hotel that served alcohol. It is also where, sometimes, an eccentric foreigner who chooses to pause can find solitude.

Though Caddie thinks she is prepared for the sea's chill, it startles. She swims the breaststroke for a few minutes to warm up, then dives under. Once she's beneath the water, it comforts like the weight of a hefty blanket. As she breaks the surface, though, old images assert themselves. Again she submerges, walking her fingers along the sandy floor. She stays under until her lungs ache. After a few gasping breaths, she sees with a shock that pale crocodiles lie stranded on the beach, waiting for her.

Driftwood. Only driftwood, of course. Crocodiles don't live in Gaza.

This won't work, this attempt at renewal. "Go drink the sea at Gaza," the Palestinians say, when they mean *go to hell.* Why did she think she could find consolation here?

She emerges, throws the sheets over her car to block the windows and, within the car's confines, struggles out of her wet clothing, into the dry shirt and pants. Then, instead of heading back to Jerusalem, she aims for Gaza City. She passes a Palestinian refugee camp, its plywood and aluminum shacks peeking from behind a brick wall. Few cars travel through the streets paved with stones and broken bottles. Almost on autopilot, she heads toward Hikmet Masri's shop. She stops to see Hikmet every time she's in Gaza. Her most reliable source, calm and articulate. Plus, he lives above his store, so she can usually find him even when it's closed.

This time the door stands ajar. She peers inside to see the

jumble of the shelves, the mix of colors and shapes crammed together as though Hikmet simply gathered whatever manna fell from heaven and dragged it in, planning to organize it all another day. Hikmet himself sits on a stool, the traditional checkered cloth draped over his head.

"Caddie! Allah blesses me in directing you here once again. What can I offer you? Today I have fresh limes and ribbons in a dozen colors. Also two volumes of a French-language dictionary and some slightly used crayons." Then Hikmet chuckles. "Or perhaps you want only a good quote?"

He pours overheated Turkish coffee from a samovar and offers her cigarettes, which she declines. His shop smells of cardamom. She suddenly feels leaden.

"And your photographer friend?" Hikmet asks. "Where is he today?"

Only then does Caddie recall that Marcus accompanied her last time she visited Hikmet, last time she inhaled in one breath the scent of cardamom and crayon and citrus together. She tries to wet her lips, but her tongue is dry. "He's not working anymore," she says. Hikmet raises his eyebrows. "Sometimes this job is dangerous," she says. "We were in Lebanon and—" She picks up buttons from a basket, rubbing her fingers over their indented surfaces, pretending to inspect them before letting them fall. "He decided he'd had enough."

"And you continue on?" Hikmet draws on his cigarette and holds the smoke a moment before exhaling. "A man is not what he wants to be, but what he must. Sometimes, perhaps, it is the same for a woman."

She pushes the basket of buttons aside. "What's been happening?"

He begins to grumble about the clashes, a noose around his neck, always followed by the funerals, which require him to close his business for a day, and then there are more clashes, more dead, another funeral. A downward spiral, he says. He pauses as though to consider the colorful phrase he will come up with, the quote so perfect she won't be able to put it any lower than the third graph. Before he can speak, though, they're interrupted by a noise from outside. Muffled, it's hardly louder than a generous sneeze. But they're attuned, both of them, to sounds of a certain timbre.

Hikmet invokes Allah's name. "Always it's something," he mutters as he tucks his prayer beads into his pocket and rushes to the street.

Caddie's knees soften; her fingernails drive into her palm. There is Marcus, with his chilled, wide-eyed expression.

She pushes him off. Too heavy.

His right shoulder slams against the door of the jeep.

His head falls carelessly at an odd angle, oh God.

She tears her gaze away from him and spots Rob staring at her with something she can't identify. Not at first. Then, sharply, she recognizes it as accusation, as if she were responsible.

She hears a woman trilling. *The blast is here, in Gaza. Not Lebanon.*

Notepad already in hand, she pushes through the shop's door in time to catch an ambulance slicing up the street, and the ululating woman lifting over her head a scrap of cloth stained with blood. On the next block, a section of wall is missing from a second-floor apartment. She looks up to see a man stumbling through the building entrance carrying a girl who looks to be about ten years old. The child's eyes are closed. Her chest and right leg are burned.

Caddie imagines this moment framed through Marcus's lens. Woman dropping to her knees: *click*. Man emerging from the smoke with girl in his arms: *click*. Close-up of girl, delicate face above damaged body, glazed eyes half-open: *click, click*. It's odd, seeing it this way—at once more focused on tiny details, and more distant from them.

Emergency workers converge on the girl, and then three men lift her into the ambulance. Others rush upstairs to the smoking apartment.

There is no surprise in the accidental explosion of a fire-bomb. Materials used to make such bombs in the Strip are old and unstable, and the bomb-makers themselves—kids, often—are trying to patch together deadly explosives the way they might, in another culture, use rubber cement to assemble a model airplane. Mistakes are common. Still, there might be a story.

Caddie jogs to her car and drives fast to the Strip's main hospital. She runs up the steps, discolored with blood, and shoves open the doors. No trace of antiseptic scent lingers in the halls; instead it smells of chickpeas, sweat and mold. Women in headscarves gossip as they cook over Bunsen burners in the hallway, while children toss jacks near their feet. A knot of men under knitted caps huddle, their foreheads nearly touching. One drops a cigarette butt to the floor and grinds it with his heel. A nurse strolls past, pushing a patient in a wheelchair, his head slumped and eyes closed as he hums loudly, tunelessly. He is shushed by one of three men who sit on their haunches around a radio plugged into a hallway outlet, listening to the news.

A tall man wearing a stylish charcoal-gray tie stands awkwardly in the hallway. He is neither Palestinian nor patient, doctor nor common visitor, but clearly an outsider, like Caddie. He is taking in everything but he's not a journalist—she's sure from that silk tie. He meets her glance. His eyes are so dark they startle. He lifts an arm as though to stop her, to ask a question perhaps. But she hasn't time. She glances away and moves past him.

Caddie knows from previous visits that the emergency room has been turned into nothing more than another ward: too many emergencies, too little space. Most new patients, whatever their conditions, are simply hustled into one of the large dorms. Nurses don't waste time trying to group them according to the type or even seriousness of their ailments. A boy whose leg hangs in a cast lies next to a comatose woman hooked up to a ventilator.

Shooting through the hallways, Caddie finds the girl in a room that holds about twenty beds, all filled. She imagines some poor soul being carted to a grave minutes earlier, and the girl taking his place atop a still warm, rumpled and discolored sheet. The family is gathering: wailing women and sullen men. Caddie backs against the wall near the girl's bed, trying for invisibility. Listening to their talk, she learns that the youth who had been making the bomb is dead. The injured girl is his sister. Her burns are severe, especially on the chest. A woman—mother or aunt—opens the child's shirt slightly to show a red mass, skin almost gone, and what's left looks crisp in places, leathery or wet in others. She is conscious. A moan emerges from far inside her.

A doctor arrives and begins an examination. Two weeping women are led from the room by the others, leaving three young men, probably cousins, to await the doctor's verdict. Before he can pronounce it, a second doctor enters, two nurses on his heels. His graying hair, and the way he holds himself, make it clear he is the senior. "She should be intubated and on IV," he tells the first doctor.

"I've ordered it."

The senior doctor sends a nurse away to check on what's become of the drip, and then examines the girl himself. He straightens. "Wait outside," he orders the remaining relatives. He glances toward Caddie, who quickly kneels beside the unconscious patient in the next bed, her eyes closed as though praying. He turns away from her and back to the girl. "The burn penetrated the subcutaneous tissue," he says.

"In one or two places." The younger doctor sounds as though he equivocates. Caddie leans toward them slightly to better catch the Arabic.

"Third degree on the chest, that's clear. She had trouble breathing in the ambulance, no?"

"She needs morphine," the junior doctor says. "Penicillin."

The senior doctor doesn't reply at first. He looks at the girl thoughtfully with large, liquid eyes. A skeletal cat prowls the ward, meowing loudly. "You know the state of our supplies?" he finally asks.

"We'll use what we have," the junior doctor replies.

Still studying the girl, the senior doctor speaks in a rhetorical tone, as if he were teaching. "Is that practical?"

Caddie doesn't understand what he means at first. She wonders if she's misinterpreted the Arabic.

"Either way, we must alleviate the pain," the younger doctor says, his tone growing peevish. "The question you raise is in Allah's hands."

The senior doctor crosses his arms and taps the fingers of his right hand. "We have twenty vials left of morphine. Penicillin is also short."

The ward is suddenly quiet; even the patients' moans seem to die on their lips. Only the doctors speak, quickly, one's voice falling on the other's.

"And you suggest?"

"Codeine."

"*Oral* codeine." The junior doctor grunts. "The corruption of our own government . . ."

"Fortunately, some nerve endings—"

" . . . means we never have enough. And for infection?"

"—are already dead. So the pain—"

"*Infection*, I said."

The senior doctor picks up the girl's chart and writes. His

voice is painstakingly slow now and Caddie has no trouble following his words. "There's been a clash with some settlers. Two teenagers and a child are on their way in right now, Ahmed. *Another* child. This one eight years old. Bullet wound to the leg. Decent chance of survival. But without painkillers, the boy may tear at his wound. Infection and death could follow. *Needless death*." He sighs. "You know this, Ahmed."

"In Allah's name, look at her," the younger doctor says.

The senior doctor looks at his colleague sadly but from a great distance, as though mourning a son's obstinate refusal to learn. "*You* can invoke Allah," he says. "But *I* have to allot the supplies." He hands the chart to the nurse. "I'll return in two hours. Let me know if there is change before then."

The child is no longer crying. She stares at Caddie with stunned eyes that hold fear—though surely, *and please let this be so*, she is too young to comprehend the sentence just pronounced on her. It must be the possibility of more pain that frightens her. Not the promise of nonexistence.

The first doctor has his back to her; he is already moving on to the next patient. "Excuse me," Caddie calls. "I'd like to talk to you about the medicine shortages." He turns. For the briefest instant, she sees a flicker of interest in his eyes. Then he looks her up and down, and scowls. "We can talk as you work, if you'd like. Or I'll wait."

"You are—who?" the doctor asks in English.

"Newspaper reporter."

"Which country?"

"America."

His frown stiffens. "You aren't allowed in here. I have nothing to say to you."

"I heard you talking," Caddie says.

"You heard? And in what language did you hear?"

"My Arabic is fine," she says, slipping back into that tongue.

"Mistakes are easy to make when it is not your language." The doctor continues to speak English. "Not your people."

"I might be able to help."

"You think we will get more money because you write that a bomb-maker's sister suffers? If it were so simple, you think our own would not have already achieved it?" He shoves his right hand into his pocket and tilts his head. His look turns suddenly softer, appraising. "You want to help? Go to an Israeli hospital and bring us back the medicine we need." He steps toward her. "But go quickly. The child can't wait."

She could do it. Get in her car and zoom back to Jerusalem. She might be able to persuade some leftist-peacenik doctor to give her the morphine, the penicillin, whatever is needed. For a little girl, a few supplies to ease her pain. Maybe even save her life.

Caddie rubs her right wrist, remembering the leather band Marcus wore at his. It was a gift from a woman whose demolished home he photographed, whose coffee he drank, whose children he admired. He'd given her back her dignity, the woman told him, so she gave him the bracelet. They called each other *habibi*, friend.

Caddie had scoffed. "A story is a story," she'd told Marcus later. "These people aren't our friends. We don't share their lives in any sense of the word. We slip in, dig up what we need and move out, fast. All that buddy-buddy stuff is only worth it if it gets you a better photo."

"Bullshit," he'd answered. "You want something more, too. Something to make us more than friggin' voyeurs."

"Us? *I* know better."

Now, watching her, the doctor's stare slowly grows hard. "I'm very busy," he says, and turns away.

Caddie studies his long, narrow back. She imagines a series of interview questions. *Have you ever been so tired you dispensed the wrong medicine? Have you ever made a mistake that cost a patient his life, and then lied to the family?* She watches him leave the room. She can no longer see him, but in her imagination, he blushes.

Still, it's difficult to leave. The girl's family has not yet returned, and she is watching Caddie with eyes that pull. It's as though she's waiting for an answer to a question.

Get too close, feel too much, and you're sunk. That's what she'd told Marcus. What she believes.

Caddie forces herself from the hospital room into the hallway and halts before a window that overlooks an inner courtyard where recovering patients sit surrounded by extended families. The floor feels gritty beneath her feet. She leans against a wall. She's done here.

As she fights sluggishness, an emaciated man moves past, one hand pressed against the wall for support. The patient's eyes are large above hollow cheeks. Each step is a labor. He's maybe twenty-five years old, strikingly young for one so strikingly ill.

The flesh is weak.

The first time she'd heard the minister say that, she thought he referred to Grandma Jos, who had been having more and more accidents as her eyesight worsened, who'd cut herself that very morning with a paring knife. And Caddie wondered, how did he know, this minister? How did he know that Grandma Jos was aging fast? Did he, as God's emissary, have God's ability to see straight into their home? Was Grandma Jos really right, with her faith that seemed so inept?

Later, much later, when she learned the minister meant something else, something obscure about lust and sin and redemption, she rejected his interpretation as overblown and unrealistic, the explanation of the cloistered. No, she'd been right from the start: "the flesh is weak" was a maxim—or, better, a protest cry—about the inescapable vulnerability of the human body. Everyone has to die—in an armchair, on the pavement, in a bed. Caddie can't prevent it.

She turns to leave and almost runs into two orderlies rushing past, pushing empty beds. "Fucking son-of-dog Zionist settlers," one curses loudly to the other.

"Any dead?" Caddie calls after them.

The orderly glances at her over his shoulder. "Yeah. There's dead."

"How many?" she asks, but he's already moving out of earshot. To her right, there is a quick movement, and she turns to see the man with the silk tie lean forward from a chair against the wall as though he, too, is waiting for the answer. His hands rest on his lap, cupping a cell phone. His dark curls contrast with his angled cheeks and chin. His mouth is a narrow leaf. A deep dimple cleaves his chin. His eyes sweep down the hallway, following the orderlies, then anchor on her. His stare is intense, yet vacant. Caddie has seen this expression before. In the woman, smelling of vinegar and sweat, who collapsed on her in front of a bombed building. In the child whose father had been shot that same day. In Sven, that afternoon.

"Something happened to you." He says it to her, even though she's thinking it of him. He speaks English with an accent. Russian, she thinks.

"Many things." She speaks with deliberate indifference as she begins walking away.

"The earth is hungry, it takes as it needs," he calls after her. "If we knew where we were going to fall, we could spread straw."

It sounds like something he has said before many times, a personal truism that is unfamiliar to her. His tone, however, *is* familiar. And he speaks as though he recognizes her.

But no. He's a stranger, just some stranger. Caddie stiffens her shoulders. "Poetic," she says. "And ridiculous. You have no idea what you're talking about."

He isn't angered by her curtness. In fact, he seems amused, maybe slightly intrigued. The way Marcus would be. He's about to speak again. She doesn't want that. She turns and strides down the hall, making her escape.

Three

Another tangled night. Dreams of childhood, and of guns.

She's a girl again, grasping a Remington by its barrel. Comforted by its solidity, thrilled by its smooth wood beneath her fingers. Then, in a single breath, she's an adult, aiming the rifle with intent to shoot. Her target is large and blurred. She's about to fire when it becomes human, with eyes. In the background, she hears the voice of a colleague talking to a reporter in the field. "So how many bodies you got? I need a count for the story. Only the warm ones, now." She hesitates a second, then contracts her trigger finger. For a moment she thinks—she hopes—she's missed. Then she knows she hasn't.

She's awakened by a sharp sense of tumbling. She rises, needing water.

She hasn't dreamed of guns in years. Not since childhood has she even held a rifle. The first time: a Fourth of July town picnic when she was eleven. The fathers organized a shooting contest at the edge of the field. She wandered there out of thoughtless curiosity, drawn along with the other kids. Someone put a rifle in her hand. At first, she didn't like its leaden awkwardness. Right from the start, though, she was a sucker for a protective arm flung over her shoulders and a bit of fatherly advice—even if it was someone else's father and only about how to hit a target. So she stayed long past her turn, as her friends were groaning, "*C'mon*, Caddie." She stayed until Grandma Jos came to take her home.

For the rest of that summer, at one house or another, she target-practiced into the gray of evening. The fathers, who soon blended into one amorphous Father, were in turn surprised, amused and, finally, appreciative of her eagerness. They taught her to identify the firing pin and the ejector of a .22-caliber bolt-action rifle. She learned how to hold it steady but not tight, how to lower her cheek, close one eye and stop breathing as she slowly compressed the trigger. She got good, damn good. She learned how to shatter a Coke bottle from fifty feet by at least her second try, every time. Eventually she discovered how much pleasure she could find in the simple weight of a gun held snug in the pocket of a shoulder. Focusing in, and controlling the wild explosion, that was an attraction. And, unexpectedly, she began to see the beauty in a rifle, in its lines and its angles and its sheen. In its bulk and its specific gravity. This surge of emotional response to a gun, she kept to herself. But she felt the fathers guessed it, and approved.

She shot the next summer, and the next, and a little of the next, the summer of her fourteenth year. That was the last of it, though. That was the summer simple praise no longer held enough appeal, the year she drifted away from the fathers in favor of their sons. The summer she stopped imagining squeezing triggers, stopped feeling gun euphoria. Until now, in a dream.

Why hadn't she ever told Marcus about her girlhood skill with guns? He would have loved that, would have made up markswoman jokes, teased her about being a crack shot.

She pulls her heavy vacuum from a hall closet and pilots it through the living room, pausing to take particular care in the corners. She vacuums the seat and arms of the couch, and then lugs it aside to clean beneath. She runs the vacuum over the carpet again and again, as though she were a penitent performing an ablution. Midstride, she stops, marooning the machine in the middle of the floor.

The phone rings when she is sitting on the carpet, leaning against the couch and trying to block out everything but her rhythmic breathing.

"Caddie?"

Immediately, she puts face to lilting voice. "Sven? My God."

"I know, I know, it's nearly four A.M. there. I'm sorry to wake you."

"Jesus! It's not *that*. It's only—what took you so long?"

"I'm sorry." He is silent for a beat. "I *have* tried you at this number. A couple days ago."

"I just got back from Nicosia. Where are *you* calling from?"

"London."

"Well, get on a plane and get back here."

"Actually," he says, "I'm thinking about staying."

"Staying?"

"Taking a job with one of the rags. Easy pics, royalty at horse jumps, all that. And no travel for a while."

"A paparazzi?" Once, she might have privately sneered.

"Fluff, yes." His voice thins. "But calm."

"That's something," she says.

He coughs. "So you're okay, right?"

"Yeah, fine." That damn word again. She tries not to let it fall heavily.

"When the hospital released you, I took that to mean you were, you know, fine."

Sven—charming, polite, company-fit-for-the-queen Sven—sounds almost embarrassingly awkward.

"It was—you were—lucky," he says. "We all—but you, a couple more inches—be careful, Caddie. From now on."

She knows. It's simply a matter of odds. She's used up too many lives. Sven, too. All three of them, in fact. She presses the phone between her ear and shoulder and crosses her arms. "Hey," she says, "what's with Rob?"

"Somehow he talked them into sending him directly to Chechnya."

"Jeez. I had to struggle to get back here."

"So you're working again? Already?"

"Yeah. Well, features . . ." She moves toward the window and pushes it open. She smells chicken cooking with rosemary: some mother preparing dinner before work, probably. Suddenly Caddie is impatient with small talk. "So listen, Sven. That driver—"

"I have no idea." Sven's voice turns abrupt.

"No, of course not." She rubs the back of her neck with one hand. "But you talked to him more than the rest of us."

"I don't *know*, Caddie."

Caddie feels the breeze shift, escaping through her apartment. The remaining air turns heavy. "Of course not," she repeats.

"I mean, *I* was the one who talked, not him," Sven says. "He was quiet. That's what I remember."

"His skin," she says. "You remember? So leathery."

"Not that it matters."

"No," Caddie says. "Right-o. I keep thinking, though."

"Yeah, I know. But you've got to let it go."

"Thinking," Caddie goes on as if he hadn't spoken. "Thinking *we* should go."

"What do you mean?"

"Back, of course. Find that driver. That goddamned driver." She hears her voice sharpen. Her words come involuntarily, like an arm raised to counter a blow.

"Caddie."

"Find *all* those assholes. *Deal* with them." What a relief. The need to say it aloud has been pressing against her, knotting her stomach. "Let them smell fear," she says.

"They *do* smell fear," Sven said. "All the time."

"More fear, then."

"Caddie. Yaladi and his men—or his enemies, or whoever it was—anyway, they're all long gone. The trail's cold."

He's right about that, of course. It goes cold so quickly there. "But—"

"Trying to find them could get us into serious trouble," he says. "For what?"

"We owe it to Marcus," she says. "You don't ignore something like this." She's angry that Sven doesn't understand. But embarrassed, too, that she has shown herself to be so underdeveloped a human as to want to personally slow-torture the ambushers. "We've got a responsibility. We—"

"That's crazy," Sven interrupts. "Our *responsibility* is to remember—and go on." He pauses and sighs. "We *will* go back, Caddie," he says more gently. "Someday."

So he wants her to wait, then. For someday. "Same road?" she says. It sounds insane to her own ears, even as she says it.

"Together," he agrees.

"We'll try to find that driver?"

"Sure," he says.

She's being worked, she knows. But from Sven, at this moment, she can permit it.

Into the silence, he adds, "I've seen his parents. They're concerned about us."

"Hmm."

"Made me feel better, Caddie, to talk to them. Maybe you should catch a flight to London, come see them, too."

"Oh."

"And you know about the website?"

"Yeah." Mike mentioned it when he came to the hospital.

"Have you taken a look? There's a shot of Marcus that I took. And lots of stuff people have written."

She hasn't gone there. But she doesn't answer.

"Some really nice tributes." He trails off. "Well . . ."

The conversation is wearing out; Caddie hears it in his voice. His comments seem disconnected from what she needs to talk about and she can't think of how to respond to him, but *she doesn't want it to be over.* After this it may be months, even years, before she talks to him again. He'll move on, send a bit of cheerful e-mail at New Year's. This thing between them, this thing they shared, will be gone, evaporated like dew, barely even a memory. And she doesn't want that.

"Take care of yourself," he mumbles.

She'd like to beg him not to hang up, to please please keep talking, but she's suddenly afraid of what might happen if she tries for words spoken aloud.

"Keep pushing forward, Caddie," he says. "It's going to get easier. It's got to." And then he's gone.

SHE WAKES AGAIN AFTER DAYLIGHT, hit by the now familiar sensation: part of her stomach has broken off and is churning within. Her breath comes fast, her fingers tremble, her tongue is as dry as a dead leaf. Moments repeat themselves: the driver slows, she hears a popping sound, feels the weight. She's aware of severed branches, a smell like creosote.

Then the effort—never successful—to shut it out, this hard, fundamental knowledge that blankets her like a needy lover when she lies, and churns at the pit of her gut when she rises, and won't let her go. Marcus is dead. Somebody killed him.

Hush, don't worry. Marcus's voice, softly, in her ear.

The first thing she noticed about Marcus, really noticed— the feature that made her begin to sneak long looks at him— was his voice. What he could do with it. How gentle and warm he sounded as he took people's pictures. It surprised her; she was suspicious at first of this quality in a war photographer. Then she saw that, along with the bold and the funny and the fearless sides, he really had a tender side. And she wanted that tenderness for herself. Greedily. The way a kid wants candy.

Caddie throws her feet over the edge of the bed, walks to the window and stares blindly at the sky for several minutes. She rubs her own arms. Then she forces herself to focus on the street below. Anya is at the corner, standing motionless as though listening to an inner sound. Crazy street prophet Anya is their own neighborhood victim of Jerusalem Syndrome, that psychosis that attacks dozens each year. Some wrap themselves in white hotel sheets and wander the Judean Desert; others rally to the banks of the River Jordan believing themselves to be John the Baptist, or squat in the Church of the Holy Sepulcher waiting to give bloody birth to the infant Jesus. Unless they become aggressive or suicidal, they are usually ignored by the authorities. As is Anya.

As always, Anya wears an ankle-length dress with wide

sleeves that intermittently slip up to reveal a tattoo of Venus on her right forearm. Her streaming blond hair is so snarled Caddie longs to shear it off. The neighbors say she's in her midtwenties; sometimes Caddie believes it and other times she can't imagine Anya is younger than fifty. Where she sleeps, how she gets her food, Caddie has no idea.

Some days Anya seems almost as normal as any stroller. Occasionally, in a rush of off-kilter intimacy, she links arms with Caddie on the street and asks after her in a friendly, concerned matter. But on most days she is full of mutterings about Christ, or Woden, a Bronze Age Norse god she has fixated on. She often stops at an intersection and preaches about visions, her own and others', the gift she says she's been given "in compensation." People never listen to the prophets of their own time; that seems to be her main theme. She sermonizes in such a friendly way that she usually draws a good-natured crowd.

The story is that Anya—perhaps a little high-strung and overly religious, but basically an ordinary newlywed then—was touring Israel with her young husband and her mother. Anya's husband was driving, her mother in the front by his side, Anya in the back. An eighteen-year-old immigrant from Ethiopia, traveling in the opposite direction on the Acre-Karmiel highway in the Galilee, lost control of his car. It traversed the centerline and rammed head-on into the rental driven by Anya's husband. In three minutes, three, including the Ethiopian, were dead.

By the time the paramedics arrived, Anya, "miraculously

unscathed," as an Israeli newspaper would report, had dragged the bodies of her husband and her mother from their car. Both heads rested on her lap. With the fingers of one hand, she combed her mother's hair. Her face was lit by the flames from the teenager's burning, overturned car. The horn on the rental car was stuck, and when they finally got it off, instead of silence, they heard her moaning: deep, monotonous, inhuman.

Anya traveled with the bodies to the hospital and remained mute for a week. When she finally spoke, it was to say she would not return to Sweden or cash in on her hefty inheritance. She became, instead, wandering Anya of Jerusalem, Anya of visions, Anya of the street. It was in a way, now that Caddie thinks of it, Anya's revenge.

Caddie remembers that the day before she and Marcus went to Lebanon, they ran into Anya near the corner. When she saw them, she clamped both hands over her eyes and began to howl, an eerie sound that came from somewhere deep. Then she turned and fled. Caddie and Marcus both shrugged it off. Psychotic episode, probably. A shame. Nothing more.

Now, though, Caddie wonders: Could Anya have had a premonition? Some vision that might hold a clue about who is responsible for what happened to Marcus, and what she, Caddie, should do about it? She starts to struggle into her jeans, tugging at the zipper, rushing so she can get downstairs before Anya moves on.

Then she halts, and plants cool fingers in the hollows of her closed eyelids. What next? She'll be looking for signs in the damned stars. What has happened to that practicality she always prided herself on? And to think she used to believe she had ideal traits to be a journalist.

Well, she still has. Some. She's curious. Has a precise memory for dialogue and faces. A facility for grasping on-the-ground politics. Gifted with foreign languages. And she looks the part, with clipped hair and utilitarian wardrobe.

But she has handicaps now. Sweet Jesus, does she ever have handicaps.

Outside the window, a breeze shakes the trees as if giving them a scolding. She moves to the bathroom and stares at herself in the mirror. She runs a finger along the ashy skin under each eye. Then she sits on the toilet seat to pull on her boots, concentrating on yanking the shoelaces tight.

JON IS ALREADY THERE when Caddie gets to the office. She should have expected him, yet she'd hoped to slip in unseen. She needs some time alone to warm up the seat again. Her office—too grand a term for this hovel—is cramped, grad-student style, with file cabinets, a bookshelf, her PC, a laptop, two phones with separate lines, an extra foldout chair. It's infinitely worse when a second person is added to the mix. The slightest movement becomes a process of negotiation. Marcus, cameras swinging around his neck, never more than poked his head in: *Let's go to your place, or mine.*

The only plus is its location, in a building where the AP,

Reuters and a couple other foreign news organizations are based. Since Caddie works on her own, proximity serves as an early warning for breaking stories.

Jon hunches over her desk, so engrossed in the *International Herald Tribune* that he is oblivious to his surroundings. He's tall, thin and neat in a corduroy jacket, his clean-shaven face as soft-looking as a boy's. He mouths something to himself. Based in Cairo with useable Arabic, he struggles with Hebrew. He works at it conscientiously whenever he's in town. He told her once it was insulting if he didn't at least try to speak the language of the people he was interviewing. She'd laughed and replied that his greatest charm, an overabundance of earnestness, was also a damned embarrassment.

Diligent, plodding even, Jon will be doing this until the day he dies. A perpetual Jerusalem fill-in, industrious, sweetly sincere and burnout-proof. She remembers three days after Yitzhak Rabin was shot, when they'd been working around the clock. He came back from Kapulsky's with a box of doughnuts and a thermos of coffee, and for a few minutes they shared that intense undercurrent of camaraderie that can grow during a break in a big story. Often followed, she's noticed, by the need to spill something personal. Something to do with life, not death.

Jon, in the foldout chair in front of the laptop, began talking between bites about his first time. Which, as it turned out, had been in a car not five minutes from the prime minister's office, a little farther down Balfour Street. He'd been sixteen, visiting Israel with his parents, and the girl was fifteen, a rebel from an Orthodox family. Her collarbone obsessed him; he found it beautiful. It happened on a Thursday right before Yom Kippur. It had been sweet and touching and everything a first time should be, even for a boy. Certainly for a boy like him, he said, shy and awkward still.

She laughed when he said that, and he chuckled himself. And Caddie thought of her own first time, with an Indiana farm boy. Arnie was his name, a muscled D-student. He'd whispered that his parents weren't home and described a plush living room couch with lacy pillows, but she'd led him to a cornfield, where she'd pulled him from sight between the rows. And there in the dirt, she'd learned two important facts. That her dreams, unlike those of her neighbors, were made of grit instead of lace. And that anticipation is nearly always sweeter than realization.

Then Jon was in the middle of saying what had happened with the girl afterward, how she didn't show up to meet him as they'd planned and how he looked for her, when a government spokesman called to tell them of a news conference and Caddie dashed to cover it and the topic never came up again.

Now she clears her throat and he looks up and his face turns self-conscious. He tries to refold the newspaper and some pages flutter to the floor. He rises stiffly. "Caddie, I'm so—"

"I know," she interrupts.

"I can't believe . . ."

She nods. Oh, to get through this part.

"Well. You look great," he says, as though she's come back from some vacation. He says it even though he's unable to meet her eyes. "You've always been tough. But," he spreads his arms, "should you really be . . . ? I mean, Mike told me you weren't to . . ." He trails off, his gaze wandering from her feet to her right cheek and then back to her feet again.

She steps into the office. "I'm ready to work, Jon. I *have* to work, in fact. But I'd like to keep it between us. It'll only be features. Unless, of course," she takes a deep breath, "a breaking story tumbles into my lap."

He laughs. "You're something. I don't know if I could . . . but *you* . . . you don't change. Okay, between us." He pats her on the shoulder and shoots a look of admiration in her general direction. It comes from a great distance, that look, a long lack of understanding, but it's what she's going to have to live with.

Besides, it's probably as much intimacy as she can handle right now. "Isn't the Foreign Ministry presser about to start?" she asks.

He nods. "I better get going. You'll be here when I get back, then?"

"Unless I think of somewhere else to go."

When Jon has left, she still feels crowded, as though someone else is sucking up the air and filling the space, as though she must keep her elbows compressed to her waist and avoid expansive movements. She opens the top drawer of her desk. A stale smell escapes. She stares at a pile of notes for an economic feature she was planning to write, before. She slams the desk shut, and with her foot she shoves the stack of newspapers she has to go through—two weeks' worth. She flips on her computer. *Leap in.* But to what?

She logs online, reads a couple pieces of e-mail, deletes the rest. Then she goes to a search engine and types in a few words. *Beirut. Assassin.* Up pops a list of books and movies and websites on the history of the Crusaders. She tries another search. *Beirut. Kill-for-hire.* No hits at all. What did she expect? E-mail contacts and a price list?

Down the hall, a phone rings, and a gravelly voice answers. It's Pete, a photographer in his midfifties. "How many are there?" he grumbles into the phone.

Hearing him, she has an inspiration. She waits until he has hung up before walking down to his office. As soon as he sees her, he opens his arms, thick and covered with white-blond hair, and pulls her in. He smells of shaving cream, a sign that he hasn't been out working yet.

"What a shooter he was," Pete says. "Away from work, he was such a jokester—I never trusted a word he said. But taking pictures, he was—"

Caddie nods.

"You?"

"I'm okay."

"You sure? Because if—"

She waves a hand to cut him off. "Listen, I need a favor."

He gestures for her to sit and leans toward her.

"Let me know, will you, when you hear of clashes anywhere."

"I always let you know," Pete says.

"No, I mean *anything*. Big *or* little."

His stare is suspicious. Photographers have to get to the violence or they've got nothing, empty negatives, a black hole, but experienced reporters wait until there's a body pile. Even then, they weigh what else is happening. After all, they can always look at the footage or photos later to fill out their copy. "What for?" Pete says. "You're not a hardware-sniffer."

"It'll get me up and running again."

He stretches his legs. "Most of these aren't stories," he says. "They're fender-benders. I dash by with my helmet and flak jacket, shoot a roll or two, and then I'm gone. No point for you."

"I'm talking a long-term project," she begins improvising, and then gives it up. She rises, walks toward the door and pauses. "Let me worry about what I take from it."

He studies her a minute. "Something calmer might be your best bet for now."

"Shit, Pete."

He shrugs. "Okay, okay. I'll let you know."

"Thanks."

She nods and leaves. Calmer, hell. What does Pete know? She can handle it; she can handle anything. Sure, maybe sometimes a few details get to her. The expressions and postures of the dead: the uncanny grins, the unnatural sprawls. The distinctive smell of blood and entrails: thick, swampy and sordid like a secret that should never have been revealed. Sometimes she gags. But then she holds her breath and keeps going. She is a stranger to easy astonishment. She can step over bloody ground for a quote, analyze a wound for its deadliness. Identify weapons and stay unfazed when they are waved in her face. She keeps her eyes on the basics: it's a *story*. Stories stale quickly; each one has to have an angle. She slips in, gets what she needs and moves out, fast. A visitor.

Still, once back in her office, she reaches into her drawer and pulls out a list she keeps of feature ideas. She examines it a moment, then crumbles it and tosses it into the trashcan. None of it interests her. But what, what? She kicks the trashcan.

And then it occurs to her: Moshe. Of course. Moshe is the perfect way to sink into a feature with a hard edge. A West Bank settler leader linked to the movement's radicals and, at the same time, articulate enough. She's been developing him for more than a year now.

She calls him at his office. "I'd like to come out," she says. "Spend a night. Get a feel for what's happening there."

"The only thing happening is that we're trying to raise good, productive children in a community of values," Moshe says, his voice thick. He always talks through his nose. If she didn't know, she'd think he had a cold.

"Great, then," she says. "I'll write about that."

"Having values doesn't make us extremists."

She imagines him playing idly with the gun he probably keeps in his desk drawer. "Of course not," she says.

She hears the door open. For a moment she doesn't recognize the man standing there. Then she realizes he's the silk tie. The out-of-place would-be poet with the Russian accent and black eyes.

"Foreign journalists have a hard time appreciating us," Moshe is saying, using an old line. "They draw rash conclusions."

"I have some flexibility in my schedule right now," Caddie says. "Sometime in the next week would be perfect."

"Well—" Moshe hesitates. "I'll get back to you."

"If I don't hear from you by tomorrow afternoon, I'll give you a buzz," she says, and hangs up.

She's not completely surprised to see the man from the Gaza hospital. Men often view female foreign correspondents as an odd breed, independent but lonely and ripe for the picking, women who took their jobs at least partly for the chance to have sex in exotic countries. These men are likely to track her down weeks, even months, after an interview, full of half-winks and anticipatory grins. Wanting her without any idea who she is: the ultimate insult.

If you happened upon a nude woman walking down the street, she imagines asking, *would you avert your gaze or slow down to stare?* He is, she decides, the staring sort.

"Yes?" she says after a moment, keeping recognition from her voice.

He stands at a distance and reaches, stork-like, to hand her a piece of paper. "The list of medicines they need." He turns to go.

At second glance he doesn't seem the predator type. He doesn't have the swagger, the extra helping of phony confidence. "Wait a sec," Caddie says. "Where'd you get this?" She shakes the paper without looking at it.

He speaks over his shoulder. "You'll see they lack very basic supplies."

"How'd you know I was asking about this?"

"That's irrelevant."

She shakes the paper again. "What if it isn't legit?" He looks puzzled. "Legitimate," she says. "For real."

He shrugs, giving her his back as he pushes open the door. "Check it."

"Wait." Finally, something in her command stops him. "A simple question. What's your name?"

"Goronsky. Alexander Goronsky."

He says it oddly, each syllable placed heavily as though he doesn't care what anyone thinks of him. As though if he ever knew how to smile, he's long ago forgotten. Darkness beneath a tightly controlled surface.

"Goronsky," she says. "All right. There's a start. Now why don't we go have a cup of coffee and talk a little more about this list of yours?"

It's a rash invitation that startles even her. But if he is either surprised or pleased by her boldness, he doesn't show it. He stares at her, nods and waits silently, looking out the window, for her to close up the office.

On the street he stays a step or two ahead, leading the way from west Jerusalem into the eastern part of the city, Salahed-din Street. He walks with head half-tucked, shoulders sucked in, feet gliding cat-like, as though he were prepared to slip through a sidewalk crack at the first sign of danger. He hesitates before the open door of Silwadi Café. Arabic music blares from a cassette player. A waiter sweeps past with a steaming tray bearing the scent of roasted peppers and sweet coffee. She expects Goronsky to ask if his choice is okay, but instead he moves unhesitatingly into the café's single room and sits at a table. After a moment, she follows.

They wait for their order silently, Goronsky looking around the room as though sizing it up. Small talk, though Caddie is usually good at it, sticks in her throat these days.

"So how did you get this information? And why?" she manages after their coffee arrives.

"It was something I could do." His face is bland.

"But how? Who are you?"

He straightens. He lays his hands on the table, each movement deliberate. She likes his long fingers. "Psychology professor," he says, failing to meet her gaze. "I'm on sabbatical from Moscow State University, doing research at Hebrew University." The way he speaks, so stiffly, conjures up an image of those words typed on a page. She can picture him practicing reciting them.

"Research on what?"

"Extremism," he says.

She smiles. "Sounds like a perfect cover."

He takes a lingering drink of coffee. "Did you ever call to find out what happened to that child?" he asks.

"What child?"

"The little girl in the hospital." His gaze is appraising, if not judgmental.

"You know—?" Caddie breaks off. "It was a story," she says. "It was about medical shortages, not one child."

"So it's only the story you cared about."

She looks away, stung by the sudden intrusion. Is it only the story? It seems to her now that that was precisely the question in the girl's eyes. She thinks of the girl's limp body vanishing into the sheets; she hears again that moan emerging as if from a cavern. It mixes with a memory of another moan. *From Marcus? No, he'd been silent. Sven? Or maybe me.*

She is, she realizes, stirring her coffee endlessly, her spoon making round after round in her cup. She stops herself, meets his stare. "What were *you* doing at the hospital that day?"

"Waiting for the director," he says.

"What for?"

"He is a political leader. I need him for my study."

She shakes her head and smiles. "Okay, let's say for a moment that you are doing a study. How did you find out so much about me? And why bother?"

"All I found out was what you were there for and where your office is located. I can do far better with basic observational skills if I have more time. And more interest," he adds pointedly. He nods toward the man behind the bar. "Take, for instance, Farid Silwadi, the owner of this place. His first love is music, but he can't pursue it full-time because of family responsibilities. His father is dead. He is the oldest son and is supporting his sister-in-law and her young child while his brother, their father, is in jail. He would love to sell this restaurant, but he can't, not anytime soon."

Caddie is intrigued in spite of herself, but she doesn't want him to see that. "So?" She shrugs. "One lazy afternoon, he told you his life story."

"Not until after I guessed the basic outline. See the sheet music lying on the bar? In the back he has an *oud*. If you come here directly before the dinner hour, you can hear him practicing. He's not bad. He wants to join a group that performs at parties for the faithful returning from the hajj."

"And the family details?"

"Again, simple logistics. He wears no ring, yet he works like a slave. Too hard for a man unattached. So it has to be that his father is dead and he has some other weight upon him besides a wife or children of his own. A woman alone is always the responsibility of her husband's family—her father-in-law if he is living, the oldest brother if he is not. That's how I figured it out, and then I confirmed it. I imagine Silwadi will sell this place a week after his brother gets out of jail."

She grins. "Not bad."

He immodestly nods. "It's a matter of focus, of combining observable moments. No trick to it."

They sip their coffee silently.

"Now your turn. Tell me something," he says. "Tell me about the look I saw on your face the other day in the hospital."

She crosses her wrists on her lap. "Don't know what you mean."

He looks into his coffee cup. "How about this one?" he says after a moment. "What made you become a reporter?"

"What made you become a psychology professor?" she asks. "If that's what you really are?"

"It's such an awful story, yours is, then," he asks, "that you won't even answer?"

"Okay, okay. Let me think. My grandmother probably had something to do with it. She read the newspaper and the Bible aloud to me in equal measure, as though both were crucial. When time came to get a job, there were no openings for Bible writers."

When he smiles, the darkness at his edges vanishes. "Then?" he asks.

"That's it. The rest is no big deal."

"No big deal," he repeats, solemn again. "The fly cannot get into the closed mouth, can it?"

It's not that he's charming. There's something in his eyes, though, something to do with his intensity. An element of risk he seems to hold within himself. He is staring at her, waiting.

After a moment, she shrugs. "And then, when I was nineteen, maybe twenty, I was working for the wire service on Friday and Saturday nights in Indiana—that's where we lived. It was still only a job, late shift, mainly recording high school basketball scores. One night a tornado hit this little town forty miles away and the news editor told me to hop in my car and fly."

Goronsky leans forward, his long fingers fluttering softly on the tabletop like moths against the window.

"I'd never been to the town before, never even heard of it.

It was dark and I started to get lost, but then I could see I was in the right area because of the snapped tree trunks, the flattened bushes. The wind made that shrill warning howl and I thought, what am I, crazy? I could drive right into the damn storm."

His stare deepens. "You were scared?"

"No." She licks her lips, remembering. "At least, that wasn't the main thing. I felt focused. I had to find my way to wherever the story was happening. So I kept driving and it kept blowing and then I heard an ambulance siren. I tailed it all the way into pandemonium, clean and simple. The county hospital. Seven dead, a dozen or so injured. I spent the night interviewing and calling in reports, then drove out at dawn to assess the damage. And there it was, everywhere you looked— smashed houses, scattered toys, as though some god had flown into a fury."

She looks up to see Goronsky watching her, and not with the fearful admiration that she's been getting since Lebanon. Again, his stare holds intimacy. Again, that recognition.

Something inside her drums like his fingertips on the table. She looks away, pretends to survey the room.

"So that's it," she says after a moment, going on almost against her will. "That's how I got addicted. A chance to find the seams. Live more than one life."

She takes a deep breath, surprised by the words, committed to stopping them. And in that second, she feels his hand covering hers. Before she can be startled, he pulls away. She doesn't look at him, and she can sense that he, too, avoids glancing at her. When he speaks, his voice is taut, controlled.

"It's how much you can take, isn't it?" he says. "How much blood and breast-beating. That's what makes a success in your business."

Caddie almost rises from her seat. He's drawing too close, this bosom stranger. She manages—just—to still the impulse to walk out.

It takes a moment to summon her will. Then she gives him a grin of indiscriminate friendliness, professional and proscribed.

"That," she says, "and how closely you follow the howling wind."

Four

CADDIE SPOTS THE SMOKE FIRST. Then she sees several dozen forms agitating by the roadside like drops of water sizzling on a skillet. She and Pete are driving down a side street, and by the time they are close enough for a wide shot—*here we have Bethlehem, scene of today's clash*—the stench of burning rubber forces its way through the closed windows. A smoldering tire sends up its signals. An ambulance lingers nearby. Pete shoves a red-and-white *keffiyeh*—a solidarity symbol—on the dash next to the sign that says "journalist" in large Arabic letters. "For what fucking good it'll do," he mutters. He backs up, points his car down an alley and parks in a sheltered area behind the Israeli checkpoint.

He shrugs into his flak jacket and tosses Caddie a bicycle helmet that belongs to his neighbor's son. "Let's rock," he says, and they move forward together, slowly at first, then a dash alongside the street where Palestinian-thrown rocks and broken glass are landing. They take cover in a shuttered gas station as an Israeli soldier fires off a round. Caddie slips in close to the building, breathing fast. A sour taste forms in the back of her throat.

"You okay?"

"Yep. Just—" Caddie hesitates, unzips her waist pouch, feels around inside. "Making sure I have everything."

Pete studies her for an extra beat, then nods and moves forward.

This fear is unexpected, damnit. She's going to give herself about five minutes to feel it. Then she's going to get over it.

She paces, the fingers of one hand grazing the rough brick wall, studying the position of the four-dozen *shabab* and the three Israeli soldiers. She needs to get a sense of where the stones and rubber bullets are likely to land; that will make her feel better. She needs to find her comfort zone within the hollow boom of tear gas, the sharper rap of rubber bullets, the whiz of hurled stones. No live ammo on either side so far. Only photographers are here, grouped near the gas pumps where they can zoom in on the clash. They exude a vague sense of indifference, a bit bored as they wait for that moment of loss or anguish that could propel their work to the front page, the top of the newscast. Occasionally they chat or someone cracks a joke.

It seems safe enough. Of course it is. And anyway, it's been five minutes. She won't regain her nerve hugging the wall.

She edges toward Pete. "This gang shot—it's no fucking good," he says half to himself as he turns toward her. "Besides, the light sucks. Over there would be better." He points his chin in the direction of the Palestinian protesters.

An ambulance pulls forward to reposition itself, and Pete dashes toward it, using it for cover. He holds his camera near his face for protection. Without thinking, Caddie follows. The vehicle shields them briefly, then turns onto a side road. For half a dozen heartbeats, Caddie is fully exposed, directly between protesters and soldiers, in line of both stones and bullets. She stretches her legs, clears the street and flattens herself against a lime-colored wall—a bakery, closed for now. She's panting slightly.

Pete hasn't paused. He keeps his back close to the shops, his camera to his eye, snapping.

Before Caddie can assess her new position, a young woman, perhaps seventeen or eighteen years old, grabs her arm. The touch makes Caddie jump. The woman holds a cucumber in one hand, which she waves as she talks in a half-crazed voice about Israeli settlers creeping to their house before dawn a week ago, dragging away her cousin and his best friend, beating the cousin and murdering the friend. "He was not involved in crime, like they say," she says. "He was a good boy, my cousin's friend. And now he dies and no one notices. It is wrong." She swings the cucumber, narrowly missing Caddie's cheek. "Can I tell you his name?" she pleads. "Only his name, to include among the martyrs?"

Could be decent. Maybe Caddie can weave it into whatever she manages to get from Moshe. But not now. She takes the woman's name, Halima Bisharat, and her address and promises to stop in to see her family next week. "We will talk more, Halima," Caddie says. "You tell me everything then, okay?" The young woman nods gratefully and Caddie turns back to the clash, aware of the intensifying fury of the protesters around her.

The "demo car" pulls up, delivering fresh stones and bottles to the protesters. Its driver, his features hidden behind a ski mask, fires a rifle into the air and draws cheers from the crowd. He fires again toward the Israeli checkpoint, then hits the gas, raising dust and sending his car skidding away. The calls to Allah, chanting and obscenities become louder. *"Allahu Akhbar."* "Kill the Zionists." God and gunfire, the combustible combination.

Pete scoots forward occasionally to grab a shot from behind the shelter of a demonstrator. But mainly he paces within his invisible safety zone. *Safety zone, what a pathetic concept. Like trying to walk between raindrops.*

What would Marcus shoot if he were here? Because he *would* be here. He sometimes covered three clashes a day—he had incredible stamina, for which he credited those boxes of raisins. He'd look for dead and wounded, of course, but also for pictures of the youngest demonstrators, the nine- and ten-year-olds. They'd argued about that, the two of them.

Why always the kids, the kids, like they're the only ones here? Why not the men?

With their sneers and pockmarked faces? No. For me, the children are the story.

She squints and can nearly see Marcus joining this dangerous dance, his hands cupping the lens the way a florist might an orchid, his face pressed to the viewfinder, staring through the lustful eye of his camera, absorbed in the poetry of the scene.

Stones arcing beneath tear-gas canisters: *click*.

Molotov cocktails answered by rubber bullets: *click*.

Night-haired boys pitched against their helmeted half-brothers on an ancient battlefield, one or two folding to the stained ground: *click, click, click*.

She inches closer to the crowd, as Marcus would. Crouches, processing the scene from various angles. An Israeli soldier lunges from behind his concrete barricade and, with the skill of a starting pitcher, hurls a tear-gas canister with one arm and a stun grenade with another. He swears in Hebrew, a long slur that sounds like a medieval curse. Caddie's eyes are watering. A Palestinian boy with a pink scar from eye to jaw-bone grabs Caddie's arm and offers a dampened bandana as protection against the acrid tear gas. Caddie ties it around her nose and mouth and inhales deeply from under the bandana.

Wrapped around her face like that, it becomes a disguise that frees her. She begins to drift among the protesters like an invisible vapor, taking in their mood. Determination, yes, but also playfulness—they are, after all, mostly kids. A heightened sense of drama, too, runs between them. One of them may die today, so these moments must be full, valiant, colorful. A boy uses a rock to scratch a hand of Fatima in the dirt and then flings the stone toward the Israeli checkpoint with a cry. Two others hold their wrists together for a moment in what seems to be a gesture of solidarity before dashing closer to the soldiers.

"Caddie!"

Three feet away from her, a bullet hits a Palestinian boy in his right shoulder. He looks to be about twelve. The force drives him to the ground and he falls with a sickening thud. He opens his mouth, but no sound emerges, and then he is hit again, this time in his groin. Blood splatters as though from the brush of a careless painter. He curls up and rolls onto his stomach. At the exit wound on his shoulder blade, a red spot appears through his clothing, then blooms like a flower, but fast like one of those speeded-up nature films.

She is closest to him, and she moves toward him. *Got to drag him to the ambulance.* Then she draws back. What she's got to do is *not* assist the boy, but pay attention to the air turning frantic with *keffiyeh*s and curses, the tear-gas stink replaced by the syrupy odor of blood, the guns of the Israeli soldiers now swinging slowly from right to left and back again. She has to be able to report it all.

Why, though, is no one helping the boy?

Finally, after what seems like a dozen minutes, several young men make their way to him and half-lift, half-drag him to the ambulance about a block away. The boy is not crying, not even whimpering, and what that costs him is etched on his face.

"Get back!" She turns toward Pete's voice and realizes she is standing six yards in the open, without cover. Four boys stoop nearby behind two burned trash barrels. She drops to a crouch and scuttles to join them. They barely glance at her, intent on their stone throwing.

Now more tear gas, more coughing. The barrel she's hunched behind is hit dead-on by a bullet; it lurches like a man punched in the stomach. Rubber-coated or brass-tipped? From the thud of impact, she guesses the former.

Her forearms are covered with bits of ash. She brushes one off, then the other, aware of her sharp wrist bones, the rubbery texture of her palms. She feels a stare hot on the side of her neck and turns toward the shops. A girl, perhaps nine years old, stands watching. Despite the distance between them, everything about the child is magnified—long lashes, tiny hands, old straw basket on her arm.

Caddie should be where the girl is instead of kneeling in the center of the street.

But she wants to be closer to the violence than that, as close as possible. This rush is unmatchable. Far better than drugs or alcohol, better than collecting quotes like spent ammo after the fighting is finished. The talcum-dirt under her knees, the suspended smoke, the wide-eyed child, the percussion of her own heart—every element in this moment is rich, and essential.

She peeks out to judge the distance of the soldiers and catches sight of a rifle pointed in her direction. She ducks back. The boys are grinning at her now. One tugs her sleeve, pulling her gently to a safer position. She scrunches up more tightly behind the barrel. Another shot ricochets off its metal side. "Bang, you dead," one of the kids teases in English, his smile friendly. She laughs back, tosses her head and closes her eyes in a mock-dead posture.

A siren fused with a woman's wail is the coda. As if the movement were prearranged, the protesters retreat like closing credits. Sometimes it goes on until nightfall, but this time they've decided to end it early, share a meal—who knows, maybe log on and read a backlog of e-mail. *Her* boys, the ones she took cover with, wave as they run off. "See you next time, lady," one calls.

"You got a date," she answers, doubting that he understands the slang.

She moves from behind the trash barrels, aware that she is in the sites of Israeli guns. The tire still smokes. Her shoes are filthy. Her damp clothes are permeated with sweat and tear gas. She wipes her face with her sleeve, eases closer to the Israeli checkpoint and scoops up a handful of ashes, dirt and a spent rubber bullet. She holds her fisted hand to her neck.

"Let's go!" She hears Pete's voice. "C'mon, it's over."

These intensified moments exist without a past or even a future. She's not ready to leave.

But it *is* over. The theater is littered and empty. Overoveroverover. She opens her hand. Some of the dirt slides down her shirt.

In the car, Pete barely contains his fury. "What the hell were you doing, running out there like that?"

She pulls the seatbelt over her lap, then throws it off. The belt—no, the whole car—feels constricting.

"You hear me?"

She takes a deep breath, searching for the words that will appease Pete. "It should be obvious," she says. "I've got to see what's going on."

"Gotta fucking get plugged, you mean." Pete twists the key violently to start the engine. "You can *see* from the wall. Christ. You can actually see from the office by looking at my stuff. You wordies don't need this."

She might have said that herself an hour ago, but now she rejects it. "I can't write it if I'm not in it. You know that."

"Screw the writing. Don't do that again, damnit," he says. "Don't run out in front like that. Not when I'm your ride."

She looks out her window, turning her head away from him.

"You got some fucking death wish, fulfill it somewhere else. I don't have time to take you to the fucking hosp—" He cuts off suddenly. Maybe thinking of Marcus, maybe thinking he's gone too far.

They drive in silence for a few minutes. Then Pete lets air out loudly through his mouth. "You even get anything you can use?"

"Quote here, quote there." Actually, Caddie doesn't think she took a single note after Halima, the woman with the cucumber. And she still doesn't know precisely what her story is. She's half-sitting on her notebook. She shoves it into her waist pouch.

"Yeah, but no bodies—not unless that one guy goes down," Pete says. "So what is it, besides a caption?"

A part of a story that eventually will pull together all her scattered pieces. Or maybe just something to drown out this craving to hunt down those Lebanese killers and castrate them, whack their balls off, one by one.

"I'll cover a couple more," she answers. "Then, don't worry about it, I'll have something to write. I'll have my story."

THREE MESSAGES WAIT on the office answering machine. The first is from the Gaza City hospital. "I am sorry, we are not at liberty to report on the status of our medical supplies. I can confirm, however, that it is a priority of Chairman Arafat's to make sure our wounded get the best possible medical care. Let me also remind you that journalists are not allowed in the hospital without having obtained prior permission. As to the status of the patient you inquired about, that information is private."

For the girl, Caddie has little hope. But, with the details Goronsky provided, she should be able to scare up a confirmation or a denial on medical supplies somehow, even without the hospital's cooperation. Maybe Hikmet could direct her—she seems to remember he has a nephew who works at Shifa.

The second message is from Moshe, who agrees to let her stay overnight with his family. "We have nothing to hide," he says. She must call him to arrange the time.

There's a pleasant piece of news. If she can toss in the experience of being in the clashes with that of being in the settlements plus an interview with the cucumber girl, it'll make a decent piece. She's on to something, and to hell with Pete. She's not chasing bullets or playing some roulette game. She's doing her job.

The third message. A man's voice. "I have an idea for dinner."

The words make her stomach tumble. She feels Marcus leaning in toward her as the Land Rover takes a turn. *I have an idea for dinner tonight.* Smelling her cheek. Flirtatious. *Dinner tonight.*

"It's Alexander Goronsky," the voice goes on. "I'm at the Mount of Olives Hotel, Room 211."

An accidental turn of phrase, one that carried an accidental echo.

She won't return his call. She has no interest in being observed by him. No interest in making herself appear available.

Pete and some other journalists pass in the hallway, laughing. "Hey, Caddie," Pete calls, his anger evaporated. "Want to get a bite with us?"

"Thanks, but I'm busy," she lies.

"Okay, then," he says. "Later."

This Goronsky, who is he? Probably a traditionalist who favors Johann Strauss, and Tolstoy. He would never take his spoon and pretend to ski down a mountain of sugar on his cereal, like Marcus did. If he even eats cereal for breakfast. Which Caddie doesn't intend to find out.

As the elevator down the hall jerks open and then closes, the voices of Pete and the others are extinguished.

Of course, dinner has nothing to do with breakfast.

Caddie holds the receiver in her hand for a long moment before dialing Goronsky's number.

HE ARRIVES AT HER OFFICE around five, too early to eat, so they begin by unspoken agreement to stroll the sidewalk. It's another loud evening: bus brakes squealing, soldiers arguing as they inhale pita sandwiches, merchants yanking down metal shutters to close up their shops. Caddie can't squeeze in a decent piece of conversation. But she doesn't mind letting any possibility of shared words be overtaken by horn blasts and radio static.

When they pause at a corner, he takes her arm right above the elbow. "What kinds of stories do you like to cover?" he asks.

It's a neutral question, but it makes her uncomfortable. What's he hinting at? A stranger's appeal is supposed to be that he doesn't know anything beyond what she tells him. A fresh start.

"The nasty stories," she says. "Two sides killing each other, me watching." She doesn't grin, giving him nothing to hang his hat on.

His cell phone rings then. He tilts his head to one side, cups the phone to his ear and listens a minute. "Okay," he says. He hangs up, stares into the distance and seems to slip away. He walks ahead, crossing the street as though he's alone. His stride is long. She hurries to catch up.

Marcus did this, too, sometimes. Vanished on me, distracted by the shadows within his negatives. But it passed. It always passed.

The hair that curls on Goronsky's forehead looks damp. His brown eyes have darkened, and she sees herself reflected there. He moves closer to her. "A release," he says, his voice so quiet she has to lean forward to hear. "That's what it is, this journalism, no? You're part of it, but it's bigger than you, more meaningful than you alone can ever be."

This time his intensity sets her on edge. "That's not quite it," she says.

"Everybody seeks the drug of risk-taking from time to time. Dangerous jobs, dangerous sports. Reckless driving. Fierce drinking. Makes life less bland." He looks directly at her. "Or dulls the pain."

She shakes her head. "It's not *my* appetite for violence that's at issue here. It's the appetite of the newspaper's readers."

He stares at her a moment, but doesn't reply.

HE TAKES HER to a new restaurant run by an Orthodox Jew who greets him by name.

"You know an odd variety of people," she says.

He ignores the comment. "You were an only child, I'd bet," he says.

"Lucky guess," she answers. "Why are you staying at the Mount of Olives, anyway? Isn't that mainly Christian tour groups?"

"Nice view," he says.

"I would have expected King David, for a professor doing a government study."

"Too formal."

"Or, security simply too tight for someone studying extremism?"

He glances away. A waiter brings a bowl of green olives, a plate of tomatoes and cucumbers drenched in vinegar, another plate of fish and fresh hummus seasoned with paprika. Goronsky fingers a piece of warm pita. "Were you close to your parents?" he asks.

"My father died before I was born."

He leans forward, suddenly intent. He's not wearing a tie this time and his shirt is unbuttoned at the neck. His shoulders are broader than she'd realized before.

She's surprised at this show of interest in her childhood. But it feels safer than his other probes. She doesn't want to talk about violence, what it means to her or what part she plays in it. On the topic of long-dead parents, she's practiced and comfortable.

"He was an amateur racecar driver." She pops an olive into her mouth. "He wanted to be in the Indy 500. But he crashed first, some minor race in Toledo. Lost control taking a curve. All I have is the newspaper clipping. And an impression, from my grandmother, that he lived hard."

Goronsky's hands are on the table, one cupped in the other. Even at rest they seem more the hands of a farmer than an academic. He has a scar on his chin, curved like a sliver of moon.

"My mother took off soon after I was born. Ditched me, basically. I think the pregnancy was an accident anyway." Caddie smiles, sips her Bitter Lemon soda. "She was a potter— when she could afford the clay and the fee for a wheel. She moved a lot, sent postcards. A couple times she sent pots she'd made, quirky shapes glazed in dark colors. My grandmother lined them up chronologically on a shelf in my bedroom. When I was nine, my mother was in San Francisco, out on a street late at night alone, and she got mugged and beaten up. She died in the hospital."

"Your grandparents raised you, then?" Goronsky asks.

"Grandmother. My grandfather was already gone, so it was only Grandma Jos and me."

Usually when Caddie tells these stories, her listeners give her a puppy-dog gaze. *A child orphan, all these untimely deaths, what a shame.* And usually she nods and thinks how easy it is to fool people into believing she's been open, merely by pulling out a stale story.

In Goronsky's face now, however, there is none of the typical pity. Just, again, that recognition.

Marcus was spontaneity and irony and a joke. Marcus was a noontime sun flooding the room, washing out its corners. This Goronsky is a single, eye-stinging beam that claims to know her even better than she knows herself.

Unexpectedly, that pleases her.

. . .

HALFWAY THROUGH THE MEAL, she catches him staring at her.

"Is it awful?" he asks.

"What?"

"The food. You're mostly rearranging instead of eating."

She looks at her plate. She's hidden the fish under the salad and hasn't touched the bread. In fact, she realizes that she hasn't eaten dinner for weeks, starting in the Cyprus hospital. The one meal she's been skipping. "I'm not too hungry," she says.

After dinner, they walk again. They do not touch, but their shoulders are close. Too close. She sits on a bench and places her backpack between them as he, too, sits. "Now you tell me a story," she says. "A story of *your* childhood."

"Hmm," he says vaguely. "You are interviewing me?"

"You already interviewed me."

"A typical Russian childhood," he says. "We went to school as a number, not a name. We sat in neat rows behind blond desks. We dressed the same, drew the same pictures, spoke to the teacher in unison." His tone grows impatient. "Sasha is the diminutive for boys named Alexander or girls named Aleksandra. You know how many Sashas were in my class? Nine. Every year, the same nine of us, growing older as one." He presses his lips together and looks, for a second, as though he is going to spit. "As one of many Sashas, I was invisible. I could get away with anything."

Although she's seen enough rage in the last few years to recognize it now, it surprises her. Even controlled, it seems out of proportion. To be invisible doesn't sound like such a bad thing. How much better than being known as the girl whose mother, plainly put, couldn't find a reason to stay.

He grows so silent that she thinks he may not speak again tonight. "I like Jerusalem, don't you?" she says after a few minutes. "The hills, the history."

He doesn't answer but leans slightly over her backpack. The intensity of his attention attracts and chills her. She's careful not to touch him, but he is near enough for her to breathe in the smell of him: a scent of sea salt.

"I only wish Jerusalem had the ocean," she says. "That's the single advantage to Tel Aviv."

His body grows board-like. He rubs his arms as though chilled and looks away. "You like the ocean, then?" he asks.

She hesitates. "I like its power."

"You've been to the seaside a lot?"

"I didn't ever leave Indiana as a kid. But later, after I was older, I spent a vacation in San Diego. For a week I collected shells and stones. Obsessive, almost—handfuls of them every day. Always looking for the perfect ones. Finally, I got over it. I gave them all away to a bum on the boardwalk."

"And since then you've collected, what? The maimed and the marred?"

She laughs, ignoring the coolness of his tone. "Essentially."

He doesn't speak for a few minutes. "I have a beach story," he says at last, his voice inflectionless. "It's about Israel. About a woman who emigrated from Russia. Do you want to hear?" He doesn't wait for her answer. "Lean back, then," he says, the scratchiness of his voice combining with his accent to set free a kind of music. He slides her backpack off the bench and scoots closer so their shoulders nearly touch, so his lips almost brush the hair that covers her ear. "Close your eyes." His words float to her.

Vera moved from Moscow to Jerusalem with her parents at the age of sixteen and got married at eighteen to a *sabra*, a nice Israeli-born boy who liked to work the land. She loved that her husband worked with his hands, that he knew every inch of her adopted country. They moved north to a village on the Mediterranean called Neve Shalot, with green fields on one side and blue water on the other. They had a son first, then two daughters. The days were a weave of salt breezes and childish laughter.

One cloudy autumn evening not long after dinner, when the baby was six months old, one daughter was three and the son six, the old woman who lived next door came bustling all in a fright and said she'd seen men, Arab men, landing a small boat on the shore.

"How do you know this, in the dark, that they're Arabs?" Vera's husband asked, but the woman insisted she did. He gave his wife a skeptical look, but still the two of them, their children and the frightened old woman hid, crowded into a tiny coat closet in the upstairs hallway. After only a minute, though, the baby began to cry.

"She needs her bottle," Vera said, because she had already

stopped nursing, thinking to get pregnant again, and her breasts were as dry as the desert.

"I'll fetch it," said her husband.

"Me too, Poppa," said the three-year-old girl.

"Safer for you to stay here," said the husband.

"Oh, she'll be fine with you," Vera said. So out they went, father and daughter, downstairs. And while they were rummaging in the refrigerator, the men from the boat burst through the back door that opened right into the kitchen. In separate, isolated notes that sounded like instrument solos, those hidden in the closet heard the girl scream, but not too loudly; they heard glass break on the floor; they heard the father pronounce a phrase of prayer in Hebrew and the intruders talk in a jumble of urgent Arabic words. The boy, the six-year-old son, didn't have enough self-control to prevent a gasp.

"Who else is here?" one intruder asked in accented English.

"No one," said the husband, and his words, clear and strong like the muscles in his arms when he worked in the fields, floated up to the hidden ones. "My wife, she is visiting her mother."

"But, Poppa," began the girl in Hebrew in her pure, childish voice.

"Hush, dear one," said the father. And the girl, of course, behaved.

Vera and her son heard the intruders leave with father and child. The old woman sank to the floor of the closet and knelt there trembling. Vera held the baby tight to her chest so she would not cry again, so no one would hear her if she did.

"Hush, dear one," she whispered over and over. "Hush or we'll all be taken. And that is what your daddy, brave and good, forever strong, does not want. That's what he was trying to tell us. Hush, dear one. Hush."

They stayed there in the upstairs closet, the old woman clutching the twigs of a broom, Vera upright and rocking her baby, her son crouched with his head lowered between his knees. They stayed so long that the boy lost all sense of how long they'd been there. He smelled his mother's hot desperation and it reminded him of curdled milk. He smelled the tangy scent of his father that came from the coat he wore for army reserve duty. The boy didn't know it then, but he would never forget those smells.

He waited for his father to return, to tell them it was okay, they were safe, the trespassers gone. He was confident his father would return. In the end, though, his father did not come, but only other men, men speaking Hebrew, saying, "Here we are, it's all right now, all right."

Vera hugging the baby, the old woman clutching the broom, the boy clinging to his father's coat. All three stepped cautiously from the closet, and even before the men spoke, the boy could read the facts in their faces. His father and sister had been shot to death on the narrow beach by their home. And as his mother lowered his sister from her chest, he knew by the way the baby lay that she'd been suffocated. That his mother had killed her trying to prevent her cries.

When dawn broke, his mother stretched out face down on the same beach where his father and sister had fallen. She waited to die too. When that didn't happen—when they re-minded Vera of her son and pulled her inside and gave her pills of calm—she packed her bags. She told her aging parents she was returning to her native land. When they protested, she said, "Yes, I know of pogroms, I know what can happen to a Jew in Russia, but in Russia there is no illusion of safety. No trickery. A mother does not unwittingly become murderer of her children, her husband."

Once Vera and her son got back to Moscow, she no longer mentioned what had happened. Not even when she found she was pregnant, she'd been with child all along on that thirsty, moonless night. Only during the birth of her fourth baby, the one all the neighbors thought was her second and probably il-legitimate, did she break her silence to howl, an unintelligible, guttural sound like waves crashing, so uncontrolled that the nurses summoned the chief doctor to scold her harshly for her lack of courage. They scolded her even as she bled onto the grayish-white sheets, even after the baby was born dead.

$\mathcal{A}$ND I SUPPOSE that was the last loss she could face, that she used up all her emotions then," Goronsky says. "Because after that, even if I kissed her a hundred times, still she could not feel that I was there. And even if I'd wanted to talk about what happened to us, she would have refused."

Caddie's eyes are open now. *Why? Why did you reveal this horror to me? I barely know you. You barely know me.*

He takes her hands. "I knew you'd understand."

She doesn't reply. She can't.

After a moment he stands. She rises, too. This time she leads the way.

At her apartment he trails her up the stairs. She unlocks the door and steps in, allowing him to follow but without invitation, without ceremony. She switches on a light in the living room.

He does not look around her apartment. He watches her as though he knows her well and has been here many times. She knows she should find this irritating, the confident intimacy in his gaze. She finds it hypnotic.

She considers offering him something to drink, rejects the idea. "Excuse me a moment," she says.

She has to be alone. Wash her hands, maybe scrub her face. Try to wipe herself clean somehow. Break the connection between them.

She slips into her bedroom. Leaves the door to the living room open a crack, not wanting to switch on any more lights. Preferring shadows just now.

In the bathroom she turns on the faucet and puts her hands beneath the water. As it spills over her knuckles, her palms, she closes her eyes, drops her head and urges her shoulders to unclench. She tries to thwart thought. A hot shiver arcs over her.

Since they left the bench, Goronsky has not spoken at all; Caddie has said only four words. But even as she dries her hands, she knows how it will be. She knows before she steps back into her bedroom that he will be there.

Their movements then are quick. It is not a celebration in

the revelation of an unknown thigh, the surprise of a new touch. It is the pull of a cord that seals a draw-bag.

He is above her, an airless night. She tastes the salt in the hollow beneath his collarbone.

The shadows that fall into the room are distinct. They slice up his body, and hers, and theirs. She turns her head into her own shoulder. She still smells of tear gas and sweat.

She looks into his face, half-darkened, and sees something in his expression that she's seen before in one war zone or another, though never this close. Something stark and fearless and terrified and desperate. She wants to turn her head, but she can't stop looking.

Then he is lifting her legs to the ceiling, bending them back toward her head and she pushes upward, needing that desperate scared fearlessness inside her, because it already is inside. The sound of breath takes over. She loses track of where her body ends and his begins. She forgets her name.

And as they merge again and again, she understands that her reporter's gift of precise recall will fail her this time. All she'll be left with is a blur. Because, for the first time that she can remember, she's not holding herself in check at all. She has abandoned the one who until now has been her most trusted friend: Caddie the sidelined, cautious observer. This time, she is so much *part* that she cannot locate *apart*. This time, there is no distance from which to watch.

When dawn shadows slip into the room, they separate. Her cheeks are wet, though she can't remember crying, and she's exhausted, as if her bones have been crushed beneath stones.

She never let this happen with Marcus. She doesn't know clearly how it happened now.

But it doesn't matter, none of it. Marcus is dead. She might have been killed with him. Chances are she *will* be killed. Later.

At this moment, only one thing scares her: the sense that something unnamed has been settled between her and Goronsky, that this unlikely coupling has linked them—no, more, lashed them together, as if with a cord of hemp that already twists and tears at her skin.

Five

IT'S AN EARLY DARK. The Egged bus is heavy with the intimacy of a bedroom just before sleep. Men speak without urgency, a woman hums to her baby, even the children have abandoned their bickering in favor of melding into their mothers. They have shrugged off their day in Jerusalem like a heavy coat and are traveling light, in the comfort of dusk, toward their settlement homes. Lulled, all, by the maternal bounce of the bus and the hushed murmuring of voices like moths spreading their wings.

Caddie is among them, among strangers. Moshe, her settler contact and the only person she knows here, sits two seats ahead with the men. Though she has covered her hair with a scarf in hopes of going unnoticed, and though the night has smudged the expressions of faces near her, she is aware of drawing sidelong glances. Everyone knows everyone on this route. These Israelis, in fact, share a bond deeper than mere neighbors, something akin to wagon-train dependency. They are part of a tapestry tightly woven with ideology and religion. She is the mismatched strand of wool—she and the Israeli Arab driver. He, at least, has an acknowledged role.

She stares out the window at the charcoal outline of the Judean Hills. The bus wheels croon. Behind her, two women laugh discreetly.

Here I am, Marcus. Hoping I still believe in this story.

"Now, now," soothes the woman next to her, wearing a stiff wig beneath her scarf. She holds out a hand, offering an open container of square Saltine-like crackers.

Christ. Caddie's been muttering aloud. And worse, she doesn't want to stop. She wants to talk and keep talking until she gets an answer, direct from Marcus. She wants to tell him about Goronsky. Not about his eyes, or his shoulders or the place where his abdomen dips into his groin or the curve of his knees. Not about how often she's been thinking of him— a constant undercurrent that surprises and frightens her. But about her own stupidity.

How did I get so suckered? Haven't I heard a million sad stories? And what about his dark edges—or is it just me, just that everything feels risky right now?

The woman sitting next to Caddie taps her on the arm and pushes the package of crackers forward. "Take one," she urges. "Something in the stomach will settle the nerves *chik chak.*"

Caddie meets her neighbor's gaze. "Widow Murphy," she says.

"What, dear?" the woman asks.

"Someone I used to know," Caddie says. "She did this, too—talk aloud to people none of us could see."

The woman pats Caddie's arm. "Happens to us all, from time to time." She sinks back in her seat and chews another cracker.

Grandma Jos was kind to Widow Murphy, as this woman is being kind to Caddie. Grandma Jos invited the widow for coffee, ignored her private asides to the air and urged Caddie to do the same. "It's Christian," she said. But Caddie defied her, rushing off to work on pretend homework whenever the old woman walked in the door, staying as far away as possible. Fear drove her upstairs. If she had too much contact with wild-eyed people, she knew, she'd become infected and turn wild-eyed herself. "Be careful, girl, because you're susceptible to instability," Grandma Jos once told her. "Your own mother was always more than half crazy. And these things run in the blood." She didn't say—she didn't have to—that this heredi-tary curse came from her disloyal, drifter husband's side of the family.

Now Caddie has proven Grandma Jos right. Though she thought it would happen later, and involve a loss of words in-stead of an overabundance of them: a graying grouchy woman, alone, unable to find the phrase she needed, beating down panic, calling out to bemused passersby in an incomprehensi-ble mix of languages, gibberish misfiring from her no-longer-useful brain. Instead, this falling into—lust, or whatever it is—has made her dumb before her time.

The story, the story must be her anchor, not a hunger for

this barely known man. She has to do what she's always done as a journalist: be here, now. Close all else off.

With effort, she turns her attention to her fellow passengers. In the front, a round-shouldered man with side curls uses a book light to read. Behind her, a young girl sleeps against her mother. Caddie pulls the notepad out of her waist pouch and begins to scrawl in the semidark: "Radio on low. Mood light, peaceful."

A sudden, sharp scent reminiscent of sweat startles her. With her peripheral vision, she sees a circle of flame jump up on the blacktop to the side of the bus. A firebomb, she knows instantly. Everything slips into slow motion. A stone the size of a fist zings through her window. It brushes by her cheek. Glass shards strike her chin, her nose. A Dead Sea sulfur odor pours through the shattered window. Scorched, chemical-laden air stings her throat.

"Stop!" a woman shouts. Her voice jars Caddie.

The Israeli Arab driver pulls to a halt and looks over his shoulder, eyes wide. She hears three sharp cracks. Then comes a long second that's sucked dry of movement, of sound. And the harsh, cracking voice of a boy: "Arabs! Get them."

The woman next to Caddie, her crackers spilled onto the floor, begins to bob her head in mumbled prayer, eyes knotted. For her, it is another time, another country, another convoy of Jews.

"No, don't touch it," implores a woman behind Caddie. Caddie turns to see the girl who had been sleeping moments before. Her face is covered in glass dust. Her mother tries to blow it off and simultaneously restrain the girl's hands.

Caddie touches her own chin involuntarily, and is surprised to see blood color her fingers.

Their bus, Caddie realizes, sits like a giant bull's-eye on the paved road. "Go, go, go," she wants to shout, as Sven shouted to their driver that day.

She doesn't, though. Her words would be useless. Running for cover may be wiser, but these men are swollen and blinded by anger. Their guns are their favored wisdom. Three push out the front door, firing shots. Two others bolt through the rear emergency exit. One woman wraps another's forearm in a flowered headscarf. Blood already seeps through the makeshift bandage. An older man shouts and waves his arms, ordering Caddie and the other women and the children to the floor. She ignores him and rises. The woman who had offered Caddie crackers grabs her arm, trying to pull her down. She jerks away and jumps from the rear of the bus.

The blaze started by the firebomb is burning down, its apricot flames knee-high. Beyond it is the dark of night.

If the attackers had other Molotov cocktails, they would have used them already. Right?

Unless they are hunched down in the hills, selecting their targets. Because now there is more at which to aim: the bus, the men outside, and her.

Can they spot her clearly from the hills, or does she dissolve into the blacktop? She touches her cheekbone, defining her own outline in the dark. If they *can* see her, they will think she's a settler. An enemy. She has lost even the pretense of immunity.

Another round of shooting echoes like a flurry of applause. But it's not as loud as the commotion within her. She has to concentrate to hear. She makes out the sound of footsteps hurtling down the road. Jogging forward, she crouches. Stumbles over a rock, barely catches herself. Scans the hills and sees the silhouette of irregular shapes—ancient boulders or angry men? Too dark to tell.

Her freebies have run out. Of that, she's certain.

Her stomach tightens. If it *is* the time, will she realize she's been hit? Another surge of adrenalin, maybe sixty seconds' worth, before shock turns to pain? Or a midstride of running and then nothing? She hopes not *that*—she'd rather know.

She flashes on an image of a woman she once interviewed, the widow of the soldier who told his commander by walkie-talkie—his last words—"I've been killed."

Her breath comes in short gasps.

She puts a hand to her hair. Her scarf has fallen off, probably back on the bus. Her backpack is there also, under her seat. And her press card, damnit. She turns to look at the bus, its brake lights an eerie yellow. She's out here alone with nothing more than a narrow notepad and two black pens in her waist pouch. But turning back seems as dangerous as going forward. And with less chance of nabbing the story.

She ducks and thinks of an animal scurrying along the road. Her heart presses against her rib cage; her cheeks are clammy. The air is heavy, as though rain waits. Staring into the dark, she remembers: *the face of that Beirut driver. His eyes, specifically. His veiled squint.* The thought propels her forward.

She's upon them so fast she nearly runs into them. A huddle of men, hidden by the shadow of the hills. They swing on her sharply, guns pointed. One fires a shot to her right. She cringes involuntarily. Another jabs her in the side with his rifle and utters something guttural she can't understand. She recognizes it as Hebrew, not Arabic.

"Hold it," she says quickly. "I'm the reporter. The one on the bus with you."

From a brew of muttering, Moshe's impatient voice emerges. "I know her. She's with me." Moshe takes her arm roughly, pulls her back toward the bus. "Though why you would come out here . . ."

"My job," she says.

"Not the place for a woman," he says. "Not the time for an interview."

In a few more steps, they are back. "They got away," Moshe announces to his fellow passengers as they climb on the bus. "They scattered like rabbits." And then the bus is awash in disappointment and disgust—just as, twenty minutes ago, it was bathed in a murmured calm. A quick inventory confirms that although some stitches may be necessary, no one is badly hurt. That does not relieve the tension. Talk boils as booted men kick glass shards into a corner.

"How many were there?"

"Which village, do you think?"

"No more! Time to put an end to this."

Caddie sits directly behind Moshe and jots in her notepad. She tries to be inconspicuous, though she probably doesn't need to, so caught up are the passengers in their shared fury as they jostle back to their seats. They've forgotten her.

After several minutes of talk unrelieved by the sound of an engine starting up, someone points out that their driver is no longer among them. Apparently more afraid of the enraged settlers than of losing his job, he has fled into the night. Men begin to guffaw; one strides to the front to drive the bus home. And now, although the mother has not resumed her humming, the vehicle is filling with a sense of satisfaction: their womenfolk and children have been attacked this evening, but they've managed to scare at least one Arab in return.

When the bus begins to move, Moshe leans back and speaks with more candor than Caddie would expect. "Slimy bastards," he says, slapping his knee. "Next time they'll kill one of us. *Again*, they'll kill one of us. We've got to get them first." In her presence Moshe is usually smooth and calm, full of pious concern for the world. But now he's forgotten she's a reporter—or no longer cares.

A man twists in his seat to answer Moshe. His forehead is as white and shiny as a boiled egg. "The devil's insects stir things whenever they can," he says, wiggling his thick fingers. "We'll squash them."

Noticing Caddie watching, he scowls and, with deliberation, turns away.

. . .

At his settlement, Moshe gets off the bus first, waits for Caddie and hands her a damp handkerchief. "Wipe the blood off your chin," he says.

She takes it. "Thanks."

He waves dismissively. "Don't want to needlessly frighten my children."

They pass together through the yellow barrier gate that controls entrance into the enclave. Before them spills a neighborhood of straight streets, orderly homes. An armed guard sitting on a watchtower waves down at them. *"Shalom,"* he calls to Moshe.

"So?" Caddie asks as she jams the stained handkerchief into her pocket. "Tonight?"

"What?"

"You're going to respond?"

He widens his eyes for her benefit. "What do you mean?"

"C'mon, Moshe. Teach them a lesson, send a message, however you want to phrase it. Because if you are, I'd like to come."

"We're good men trying to protect our families."

His voice has changed since he got off the bus. This is the modulated Moshe that she must get beyond, the wallpaper she needs to peel off. "I was with you tonight," she says. "I survived it, too." She stops then, halted by a sudden clarity about what she needs to write. "Revenge is a physical craving, like for food or sleep," she says. "Your mind may say you don't need it, you don't want it. But your body insists you do."

He stares with candid curiosity. It surprises her, too, frankly, this intensity that unfolds as she speaks.

"Let's discuss it later." Moshe's tone is removed now. "I don't want to worry my family." Then, with a cautious sideways look, he turns and strides away.

She's glad to follow a few steps behind, caught up as she is in this idea. A rush of excitement moves to her chest, her cheeks.

She's been a fine reporter, sure. She can smell a lie, nail the lead in a second, find a fresh take on yet another tragedy. She's an attentive listener and can get anyone to spill his stuff during an interview. But those barriers that she's put up, necessary barriers, may have sometimes, she sees now, gotten in the way of the story.

Maybe this time she can write something that will compensate for the other half-stories. A piece that will show intimately how violence shreds sleep and appetite and memory, disfiguring those it leaves behind. A story that will get close enough to give vengeance a human face. Maybe that's what she is supposed to do with all this anger and frustration and loss.

The door to Moshe's home is slightly ajar. The noise of children floods out. Moshe reaches out to touch and kiss the *mezuzah.* "*Shalom,*" he calls as they step inside. They enter a living room illuminated by a single hooded lamp. One worn couch, two overstuffed chairs. A child's Torah in a corner, along with a rusted Tonka truck and a homemade doll with brown yarn hair. A small face peeks around the corner, stares at Caddie, then disappears. "Ah, I smell dinner," Moshe says in such a sitcom voice that Caddie wants to groan aloud. After a moment, a woman comes in wearing a chocolate-colored skirt that reaches her ankles. A vibrant, multicolored silk scarf covers most of her auburn hair, making her seem a reluctant frontierswoman. Moshe looks past her as he says, "My wife."

Caddie remembers Moshe telling her that this wife was born in the States, Massachusetts, she thinks. "Hi. I'm Caddie. And you're . . . ?"

"Sarah," says Moshe, as though she can't be trusted to pronounce her own name. Caddie would stomp on the foot of such a husband, but Sarah doesn't react. "I'm going to get cleaned up," Moshe says, and leaves them alone.

"Thanks so much for having me for the night," Caddie says.

"The night?" says Sarah. "Of course." Her scarf is tied under her hair in a large knot like an unnatural flower blooming at the back of her neck. Three children hover. A long minute inches by. "We'll eat soon," Sarah says. "Would you like some water? Or juice?" Her voice is soft but hoarse, like a heavy smoker's.

"Water would be fine."

Sarah motions Caddie into the dining room, where the table is set, then excuses herself. A few moments later one of the older boys, maybe twelve, with the onset of acne and a refusal to meet her eyes, brings Caddie a glass of water. She takes a sip. Lukewarm, it slides down her throat reluctantly. He silently stands before her, arms hanging limply. "So," she says, "how long have you lived here?"

"Year." He's looking at her right ear. "About."

"And before that?"

"Kiryat Arba," he names another settlement.

"Are there many children in this neighborhood? Do you go to *yeshiva* here?"

Two questions at once have been too much. The boy looks at his feet while nodding quickly, a gesture that could mean anything, then slips out of the room.

Within minutes, the family begins gathering at the table. No one introduces her. Only the little ones even glance at her directly. "Sit, sit." Moshe speaks to her in a large voice, gesturing to an empty chair.

Caddie counts the children—seven—as they follow Moshe's lead in intoning a blessing. *"Baruch ata Adonai Elohainu . . ."* Their faces remind her of marshmallows: pale and spongy. She takes a few bites from her plate, then looks around in vain for salt or pepper. The food, by appearance, texture and flavor, is tasteless and unrecognizable. But no one asks her if she needs anything. She pretends to eat. She's not hungry anyway. She wonders if, despite all these children, sex between Moshe and Sarah is as bland as the food; then she banishes the thought as Moshe asks each child in turn what he or she has learned that day and they rise to their feet to tell him. The younger ones recite phrases from the Torah; the older ones reflect on their meanings. Only the baby is exempt. Moshe strokes his wispy beard and nods as each one speaks. His smile is subdued, but his eyes speak of pride. This ritual, Caddie suspects, is his primary contribution to child-rearing. Sarah looks up from her plate only to spoon food into the baby's mouth.

After dinner, Moshe nods at his wife as he leaves the dining room. Caddie jumps to follow him, but he steps into a room and closes the door firmly behind him. The bathroom, perhaps? She returns to the dining table and starts to help clear it until the oldest boy, looking like a bird ready to give flight, waves his arms and mumbles something about *kashrut*. Of course. As with every religion, there are laws, and in this case they concern separation of dairy and meat products. Special flatware and dishes, special sinks and special sponges, dish towels and drain racks. There can be no merging. If a mistake occurs, whole sets of dishes may have to be tossed. They don't want to bother explaining and then checking to make sure she does it right.

She returns to the living room. There are no books or magazines, so she sits, then rises to look out the window. She opens a hall closet, looking idly for Moshe's rifle. He has one stashed somewhere, she's sure. At least one. But this closet holds only coats.

She takes a few steps down the hallway. "Moshe?" No one answers. In the kitchen, Sarah and her children are still washing dishes. Caddie tentatively opens the door that Moshe disappeared behind. It leads to a small mudroom and, beyond it, the street. Moshe is gone; he's given her the slip.

She eases out the door. The settlement, surrounded by barbed wire, is stripped down like a version of a toy town with blacktop streets, a gas station, a playground. The identical five dozen red-roofed houses look spacious by Jerusalem standards. No obvious clues as to where Moshe might be.

Outside one home, a light is on, and a woman kneels over a planted pot by her front door. *"Shalom,"* Caddie calls as she approaches. The fact that she's passed the guard and is inside indicates she is an invited guest, and that should give her some measure of acceptance. She hopes it's enough.

"Shalom." The woman straightens, but she's hesitant, searching Caddie's face.

"I'm Catherine Blair." Caddie holds out a hand. "I'm visiting Moshe Bar Lev. He's gone to a meeting and I'm supposed to be there, too, but," she shakes her head, touches one hand to her forehead and smiles, "I've forgotten the house number." She waits. The woman says nothing, glancing down at a handful of herbs she holds in her hand. "Do you know, perhaps?" Caddie asks at last.

The woman shakes her head slowly. "Why don't you ask Sarah?"

"Of course. She was busy with the children, so I thought— but now I guess—" She motions toward Moshe's home.

The woman nods. "That would be best."

Caddie staves off a moment of doubt. These endless awkward requests, this shuffling around in foreign neighborhoods and living rooms, this thrusting of herself into settings where she's so clearly the outsider, if not the enemy. Why does she do it?

She once thought that she'd become a journalist out of an entirely personal impulse: the need to observe people who were, on some level, more *real* than she. People who enmeshed themselves in a community instead of observing it. Who kept address books with names of friends, not contacts. Who shared confidences, talked about feelings, groaned about getting together with family on holidays. People she might have been. People she still might be under certain carefully controlled circumstances—though she doubts it.

Right now, though, she's not interested in comparing herself to others, or in imagining a different life. She wants the story. And the story, undeniably, is taking place beyond her reach.

She walks back to Moshe's house, feeling the neighbor's eyes upon her. The phone rings as she enters. Hearing the murmur of a girl's voice, she strains to listen but can't make out a word. After a few minutes, she peeks into the kitchen—no one there—and begins to walk down the hallway, calling out, "Hello?" No one answers. All doors are shut. She raps on one. The oldest boy opens it, the boy full of elbows who fled at her questions.

"Sorry to trouble you," Caddie says. "I was looking for your father. Or mother."

The boy's eyes, fastened somewhere to the right of her cheek, widen as though she'd asked whether he drinks wine for breakfast. Without a word, he walks down the hall through the kitchen and slips into another room that must be a walk-in pantry. He closes the door in her face.

She raises a fist to knock there, too, but before she can, Sarah opens it and comes out, wiping her hands on her apron, her eyebrows raised in question. The son follows, and hurries away.

"Still working, are you?" Caddie asks. "Don't you ever long for a microwave or dishwasher?"

Sarah's smile is so slight as to resemble a grimace. "We set our priorities, Moshe and I."

"Yes, Moshe," Caddie says. "He forgot to tell me where the meeting is. Can you direct me?"

"Meeting?" Sarah shrugs. She reaches in her apron's pocket as though looking for something, but comes out empty-handed.

"Wherever they usually meet, then?"

"He'll probably be home soon."

"I really can't miss this," Caddie says. "I'm working on a story, and I need it to be—"

"I can't help you." Sarah's tone is disinterested.

Sarah: a woman married to a man who won't even let her introduce herself. Gravity already defines the shape of her cheek. Her thick lashes, which might have been glamorous, are camel-like. She would never do anything her husband might not like. This avenue is useless.

"Well, then," says Caddie, "maybe I can help *you* with something?" Her gesture includes the whole kitchen. Sarah's expression is startled, uncertain. "Better than sitting around." Caddie offers a smile. "Surely you have something even a goy journalist can do?"

Sarah studies her a moment. "I'm getting ready to make bread," she says finally. "I'm always happy for an extra set of hands."

Bread-making. Oh, great. But Caddie follows Sarah into the oversized pantry, which is also a workroom. She dusts her hands with flour and begins kneading, tentative at first. Then she uses greater force. She punches the rubbery dough, throws it onto the table and pounds it. Her fisted right hand grows rhythmic, unyielding, furious. The dough will have to amend itself, not Caddie. The dough will have to give up.

Caddie notices Sarah watching with the same curious expression Moshe had during their walk home from the bus. She eases off the kneading.

"I heard about Lebanon," Sarah says abruptly. "About what happened to you there."

It's a sideswipe Caddie hadn't expected. "How—?" Caddie breaks off.

"Moshe." Sarah looks down, avoiding Caddie's eyes. "He says it must have made you more sympathetic to us."

So that's what Moshe thinks, is it? That's how she got permission to spend the night here. Still, being ambushed and almost killed didn't boost her credentials quite enough, did it? Wasn't good enough to get her into that damn meeting. And if she says, oh yes, now she can understand so much more clearly how the settlers feel, how attacked and beleaguered, will Sarah then tell her where the meeting is? Wasn't she thinking, only a few hours ago, that she would do anything, say anything, to gain access, to get this story?

Well, on second thought, that's a hunk of meat she's not going to chew.

Caddie begins to ask questions, half-idly, like a tennis pro warming up: Where do the kids go to school? Where does Sarah do her shopping? How did she meet Moshe? Then she makes it a little lower and deep to the backhand. Was it hard to adjust to a constant undercurrent of tension? How are the children affected? Does she ever have moments of doubt, when she sees it from another viewpoint? Moshe would handle these questions smoothly, a simple lob with no real glimpse of what he thinks. Caddie waits for Sarah's response, hoping she'll dump one into the waiting net.

"This place is as connected to me as my arm or leg," Sarah says, her voice expanding to fill the small room, taking on a richer tenor for the first time in Caddie's presence. "Four of my children were born in this home. No one will drive me out. I *will* fight if I have to. So will most of my neighbors."

Four children born here? Sarah's son said they'd lived here only a year. Of course, the habit of sources to stretch the truth is one of the few facts of this beat. Caddie doesn't bother to challenge her. After several minutes of silence, Sarah coughs and asks Caddie a few questions, all containing the word *not.* "Are you not married? Do you not want a family?" It isn't disapproval she exudes exactly. More the sense that Caddie is an alien creature, beyond understanding.

"Time to let them rise," Sarah says at last, covering the loaves with damp rags. They move into the pristine kitchen and Sarah puts on water for tea.

Caddie sits at the table. "I understand you're not going to tell me," she says, "but I know that *you* know where they're holding this meeting." Sarah, expressionless, brings the sugar over to the kitchen table. "I could tell by your eyes. You're an awful liar."

A brief look of bemusement slides over Sarah's face and, for a second, she looks younger. "That's what my husband says, too."

"It's not a bad thing, to be a lousy liar."

Sarah waves her hand as though to brush away the charge. "It implies naïveté."

"You're not naïve. You can't be, if you live out here." Caddie runs her fingers through her hair. "This isn't an easy life, but you meet it head-on. You've made a place for yourself."

"I love it here."

This settlement jammed in the midst of hostile territory is not a place Caddie could stomach for long. She is aware, though, of a tightening in her chest, a distant ache, a desire she doesn't even want to name. Things seem simpler here, somehow. You get married, have a family, choose a side. All of it with conviction. All of it for life.

One of Sarah's daughters, about ten years old, comes into the kitchen and sits near her mother.

"Isn't there anything you miss from the States?" Caddie asks Sarah. "Something from childhood?"

"Nothing important."

"Okay, unimportant then."

Sarah gazes out the window, though it is now too dark to see anything. Then her eyes settle on her daughter's face. "Dunkin' Donuts."

"Food groups of our childhood. For me, it was beef jerky. Long sticks of it, from the corner store," Caddie says.

Sarah smooths her scarf with one hand. "When I was twelve, I wrote a poem about Dunkin' Donuts."

Caddie clears her throat. "A poem?"

"I remember, Ema," the girl says. "You won a twenty-five-dollar savings bond."

"Pretty silly, really." Sarah sounds as if she already regrets having said anything this revealing in front of a stranger, a foreigner.

"No, no," Caddie says. "It's just—unexpected. You remember any of it?"

Sarah grimaces, shakes her head.

"I think *I* do." The daughter giggles. "I remember the end.

The powdered, the glazed, the jelly stick.

Each could be my favorite.

But dear Dunkin' Donuts, best of all,

Thanks for making that crème-filled ball."

Caddie chuckles, which seems permissible.

Sarah laughs, too, then shakes her head. "No more talk of doughnuts." Her voice holds finality but her face, Caddie notices, looks softer, her cheek and mouth muscles more relaxed. "Ruthie," she says, stroking her daughter's hair, "you get to bed."

The daughter kisses her mother, but lingers. The three of them are still at the table when Moshe comes in. He seems surprised to see Caddie sitting in the kitchen with his wife and daughter. He looks at Sarah carefully. Sarah rises, asks him how he is and begins to clean up the tea glasses. It is clear the women's conversation is finished.

"So?" Caddie asks Moshe.

"We've decided on a letter to the prime minister."

"I'd hoped to attend any meetings." She allows some irritation into her voice, but she can't show him how pissed off she is or she'll get nothing at all.

"It was a closed session," he says. "I can tell you about it, though. We talked, we formed a committee, we took a vote. We'll write the letter tonight and then we'll collect signatures."

"That's all? A letter?"

"The prime minister governs a coalition. The right sort of pressure from us could trigger a no-confidence vote. I think we'll be heard."

It sounds as unconvincing as a spokesman's sound bite. "I expected a more direct warning," Caddie says.

Moshe raises his eyebrows, ostentatious in his amusement. "You've been persuaded by some caricature of us as Orthodox Tarzans, swinging from trees, eager to claim an eye for an eye." He tilts his head, a half-smile sweeping briefly over his face as though he enjoys that unlikely image of himself. Then he shakes his head and goes on, "Actually, we're very reasonable. All we want is safe roads. Our Israeli military and political machine can accomplish that, if called upon."

There's a soft knock at the door. Moshe opens it to a bespectacled man so thin he seems to drift within his clothes. "This is Joseph," Moshe says. "We are drafting the letter together. You are welcome to stay with us, if you want to see us *in action*." He chuckles.

Joseph looks more like a Talmudic scholar than a social activist. The *tzitzit* of his prayer shawl hang below his shirt. He doesn't meet her eyes, and she knows better than to offer him a hand to shake. When he speaks, she can barely hear him. He and Moshe talk about language, about words from the Torah that will best remind the prime minister of his responsibility to his people.

It's an intellectual exercise, nothing more. To believe this will change anything is delusional. But who isn't, in this region, deluding himself about something? Still, she doesn't want to see some sanitized version of justice. She wants to see *getting even*.

Caddie listens for ten minutes, then excuses herself and goes to the bedroom she is sharing with two of the daughters. Lights are out, the girls asleep in one bed, leaving the other for her. She slips out of her jeans and into sweatpants. Despite the open window, it's stuffy in the way of overcrowded places, too hot to lie beneath the covers.

She stands for a moment over the girls, about four and six years old. How similar they look at this age. She wonders when their faces will begin to betray their differences. She's seen it before, usually by adolescence—a way of pursing lips or folding arms, a certain shine in an eye. Subtle indicators that reveal to the attentive observer which child is defiant and which is innocent; who is quick and who slow-witted. Perhaps, even—though she's never looked for this trait before—

what sort of bravery a child has: the kind that would allow her to avenge a killing, or permit her to turn away.

For the moment, though, these characteristics are submerged. The younger girl murmurs in her sleep and rolls closer to her sister, her face smooth. How secure they still feel, falling asleep each night to the same sounds within—quiet breathing in the crowded house, the sighing of the walls—and the same sounds without—the crackle of walkie-talkies as the armed and watchful settlers carry out their patrols.

BREAKFAST THE NEXT MORNING is rushed and foggy—both Moshe and Sarah are up, although only Caddie will take the dawn bus into Jerusalem. Moshe hands her a copy of the letter he says will go to the prime minister. He worked until two, or so he claims, though he seems damned perky. Caddie's legs ache and she longs for a strong, hot cup of coffee. She won't allow herself to think of this visit as a waste. But she missed an opportunity, no denying that.

Sarah gives Caddie herbal tea and a pumpkin muffin for breakfast, then hands her another muffin and a banana for the bus ride home.

"I look forward to seeing what you write," Moshe says, his tone formal.

Caddie doesn't reveal that she won't write anything yet. "I may call you with some questions. And I'd still like to sit in on one of your meetings. Get a firsthand view of your decision process."

Moshe acts as though she hasn't spoken. He takes Sarah by the arm and they walk her to the door. "*Shalom.* Safe trip." His voice rings out, falsely hearty.

Caddie glances back once. They stand together, waving, as she heads toward the bus stop. A sham of a tableau. It disturbs her. She thinks about Goronsky, and about the danger of promises between couples. Deep and lasting is only a momentary trick of the light, she suspects—everything in her life so far would back that up. Maybe those who try to make vows end up with a lie—or monotony, and that's just as bad. Living a consistent, predictable life is deadly, she knows from her teenage years. It would have killed her long before she met up with any ambusher in Lebanon.

The bus grumbles to a stop. She settles into an empty seat, joining fewer than a dozen settlers headed into Jerusalem early. The hills that rise next to the road seem, this morning, timeless rather than terrifying. The tawny dawn desert is pristine, cheerful even. Enviably wiped clean of yesterday's losses and sorrows.

Six

WHEN SHE ARRIVES HOME from Moshe's, there he is, leaning against her apartment door. She opens her mouth to speak, but fine sand seems to coat her throat, making it impossible. She nods at him silently and he straightens. His eyes are nearly black this morning. His shoulders are wider and higher than she'd remembered. She feels him watch her as she shifts the mail into her left arm, unlocking the door. She knows she's breathing too quickly. She's aware of his eyes slipping from her hands to her face and back down. She notices, again, that salt-and-wind scent he seems to carry.

She swallows audibly, embarrassingly. "Want to come in?"

He clears his throat. "Would it be uncomfortable?"

"Of course not." She hopes it sounds casual. He nods and lowers his face so his eyes are washed out, but she catches the expression of satisfaction on his lips. She's not sure she wants to please him. "I've got to get to the office. But I need coffee first."

Maybe it's her abrupt tone that causes him to revert to formality. "My visit is too much trouble right now?" he repeats.

"You can drink coffee, too. If you want." She pushes open the door. "Or not."

He glances away, toward the building's central stairs. "I thought—since you weren't home last night—"

Damned awkwardness. She works at making her voice lighthearted. "For God's sake. Come in."

She steps aside and watches him enter. The first time Marcus came to her apartment, he switched on all the lights, walked around and studied her possessions from different angles, his head tilted slightly, his attention taut, as if he were preparing to take a still life. He kept silent. Sometimes he touched things, but so carefully as to leave them unmoved. Occasionally he paused to scan her face, and she had the sense that he was assessing her freshly based on what she owned, what she didn't. The way he carried out his inspection, it became a sort of undressing.

This is Goronsky's second visit to her apartment, and neither time has he glanced at anything. It's as though her physical surroundings are irrelevant, or else thoroughly known. His eyes stay on her.

She takes a deep breath, giving him her back as she closes the door, and turns to find herself in his arms. She stiffens for a second, then wills her brain to be still, go blank. She wants—painfully wants—to let everything go and drown herself in the ocean in front of her, to sink into this man who won't be shocked by the things she's seen and touched, the things she can't forget.

Somewhere in the midst of their merging, he pauses and smooths her hair away from her face. "There's nothing to be sorry for," he says. Only then does she realize she was apologizing aloud; she doesn't tell Goronsky the appeal for forgiveness was not intended for him. For Marcus, maybe, though she's not even sure about that.

She loses track of time and can't say how much has passed before they roll away from one another. She only knows she must break this addiction before it gets dangerous, if she still can. "Now for that coffee," she says.

"I'll help."

"No." She pulls on her shirt, tugs on her jeans. "Stay."

She picks her mail up from the floor and takes it with her to the kitchen. She puts everything down except the most tempting piece: a package from London with the name of Marcus's parents in the left-hand corner. She feels its weight and rests her hand on the manila wrapping for a moment before she puts on coffee. Glancing through the wide opening from the kitchen to the living room, she sees Goronsky, dressed now but with shirt unbuttoned, extended on her couch. He seems so at ease that it startles her. "Make yourself at home."

He smiles. "Thank you."

She has that sense, again, of being at a loss for small talk. "It's percolating." She gestures behind her. "I'm going to look at my mail." Then she grimaces. Why does she feel the need to explain this to *him?*

She positions herself at the kitchen table out of Goronsky's view. Again she lingers over the package from Marcus's parents. She's never met them. Sven must have given them her address. Perhaps Sven told them about talking to her. Perhaps they are sending something intended to soothe, to dissuade her from any plans to return to Lebanon.

"How do you want your coffee?" she calls, still staring at the cursive handwriting on the package. Goronsky doesn't answer. "Hey, you there?" She returns to the living room. He's asleep, but holding himself tightly in his slumber, like a soldier on a battlefield, full of distrust, ready to leap up at any minute. Marcus slept sprawled—as if he were an accident victim, she told him once. Every part of him exposed, unafraid.

She should shake Goronsky awake, send him on his way, then go to the office. Instead, she sits in a chair across from him. She watches him, which is so much easier to do when his eyes are closed. The night he was here, she didn't watch him sleep. She can't even remember if they *did* sleep. If she dozed at all, it must have been blitz-like, consuming, a crossing over into a lost moment before slipping back into wakefulness.

One arm is tucked close to his body. The other arcs over his head, the hand palm-down. She notices again his fingers, long and narrow like a pianist's. The lines of his muscles beneath his shirt. His neck above his collar. She feels a flash of heat, low, and she looks away, concentrating on slowing her breathing.

She turns back to watch his face, a merging of feminine and masculine, curved and chiseled. She doesn't think she'll be found out—he seems so thoroughly gone. She inches closer. Above his square chin, his lips are parted. They flutter as though beginning to form a word. His eyelids are like sun on icicles, translucent. His pupils dart beneath them.

His hair is unnaturally soft, like a child's. She recalls it brushing against her neck and puts her hand to her own collarbone. The stubble on his cheeks is stiff; that she remembers. It left a rash on her face. She considers stroking his cheek now, touching his lips.

She drops her hands instead, squeezes the padded surface of her chair and waits for the impulse to pass. Then she leaves him and goes to the kitchen, to the waiting package from Marcus's parents.

The way it arrived, wrapped in brown paper, strikes her as funereal. But she caresses it as if it were a present. Then she can't delay any more: she rips it open. Inside is a journal—one of the four or five Marcus kept, each with a different cover. She never looked in them. Sometimes when she spent the night at his place, she awoke to find him at the kitchen table, hair sticking up in funny places, photos fanned out on the table, glue and scissors and a pen at his side. He didn't jump up or act embarrassed, just closed the notebook and gathered his stuff, grinning all the while, talking about the predawn light or the universal language of morning garbage trucks. When she'd ask, "Whatchadoin?" running it all together to make it casual, he'd make some vague reply or change the subject. And she'd let it go. Because this was, after all, the kernel of their relationship. No crowding.

Holding the journal in her hands now, Caddie's stomach coils. The enormity of this violation of Marcus, her possessing his private journal, brings to mind other violations since he died. Violations of his memory and his work—the piece in *Newsweek* that felt so false, including the photo of him, when what he would have wanted was a photo *by* him. And violations of his limp body. Gripping the journal, Caddie sees the vision she'd buried almost the minute it occurred. Out there on that dirt road, after it happened, somebody pulled up in a pickup, somebody brave or stupid, she never found out which. Their driver, that pockmarked man with his squinty eyes, seized Marcus's shoulders while Sven, his face half-averted, hauled Marcus's feet, and together they lugged him to the back of that passing truck. Such a violation, the way they clutched his body, letting their hands fall anywhere they could get a grip, squeezing their fingers tight. That driver, especially, so close to Marcus's face.

It matters, even now, that the driver handled Marcus like an ungainly piece of furniture. Though it shouldn't, since clearly that wasn't Marcus anymore. This was the first time Caddie had ever experienced it in quite that way—someone *with her* the moment before, *with her* so intimately she could imagine licking the sweat from the pulse points on those perfect wrists of his, and then so gone, so not Marcus.

She'd stood beside the Land Rover stiff, immobile. And Sven had come back and led her into the front seat—no, more like lifted her. That's the last moment she remembers before the hospital in Cyprus.

She missed Marcus's burial. She missed the memorial service. If only she'd had the presence of mind to get the name of their driver, or even of the driver of the passing pickup truck. Or if she'd written down exactly where they were at the time of the ambush. That way, she could go back there again— alone, if she had to.

Goronsky, she sees from the kitchen doorway, is still sleeping, so she returns to Marcus's journal. She hesitates, then opens the note on top, a sheet of creamy paper folded in half.

Dear Caddie, Thank you for your letter after our son's death. My husband and I know your loss, too, is great. We thought you might like this. Please find us when you next come to London. Sincerely, Marilyn Lancour.

She tries to picture Marcus's mother wrapping this journal, this piece of her son, to send to a woman she'd never met. Marcus kept a photograph of his mother, but it's a blur in Caddie's memory. A smallish woman with blond hair, maybe. Or was it brown? She tends to forget the details of people's framed family photos, which always look so similar.

Surely his parents—his mother, at least—decided to give Caddie this journal for some reason. This one in particular. She goes to the sink to get water, then lifts the journal. It's the size of a school binder and surprisingly soft, covered with rust-colored leather. She lowers her face to inhale, hoping for a scent of Marcus. There is none, of course. He had no scent, he always told her. Skeptical, she'd sniffed his shirts a couple times and, in fact, found nothing except the smells of the places he'd been. No matter how he ran and lifted and perspired, he remained remarkably without odor.

Curiosity finally wins out over respect for the dead—as maybe it always does—and she opens to the first page. A photo of her, standing among five men holding Kalashnikov rifles. One appears to be leering; the others look serious. She is grinning jauntily at the camera. Underneath the photo, in Marcus's scrawl: "Catherine. March 1998."

So this is one of his later journals, begun a little over two years ago. She'd nearly forgotten that quick trip into the southern zone of Lebanon. She can't remember the story she'd been chasing, but she does recall the two of them stopping at a roadside stand, sharing a warm Sprite, leaning into one another and laughing over nothing: the dust that had settled in the hollow at the base of her neck, the tickle of the soda bubbles in her throat.

She studies the photo again. Beneath the date, he had jotted something else: "It's not war she's wary of."

Sitting baldly on the page, those half-dozen words stop her breath. They look like an indictment. They remind her of the conversation she and Marcus had in the hotel bar the night before the ambush, when he told her she'd never settle for real life.

But they'd agreed, she and Marcus. They'd agreed on keeping their relationship casual. On not wasting time talking about it, or even considering it too closely. And on keeping it hidden as much as possible from their colleagues. It had been a mutual call, she's certain.

Her hands, she notices, are shaking.

She can't do this now, not with anyone else in her apartment, and certainly not Goronsky, even a sleeping Goronsky.

She rises quietly, goes to her bedroom and stuffs Marcus's journal under her bed. Then she calls Jon to check in.

"Hey," Jon says. "Did you get my e-mail? I was hoping to hear from you. Did you pick up anything from your settlers on the trouble?"

"What trouble?" She should have logged in, read the news.

"Last night."

She draws in a breath. "Bus attack, that's all I saw, but don't mention it to the foreign desk, okay? No dead, no big deal. I'm going to use it in a feature, and I don't want Mike coming down on me, handing out more rules about what I am and am not allowed to cover." She pauses. "What are *you* talking about?"

"A couple things. A house was torched in a Palestinian village near your buddy Moshe's settlement. And just outside Jerusalem, a Palestinian woman and her daughter were gunned down in their home. They were from an old Jerusalem family whose sons are supposedly Fatah fighters, half of them in jail. Silwadi is the name, I think—something like that."

"Sounds familiar," she says.

"Anyway, in both cases the Pals are blaming your settlers."

"Stop calling them mine."

"The Israelis deny it," Jon goes on. "Internal disputes between the Arabs, they say. Nothing to do with them. But I thought you might have heard something."

Her cheeks flush hot. "Shit, Jon." She can't believe Moshe's group is behind the two deaths, but torching a home is another matter. She wonders if Moshe pulled a fast one.

"Hey, don't worry about it. I'm just doing a couple hundred words and I thought maybe."

"Let me make a couple calls," she says in a rush. "I'll get back to you."

She dials Moshe's office, gets the machine. She won't leave a message. He might not return her call, and he'll be rehearsed if he does. She'd rather catch him off guard.

As she hangs up, the doorbell rings. It's Ya'el, purse slung over one arm, her expression determined. Caddie flushes. When she last saw Ya'el two days ago, Caddie was walking in from covering the clashes—distracted, soot on her pants, hair in disarray. Ya'el looked at her strangely but didn't, thank the heavens, have time to talk.

Now Ya'el gives her a hug. "I drove up for lunch break and saw your car. Come on up and eat with me, okay?" Then she sees Goronsky, who is sitting up, buttoning his shirt. "Sorry. Am I bothering you? Barging in, bad timing . . ."

Goronsky offers an unembarrassed smile.

"I met him on a story," Caddie says, introducing him. She doesn't try to explain what he is doing sleeping, disheveled, on her couch at midmorning. She doesn't *have* an explanation for that. "My neighbor, Ya'el Givon," she says to Goronsky, glancing at him briefly, then looking away.

"Forgive me for falling asleep," he says. He rises. Caddie watches him stretch his arms.

"Yes, it's pretty unusual to find someone snoozing on Caddie's couch," Ya'el says. "Sometimes I think *Caddie* doesn't even sleep here. She's always running around, one story or another." She laughs. "Where's home?" she asks Goronsky.

"Good question," Goronsky says. Then he doesn't say anything else, his gaze resting in some middle distance.

Ya'el gives Caddie a raised-eyebrow glance. "So?" she prompts Goronsky after a moment.

"I was born in Moscow."

"And what do you do?"

Caddie wants to hear him say he's a professor again. She wants to see if she believes it this time around.

"Sorry for being nosy," Ya'el goes on after a long moment, but it doesn't sound like an apology.

Goronsky rubs his forehead as though trying to soften the creases. "I'm a professor." It still sounds like a lie.

"Of what?" Ya'el asks.

Goronsky studies Ya'el. Caddie wonders if Ya'el has the same sense she did the first time, of being absorbed by those eyes, but Ya'el's face shows nothing.

"Psychology," Goronsky says.

"Really? With which university?"

"Moscow State University."

"Hmm. How long have you been here?"

"Eight months," Goronsky says. The answer is a surprise. They never talked about it, but Caddie had assumed, somehow, that he'd arrived more recently.

"And you're here because . . . ?" Ya'el asks.

Goronsky's cheek muscles are starting to look strained. Not everyone is accustomed to neighbors like Caddie's, who consider everyone's business their own.

"Ya'el," Caddie says, a warning in her voice, but Goronsky waves his hand.

"I'm working on a study," he says slowly, "for the Russian government."

"On psychology?"

"On extremism." He enunciates each syllable precisely.

"Extremism." Ya'el studies him a minute.

"Yeah, and now—" Caddie begins, but Ya'el ignores her.

"You go around psychoanalyzing the right-wingers?"

He shrugs. "Both ends of the spectrum. The people we call extremists often start out like us. Then something happens to them, something they feel would be immoral to ignore."

"So they're more *moral* than the rest of us?" Ya'el laughs.

Goronsky shrugs again.

Ya'el turns to Caddie. "And what are you interviewing him for?" She smiles, but she's being annoyingly persistent.

"He was able to provide some information I needed on medical supplies at the Gaza hospital," Caddie says. She sounds formal, she knows, and defensive. She hopes Ya'el will take the hint and leave.

"Medical supplies?" Ya'el's voice rises in surprise. "So it's not only psychology that interests you?"

A look of impatience floods Goronsky's face for a second before being replaced by a smile. "It's broad," he says.

"Must be." Ya'el is usually so warm—too quick, in Caddie's view, to treat strangers as family—but now she's cool, slit-eyed.

"Ya'el," Caddie says, "how about some coffee? Or do you have to get going?"

Ya'el shakes her head. "So, how much longer will you be in Israel?" she asks Goronsky.

"Not sure yet." Now, instead of speaking slowly, Goronsky runs the words together. "You have a young child, I take it?"

The non sequitur seems to surprise Ya'el as much as it does Caddie. She hesitates before answering. "Two, actually." Now her look, Caddie sees, is even more cautious.

"And you are a bookkeeper? An accountant?"

"I work at Bank Leumi," Ya'el says. "I help new customers, usually people who have recently made *aliya*. You know what that is?"

"Of course." Goronsky sits down again and looks at Caddie. He is suddenly—but clearly—oblivious of Ya'el. Caddie has felt flattered by the way Goronsky seems to shut out everything else when he focuses on her. In front of Ya'el, though, it's embarrassing.

Ya'el looks back and forth between them. "Well," she says, and she draws the word out. "So since you have company—or is this an interview?—well, anyway, you probably can't—"

"Actually, I've just spoken with my office," Caddie says. "I've got to make a couple calls and rush in. Sorry."

"Hey, it's okay," says Ya'el, her voice finally warming again. She steps closer to Caddie and half-turns her back to Goronsky. "So we didn't get to talk after you came in from some godforsaken clash the other day. What are you working on, anyway?"

Caddie considers trying to explain briefly the story she envisions, the effect of violence, the context, the layers. "Settlers," she says, opting for simplicity. "Spent last night at a settlement with a family."

"Sounds like a nightmare," Ya'el says. "Sleeping with our fringe element."

Caddie shrugs. "It's an interesting time. They're like cornered animals right now."

Ya'el's eyebrows rise. "That's what's dangerous."

"It's manageable."

"You're out of touch with what's manageable," Ya'el says.

"Well, don't worry," Caddie says. "The settlers haven't exactly warmed up to me. They aren't letting me in much."

"Good." Ya'el hugs Caddie, puts a hand on the doorknob but then doesn't open it. She looks again at Goronsky. After a moment she clears her throat. "Come see me later, okay?"

Only after Ya'el is gone does Caddie realize it might have looked odd—Ya'el leaving, but Goronsky making no move to go. He heads into the kitchen now and she follows. He opens a cupboard door and pulls out two cups as though he already knows where they are. He pours coffee for himself, and then for her.

"I have this connection to Gaza and the West Bank, too," he says speculatively, as if continuing a conversation. "I grew up with snow on the boulevards, but it turns out I was meant for those dusty alleyways. The curses and wails. The frank emotion." He sits at the kitchen table and stares at his hands. "That honesty. I could never emulate that. Still, it attracts me." He blows across the top of his coffee, then drinks. "You want to join one of these settler patrols? Be there when they do their justice?"

She hadn't mentioned patrols to Ya'el, had she? "How," she asks, "did you guess all that about Ya'el?"

"What, the child, the job?" He shifts his shoulders. "She had a stuffed toy and a calculator sticking out the top of her purse. Then I saw her stroking her fingertips with her thumb, as though they ached." He smiles. "I *wondered* where you were in the middle of the night," he says.

Though he says it matter-of-factly, her breath quickens. She watches his hands embracing the coffee cup. He has a small scratch near one knuckle. She turns away with effort, opens the refrigerator, stares in blankly, then turns back. "How long were you there? At my door?"

He sweeps the table with his palm as though wiping away invisible crumbs. "You know what I told you the other evening? About my family? That was the first time I ever told anyone."

She shakes her head. "No."

"My mother didn't want to talk about it, not ever," he says. "And no one asked me about my father when I was growing up. Why would they? A fatherless boy was common in my neighborhood. People stayed out of one another's business."

She feels him gauging her reaction, and hopes her expression shows the full measure of her skepticism. "So no one knew?" She doesn't want to let him turn this into a "first time" with all that emotional responsibility.

"Ludmilla Federova knows," he says. "She's my supervisor at the university. She has a long acquaintance with my mother."

Caddie reaches into her refrigerator and pulls out a juice bottle. She can't believe that she's the first. The story was so smoothly told, so practiced.

When she turns back, Goronsky is holding a spoon between two fingers like a cigarette.

"I used to smoke," he says. "It's not only the nicotine. There's something about holding live fire between your fingers. Bringing it close to your face. *Owning* it." She watches him wrap both hands around the spoon as if smothering a cigarette. "But only for a few moments."

"How long were you waiting outside my apartment?" Caddie leans against the open refrigerator door, waiting.

"I'm planning a trip to Lebanon," he says. "I thought you might want to go with me."

"What," Caddie tightens her hold on the juice bottle, "the hell are you talking about?"

"Three, four days in Beirut. For my study."

She shoves the juice back unopened and leans in to study the mustard, the jar of pickles. To block her face from his view.

"You have things to do there." He says it like a fact, not a question.

"I have," Caddie closes the refrigerator, "a call to make.

And work to get to. Finish the coffee. If you want. Then let yourself out."

She doesn't wait for his response. She goes to her bedroom, trying to slow her breathing. She picks up the phone, misdialing Moshe's office once before she gets it right. This time he answers. "I hear from you so soon?" He doesn't sound surprised.

"What's with the house burning?" She sounds angrier than she wants to, Caddie realizes as soon as she's spoken.

"*What* house burning?"

"C'mon, Moshe." She makes her voice reasonable. "Settlers set a house on fire in the village to the north. The same village that your neighbors were blaming for last night's attack."

"Caddie, I'm beginning to be insulted by your insistence on linking me to acts of violence that occur anywhere within fifty miles of my home." Mock outrage in his voice.

"Perhaps your committee decided upon a dual action?" Caddie asks. "A letter to the prime minister *and* a punishment for the village?"

"Don't you know yet that most of these stories are invented by the Arabs? I can't think of another people anywhere who, given the situation we live under, would show such restraint."

His voice is too smooth, his outrage too practiced. He's lying, but she's got to come at this right or she might as well hang up now.

"You put me in a tough position, Moshe, by not letting me attend that meeting."

"Closed session. I told you."

"If I'd seen it myself, I'd know what happened. I could speak with authority."

"All of our meetings are closed, as a matter of course."

"As is, I have no proof."

"That way, everyone can speak freely."

"Now it's your word against theirs in the copy."

She's working Moshe so hard that she's almost forgotten Goronsky. Almost. Now she feels his presence as palpably as a sharp change in temperature. He's come into her bedroom and is standing behind her. Part fear, part anticipation rolls through her. The same feeling that comes when she's covering the clashes.

He's looking at her hair. She thinks he might touch it. She resists the temptation to go into the bathroom and lock the door. She walks to the window instead. She focuses on Moshe, who is in the process of saying no in different ways. No one at last night's meeting would have agreed to include an outsider, particularly not a journalist. And no one would have violated the decision reached during the meeting. No one would take aggressive vigilante action. It's a dust storm of words. She has to stop it.

"I know there were people who were interested in revenge," she says.

"They lost the vote."

"Fine, then, let me be there. For everything, not only the moments like your kids reciting what they've learned during the day."

Moshe sighs.

"I need to see how you handle attacks," Caddie says. "How you argue these things through. And how you go about protecting yourselves."

"Caddie—" Moshe begins, and she can tell from his tone he's going to be negative, so she doesn't let him finish.

"You can't be afraid of people knowing you, Moshe. In fact, it's to your benefit. The more people who understand your position, the greater your advantage."

"Caddie," Moshe says, "we aren't responsible for burning down anyone's house."

"I need," she says, "to witness the process."

She hears him take a sip of something. "Getting you into a meeting," he says. "That's a long shot. Long, long."

Damn. She can decipher that tone.

If Moshe won't be the source, maybe he could be the conduit. "What about a series of interviews in the settlement?" Caddie asks, thinking aloud. "That could give me a full range of opinions and you could still have your meetings private. If you urged your neighbors to talk frankly to me, I think they might."

As she's speaking, she notices Anya on the sidewalk below, walking woodenly, turning her head from side to side as though searching. Her hair is in disarray; the front of her shirt looks stained.

"Let me see what I can do," Moshe is saying. "I'm not promising. We'll talk next week."

"Good." But even as she hangs up, she knows this will

come to nothing. She's going to have to find another way to gain access to the settlers who are patrolling the night, burning homes, harassing their enemy-neighbors.

Anya is looking up toward her window, squinting. She spots Caddie, and suddenly she opens her mouth wide, as though yelling a single word. Her face creases in apparent pain. She turns and rushes out of sight.

Caddie steps quickly away from the window. It's Anya, she reminds herself. Poor, disturbed Anya. Exactly what she and Marcus said to each other before Lebanon. Nothing more.

Goronsky is behind her. "I know why you want this so much," he says.

"Want what?" She faces Goronsky.

"To be with the settlers." He brushes her hair out of her face. The skin on his fingers burns like sandpaper. "It's a relief, isn't it, to be immersed in *someone else's* fury?" She smells the coffee on his breath. "And they wouldn't scare you, would they? All cats are gray at night. An old Russian proverb."

She backs away. She wants him to quit talking. She needs to get to the living room.

"I once saw a man shoot another point-blank," Goronsky says in a voice so distant from emotion that it brings her to a halt.

"Right-o," she says.

He ignores her arch tone. "They faced each other. The one with the gun was standing, the other kneeling with his back to a parked car, only three feet between them. And another three feet between them and me."

"For your government study, this was?"

"Their knowing came about thirty seconds before the shot was fired. It was clear then that there was no turning back. Fear flooded the face of the kneeling one, a runny, liquid kind of fear, painful to watch. The one standing, he had this implacable expression, but he had fear, too. His was hard and sharp. They were scared of the same moment. Of the border each was about to cross."

Goronsky is concentrated on somewhere Caddie cannot see. "So what happened?" she asks, half-believing in spite of herself.

Goronsky seems to refocus then, and looks at Caddie with surprise. "He fired."

"And where, exactly, did this happen?"

"Time passes," he says, "and still it doesn't turn into a memory, not in the normal way. In my mind, I'm first one of them, then the other. The shooting itself remains frozen in perfect focus. Like a photograph. Often, it seems more crucial to me than my own history." He spreads his arms in a palms-up gesture. "So you see, I understand."

A flush of confusion washes over her cheeks. The way he refers to a photograph gives her the sense that he's talking about Marcus.

"I can get you what you want," he says.

"If you mean Lebanon—" she begins curtly, but he interrupts.

"This time I mean the settlers. A nighttime patrol."

She gestures dismissively.

"I got the list of medicines, didn't I?"

"How, exactly," she asks, "does a professor get hooked into a renegade settler movement?"

"I'm studying the psychology of extremism," he says patiently, as though explaining the constellations to a child.

"So?"

"I meet these people." He shrugs and gives that smile, surprising, self-deprecating. She resists it.

"I meet them, too, Goronsky."

"I've managed to build relationships." He steps closer. The sudden charge between them makes her slightly dizzy, empty of breath. "I can get you on a patrol," he says. "Why not trust that, use it? You want me to set something up?"

No. Absolutely not.

He puts his hand lightly on her shoulder, barely touching it.

A patrol. Her thoughts come haltingly, as though her brain is taking a nap. A patrol with the settlers would give her the story. And she won't get that kind of access without help from someone.

He slides his hand to her elbow, then to her hip.

"No." She steps away and brushes back her hair with both hands. "No. Thank you. I'm all set."

He straightens. They stand unmoving, inches apart. "Okay," he says after a moment. "If you change your mind, let me know." Then he surprises her. "You need to get to work," he says. He heads down her hallway toward the front door.

She wants him to go. She's glad he is leaving.

"Wait," she says.

He pauses.

"You know what you said about reporters prying into other people's lives basically to escape their own?" she says. "That's a cliché." She tries to force herself not to blink, like in the childhood staring contest.

"Okay," Goronsky says after a long moment.

He turns. She hears the door close behind him. She is relieved to have escaped his intensity, the way he crowds her. But she notices the scent of sea seems to linger in her apartment. And while she pulls on her boots—only then, only briefly—she allows herself to remember the way his eyelids looked while he slept.

Seven

"So he says his unit's headed somewhere dangerous next week, he won't say where, of course, but he wants to point out that maybe I should consider *that*, surely *that's* more important than whether or not my kids see him in his boxers." Ya'el, legs crossed in the passenger seat, gives a subdued snort and waves her hand as though shooing a fly, then glances sideways. "Caddie! You listening?"

"Yes." *Sort of.* But a million preoccupations swoop like bats through her brain. Driving, for one thing. She's headed to the mechanic's shop so Ya'el can pick up her car, and it's in southeast Jerusalem, where the roads are particularly pockmarked, the traffic especially crunched. Horns blare at all sides for no reason other than general frustration. A gunshot goes off behind her, making her jump even as she knows it's not a gun, just a taxi backfiring. She grips the wheel.

"The tired old last-sex-before-I-die line," Ya'el says. "Like every woman in Israel over the age of fourteen hasn't heard that message a million times."

And then there's the message Rob left on her machine yesterday afternoon: "Hi, Caddie. Guess what?" Followed by static and dead air. Cut off before the punch line. *Guess what?* It's the first time she's heard from him since Lebanon and she must have replayed his voice half a dozen times, lingering over the few floating words, imagining his next ones.

Guess what? I think we should go back to Beirut together. Guess what? It's time for us to grab those thugs by their short hairs. Guess what? I'm finally ready to smell their *blood.*

"What I really want, of course, is to *connect* with somebody. I don't mean just in bed," Ya'el says. "For what I want, he has too much swagger."

"Hmmm." Swagger. That's what the protest boys have: swagger and bravado. It's been two days since Caddie has "been out"—the euphemism for going to cover the violence. Two days since she's stood next to the protesters as they shoot marbles with slingshots, tolerating the tear gas, feeling dread punch from inside her stomach like a trapped creature. This morning she has an appointment to interview Halima, the cucumber girl. But afterward, she'll find some fighting. Perhaps in Hebron, where a funeral is scheduled. When she calls Pete on his mobile, she wonders if he'll tell her what's going on where, or if he'll say, "Nothing cooking, Caddie," as has been his wont lately. Maybe she'll call one of the other photographers instead.

"And it all lacks playfulness." Ya'el is still complaining.

"For him, it's sex as an act of desperation. A distraction from hopelessness."

Caddie leans forward, her attention suddenly snagged. "Desperate?" she says.

But Ya'el switches topics. "Oh well, he's too Orthodox for me anyway. By Jerusalem standards, I'm a heathen." She sighs. "Here I am, in great condition after the divorcee's diet, and what do I get? I've got to face it: I'm a firmed-up old lady with two kids. And I love them, but I had them so fast, so blindly, that sometimes it seems like one long birth broken only by nausea and nursing. God, I should have held off. The way you have."

"Held off. Yeah, right." Caddie makes a face and Ya'el laughs.

"No, really. I think, someday . . ." Ya'el says.

Caddie stops listening. She *knows* all about the emotional buzz of having kids. She's *seen* the look on Ya'el's face when she pulls one of her daughters close. And sure, she's felt a quick stab, a glimpse of possibility. In weak moments, she's even wondered if having a child might save her from herself somehow, plant her in one place, solidify her.

But those moments are short-lived. What sticks with her longer is the diminishing power of motherhood, the way choices seem reduced. Moms either erase part of themselves, as Grandma Jos did, or flee, like Caddie's mom.

Without doubt, getting quotes from children is far preferable to having them. That's exactly what she told Marcus one early dawn when the yielding light coming in through the windows lent itself to dreamy visions and he wanted to talk about kids. Caddie refused to succumb to the mood. "No way, no, never," she said, slipping out of his grasp, rolling away to get a drink of water, silent a few moments and then changing the subject, her mind moving from birth to death, reminding him of the severed leg they'd seen on the field the day before, a suicide-bombing victim, the limb turned into an object so disconnected from life that Caddie had trouble imagining that it had ever been part of a breathing person.

Now Ya'el reaches to touch Caddie's arm. "You okay?"

Caddie realizes her eyes are moist. "Dust in the air. Makes my eyes water. That's all."

"Dust?"

"Absolutely." She reaches for her bottle of water, takes a sip.

Ya'el stares at her another moment, sighs, then throws back her head and sings out the window, "I need a lover that won't drive me crazy."

"Who," Caddie corrects.

"What?"

"Never mind."

Ya'el slouches in her seat and fiddles with her purse. "And speaking of men."

Caddie glances her direction. "I know. You don't like him." She doesn't have to say the name. Even though they haven't spoken about him since Ya'el met him three days ago, Caddie knew this was coming.

"It's not a matter of like or dislike, Caddie," Ya'el says. "*Anyone* can see his posts are not well planted."

Ya'el would be more sympathetic if she knew Goronsky's story. But Caddie cannot share it with her neighbor. What he told her that night belongs to her.

"He's manipulative," Ya'el is saying. "And angry."

Besides, if Ya'el were clued in to the intimacy of that conversation, she'd probably guess all the rest. Caddie doesn't want that.

"Maybe you don't see it," Ya'el is saying. "I remember after my brother. You lose someone that way, it throws off your judgment for a while."

Caddie hits a pothole and releases a loud, frustrated breath. "My judgment's fine."

"I don't think so. Because this is as obvious as a mountain in the middle of a highway. Steer clear of this guy, you hear me?"

"Ya'el. You meet him for, what, ten minutes? You think you've got a complete reading? He's not a beach book, you know."

"I ask him a simple question, and he gets nervous; I ask another, and he gets mad. He's focused one minute, distracted the next." Ya'el turns to look at her. "Shit, Caddie. You're not in love with him, are you?"

In love. The mad thing that springs from indecipherable logic and runs on its own internal steam. The thing that leaves her more exposed and exhilarated even than covering the clashes. Caddie sucks in two small, careful breaths. "Maybe he got tired of your endless questions, Ya'el. You wouldn't let go of him. He's a professor, for God's sake, and you treated him like a terrorist."

"I don't care what he calls himself. After a few decades living in Jerusalem, I recognize the wild-eyed ones from a hundred meters. The ones who turn dangerous if you get too close."

Caddie is aware of her hands tightening on the steering wheel. Yes, Goronsky *is* a little wild-eyed. Who can blame him? And maybe that's part of the draw.

Is that *in love?* She'd like to know. But Ya'el is not the one to ask.

"What about Mr. Gruizin?" she says to change the subject. "He paints red on the mailboxes to save lives, for God's sake. Is that unbalanced? Or me. Can you, with your extensive powers, tell that *I'm* another Anya in the making?"

Ya'el doesn't return Caddie's grin. "Since you bring it up, what's with this pervasive need of yours to see the bullet come out of the barrel? You didn't used to be like that."

Caddie scoots closer to the driver's-side door. "I don't know what you mean."

"I've seen you coming in, day after day, black from the ashes, reeking like one of your photographer friends. I smell it in the stairwell." Ya'el shakes her head.

"And what do you suggest I cover, Ya'el? Political discussions in the Knesset? Archaeological excavations? Maybe religious holidays?"

"You used to, when I first met you."

"That was a different time. The violence is the story now." Caddie pulls up in front of the mechanic's shop where Ya'el's repaired car is waiting. Ya'el makes no move to get out.

"Okay," Ya'el says, "then cover it. But why obsessively?"

Caddie squeezes the steering wheel. For the adrenalin hit, damnit. Which is—as long as she survives—no more harmful than a nightly drink or a daily cigarette. But she won't get into a discussion about that.

"This is what reporters do, Ya'el." She bites her bottom lip, willing herself to stop before she says more.

"If you don't have a camera in your hand," Ya'el says, "you don't need to be there all the time. *You* told me that."

That was then. Now she's living with the privilege of having survived.

"You know shit about this," Caddie says. "You work in a *bank*, for God's sake."

She stops, sucks in her breath. She and Ya'el move carefully around their differences; they always have. They don't speak this way to one another, not ever.

Ya'el looks out her window. She turns toward Caddie. "Okay. *Your* story. *Your* friend."

Caddie knows she should apologize, but she can't find the words. After a minute, Ya'el shakes her head. She gets out of the car, then leans down to stick her head through the open door. "Be careful today," she says a little stiffly.

"Yeah." Caddie nods her head several times. "Yeah, thanks."

Ya'el turns, and the door clicks closed.

WITHIN MINUTES, Caddie is past the Israeli checkpoint, into Palestinian territory, and taking deep breaths. She loves Jerusalem, loves how her own carefully tended neutrality stands out against its biases. But today, what a relief to leave behind the city's adamant judgments. Being alone, headed down a West Bank road, feels like a holiday compared to Ya'el's interrogation.

She soon reaches a narrow dirt track that climbs to a hillside village. Amber marshmallows of dust rise from the car wheels. She rounds a corner to find a gray-haired goat blocking the road. She taps her horn. The beast answers with a stubborn stare.

Before she can get out of the car to shoo him on, half a dozen kids sweep from around the side of a house. The tallest one eyes her suspiciously, but the rest are smiling. Two who look to be about seven years old, already accustomed to the obstinate arrogance of goats, move to one side of the animal and expertly drive him out of the way. They swat at his behind as though it were a fly and call out from somewhere deep in their throats.

"Shukran," Caddie says out the window. "I'm looking for the home of Halima Bisharat."

"We show you, we show you," one boy says. He opens the back door of her car and climbs in. A friend joins him. He directs Caddie to turn right, then left. "There is house."

Caddie parks, thanks the boys again and swings out of the car. She pauses to squeeze her left hand into a tight fist and make a wordless wish for a good interview. She wills herself to become immersed in the stink of donkey manure and exhaust fumes and sweet rotting fruit. In the competing tastes of dirt

on her dry lips and the sweet tea she knows will soon be offered. In the village's background music—a thick hum of
women and children—that comes from nowhere in particular
and seems to hover near her like kicked-up earth.

She wills herself to have better luck than she did at Moshe's.

A small group of children, boys and girls both, is playing a
homegrown version of cowboys and Indians—soldiers versus
martyrs. One, the "martyr," is splayed on the ground pretending to be dead. "*I* want to be killed next," another boy says
peevishly as Caddie approaches. Several break away from their
game to circle Caddie curiously. A middle-aged woman with
a basket balanced on her head pauses to stare.

Half the homes are little more than concrete boxes with
corrugated tin roofs held in place by piles of discarded tires
and cement blocks. The others, Halima's included, are sprawl-
ing by comparison, spread over several rooms and built of
pink-tinted limestone. They were clearly constructed in times
of relative calm and have managed to survive despite the fre-
quent house demolitions carried out by Israeli troops.

Halima opens the door before Caddie, surrounded by the
boys, can knock. Halima holds a baby. Caddie didn't think this
girl was a mother. Even though she's about seventeen, which
makes her old enough to have been given in marriage and
borne a child or two, she doesn't have a mother's eyes. Her
gaze is too lacking in caution.

"Welcome, welcome," Halima says in English. She seems
to sense Caddie's unasked question. "This is my cousin." She
bounces the baby. "And this is my mother." Behind Halima

stands a woman who smiles shyly. Her face is tan and wrinkled. Her hands, which she holds tightly in front of her, are red, as if they'd been scorched with boiling water, but Caddie can't tell if it's an injury or a birth deformity. The woman nods welcomingly, gestures Caddie inside and then retreats.

The boys start to enter behind Caddie, but Halima stops them. She speaks too quickly for Caddie to catch the words, though the meaning is clear. Grumbling, the boys back away and Halima closes the door.

"Sit, sit." She gestures to a deep brown velvet couch with a look that communicates this is a possession of some pride. Above it hangs the framed painting of a young man. "My father," says Halima, following Caddie's eyes with her own. "He used to own a furniture-building factory." She emphasizes the word *own*. "He died two years ago."

"I'm sorry."

"He'd been ill a long time."

The mother returns now, carrying a tray as if it were a cushion of jewels. It is crammed with eight or nine plates of salads, olives, hummus and pita. She sets it down, then disappears and returns with another tray holding cups of tea.

"Eat. Drink," Halima says, handing her mother the baby.

Caddie smiles at the mother and sips the tea. She is surprised to be here alone with Halima, her mother and the infant cousin; she's surprised that the women have not been relegated to a corner of the room by the assortment of males who would, in most clans, insist on being present, and then take over. Even though the father is dead, she would expect uncles and cousins.

But she's far from displeased. With the men, there is so much rhetoric to be gotten through; with the women, usually less so. "Tell me about that night, then, with your cousin and his friend," she says.

Halima begins to describe settlers who come in cars to the village. Her expression is cautious. Caddie, taking notes, nods encouragingly. "Some nights they hurl stones at our house," Halima says. "One night they tried to throw gasoline at our neighbor's home. My uncle and two of my cousins ran after them with sticks, yelling. Finally they fled." She shakes her head. "It is what we know to expect."

"Eat, eat," says the mother. She is watching Halima speak. Pride and concern dart, in turn, across her face.

Caddie takes a bite of pita. "How long has this been happening?"

Halima looks around as though to find the answer written on a wall. "Even when I was very young, it happened. But not as frequently as now. Now, every few days, they come through again. Still, you can't live in fear. That's what Walid used to say."

"Walid, he's your cousin?"

Halima nods.

"What happened that night? The night Walid was taken, and his friend was killed."

Halima's voice is delicate, precise—a wonderful singing voice, Caddie suspects. "Walid and Nazir were sleeping outside on the roof; it was hot. Walid's wife and child were inside. Walid woke up when he heard a noise. He shook Nazir and together they went down. Someone captured them from behind," Halima makes a grabbing gesture, "and blindfolded them. Walid heard men speaking Hebrew. Three of them, he thinks." Halima watches Caddie closely, as if to make sure every word is recorded. The mother pours more tea.

"They pulled Walid and Nazir into a car," Halima goes on, "and drove them around for something like twenty minutes. They weren't able to talk, but Nazir squeezed Walid's hand. Then my cousin was thrown out of the car, still blindfolded. He had cuts, scrapes and a broken arm, but he was able to pull off his blindfold and get help."

"And Nazir?"

Halima braids her fingers together, unknots them, then braids them again. "We don't know exactly. Only that his body was found early the next morning, dumped outside Deheishe. A stick had been shoved into one of his ears, his chest was like pulp, his right arm broken." Her tone is incredulous as well as bitter.

The door opens then without anyone knocking. A man strides in, tall, mustachioed, with a middle-aged spread at his waist. *"Ahalan."* He smiles broadly, nodding his head forcefully. "Welcome, welcome. I am Ibrahim Issa. Brother of Halima's father."

Halima is blushing; she's been found out. There can be no secrets for long in a village this small. Caddie wonders what repercussions Halima will face for bypassing the family's men. She rises to introduce herself.

"Sit, sit," Ibrahim Issa says. The mother brings him a cup of tea. *"Shukran."* He exchanges a few words with her, then turns to Caddie. "You are here to report on the terrorism we face?" he asks in Arabic.

From that phrase, Caddie knows she is in the land of rhetoric. Damned rhetoric: such a thin slice of the truth that, to Caddie, it has begun to seem obscene.

"You have heard of the Silwadi case?" he asks. She can't place the name until he mentions the woman and her five-year-old daughter shot in their home. The killings Jon told her about. She nods to show she knows of it. "The Israeli settlers forced the grandmother to go outside," Ibrahim Issa says. "Then they shot the mother, Randa, and her child, Salwa." He goes into the back room and returns with a color poster showing the slain girl. She is dressed for her funeral, her eyes closed and, since the wounds of "martyrs" are not cleaned, a finger of dried blood coming from her mouth.

Posters, so soon. Victims Salwa Silwadi and her mother are clearly already part of Palestinian lore. "It's very sad," Caddie says. And it is. But she has to redirect the conversation back to the reason she's here. "Your family has its own tragedy. Halima was explaining it."

"Yes. Halima." Ibrahim Issa's voice sounds thoughtful and threatening at once. Caddie looks at him for a long moment, and then turns to Halima.

"Can I talk to your cousin?" Caddie asks.

Ibrahim Issa shakes his head twice.

"He doesn't want." Halima switches to English, looks apologetic and exchanges a glance with her mother, who hovers on the edge of the room. "After the killing, Walid stopped going to school," she says, moving back into Arabic. "It has been two weeks now and he will barely talk, even to us. We used to be close, he and I. He has no trust left. Sometimes I think not even for me." She glances at her uncle, who is watching her and taking long drags on his cigarette. "My mother is taking care of his child now. His wife has gone back to her parents."

"For a visit," Ibrahim Issa says. "She will return."

Halima shrugs in a way that shows she is not sure. "I used to think he would get better," she says. "I used to hope many things. His arm heals, but the rest of him gets worse."

"That's why I'd like to interview him," Caddie says.

"I wish he were angry like the rest of us," Halima says dully, "but he's—" She looks again at the painting of her father. "It's as though he's gone."

Caddie reaches out to touch Halima's arm. "Sometimes an outsider can draw someone out even when family members can't."

Ibrahim Issa stamps out his cigarette and leaps up as though no longer able to restrain himself. He chops at the air with his hand. "No outsider can accomplish this. Certainly not—" he hesitates, looking from Caddie's feet to her face, "not you. Impossible." He walks once around the room, his long strides better suited to pacing a field. "Walid doesn't even know Halima is speaking to a journalist." He gives Halima a quick and reprimanding look. "Walid would not be happy."

"Walid would be proud if he had heard Halima," Caddie says. "How well she has explained herself."

Ibrahim Issa turns to Caddie with a hard and fabricated smile. "And you have heard her answer about talking to her cousin. I must ask you to let go of this request. The topic is at a close."

The silence then is awkward. Halima's mother pours more tea for Ibrahim Issa and urges Caddie to put food on her plate. The baby must be sleeping in a back room.

"Did Halima tell you what happened to her grandmother six months ago?" Ibrahim Issa asks after a few moments.

Caddie shakes her head as Halima sinks into her seat, withdrawn but watching her uncle politely. Ibrahim Issa warms up slightly as he recounts how the grandmother got angry at some trespassing settlers, charged at them with a stick, fell ill the next day and died. "They killed her, as they did Nazir," Ibrahim Issa says intently. He waves toward Caddie's notebook, as though ordering her to write it all down. She jots a couple words and looks up in time to catch the disappointment in his eyes. If she were with a television cameraman, he wouldn't pay attention to whether or not she was writing every word he said. He'd be buoyed by the belief that the camera was recording it all.

"So what are you going to do about all this?" Caddie asks. "The harassment, the kidnappings?"

"What *can* we do?" Ibrahim Issa responds, his face wide open, sky-like. He spreads his arms. "It is the Israelis who are so well armed, not us."

But she knows. Responses can be made. Bombs assembled, weapons gathered. Suicide bombers can be recruited, ambushes launched. Otherwise, the men lose face. She leans forward. "Revenge," she says quietly. "Don't you want to retaliate? Don't your victims deserve it?"

Halima rises and takes a step toward Caddie, but Caddie doesn't glance her way. She doesn't want to be restrained. She notices she is squeezing her own knees, and forces herself to loosen her grip. "You have meetings, don't you?" she asks. "In the mosque? In one of your homes?"

Ibrahim Issa lights another cigarette, his face rigid. "You speak, perhaps, of one of the factions. I'm with those who follow Arafat."

"I'm talking realities, not factions." Caddie scoots even further forward on her seat. "You can't let them keep getting away with it. Don't you have to do something, if only to honor the memory of those killed?"

Ibrahim Issa leans into his chair, away from her, and stares as though she were distasteful.

"There's a moral imperative, isn't there," Caddie says, "to respond when attacked?"

Ibrahim Issa clears his throat. "Even if what you suppose is true," he says deliberately, "tell me, what would you do with this information if you were to hold it in your hands? You would write it in the papers? It would find its way to the Israeli prime minister's coffee table? Do you think that is something we would want?"

Caddie feels her blood rush to her cheeks. She stares into

her cup. All Halima sought was a simple interview. To tell her story and maybe help her cousin somehow. It had to be humiliating, turning to a foreigner, then finding the only interested one was American and *female*. No wonder she didn't want the family's men to know.

Now that reporter has disgraced her. Caddie is acting like some naïve neophyte who is trying to find out the date and time of the next Palestinian strike against Israel, and who seems to actually expect to be told.

Caddie places the cup carefully in its saucer. "Of course. I understand."

Halima sits back down and gives her a quick smile, vaguely sympathetic, but says nothing. Ibrahim Issa's lips are sewn tight. Halima's mother has retreated and Caddie hears the baby crying somewhere out of sight. It's the only sound in the room.

A swell of nausea rushes over Caddie. This is probably the clumsiest interview she's ever conducted. After what she's just done, it would take a stroke of enormous luck—no, more, a miracle—to give her the kind of access she's looking for here.

She searches for an inappropriate question to break her inner tension, but cannot even start to think of one. Instead, the question is for herself. *What the hell were you thinking?*

She rises, signaling her readiness to leave, and feels their shared relief, palpable and alive. "Please forgive my bluntness," she says, addressing Halima. "I want to thank you for your time."

"But will you write about it?" Halima asks. "About what happened to my cousin?"

"I will. It'll be a few more weeks. But I'll mail you a copy, or drop one by sometime."

"Mail is fine." Halima trails Caddie to the door. Ibrahim Issa remains sitting. "My uncles tell me to forget it, leave it alone," Halima says out of earshot of Ibrahim Issa. "Live your life, they say. Go to school, help your mother with the baby and wait for better times. *Better times*." Her tight expression is half-smile, half-grimace. "Well, maybe they are right. Maybe that's all someone like me can do."

"It's not," Caddie says. "It's not all you can do. It's wrong to simply let things happen. If you do nothing, it's like killing your cousin's friend all over again."

Halima is silent for a moment. She looks at Caddie sadly. Then she extends her hand. "I am sorry," she says. *"Ma'a sal-ama." Go without fear.*

Outside, the dirt track is empty. The boys have abandoned their martyr game and moved on to some other amusement. Caddie's legs are rubbery, her arms overcooked spaghetti. It takes an act of will to get into the car, pull out her key and put it in the ignition.

She's done here. She might as well call to find out where they are clashing. She cups her cell phone in her left hand and takes a deep breath.

Then, without conscious thought, she presses down the number three button, the one with the letters "d-e-f" on it. The button she programmed, long ago, to dial Marcus's cell phone number automatically.

She assumes it will be disconnected. But she hangs on

while it dials and rings. After the fourth ring, she hears his voice: "Marcus Lancour," and then the beep to allow her to leave a message. She hangs up, then dials it again, and listens to him say his name once more. This time she leaves a message. "Marcus," she says. She can't imagine what else to say. Or, more accurately, everything she would say sounds ridiculous even as it runs through her mind. "Marcus," she repeats. Then she hangs up.

WHEN THE PHONE RINGS that evening, for a split second Caddie imagines—lets herself imagine—it's Marcus returning her call. She invents his banter: "You missed three incredible stories today, kiddo. I don't know why that paper keeps you. Luckily, you have me. I'll be over in ten minutes to fill you in on the day's disasters."

She takes a deep breath before she answers. It's Mike, her foreign editor.

"Glad I caught you at home. How you doing, Caddie?"

"Fine, Mike. I've told you that by e-mail about a dozen times."

He laughs. "Listen. It's been two weeks."

"I don't know what you're talking about." Though she does.

"New York."

"Oh." She shakes her head, and even though he can't see her, he catches her tone.

"Hear me out," he says. "It's mainly reporting, only a little desk work."

"I'm still not—" she begins, but he cuts her off.

"You'd travel abroad and in the States. Features and breaking news. We'd use your experience. There's a pay raise, not enormous but something. And a title. Special correspondent."

"Special firefighter, you mean. Parachuting into places I know squat about and writing shallow pieces. Thanks very much, but—"

"I'm not," Mike interrupts, "going to let you dismiss this out of hand. This is a terrific career move. Think about it. Think hard. Then call me with the right answer."

"I can tell you now. I don't want the job." She takes a deep breath. "Not right now, at least."

"What are you waiting for?"

She doesn't answer.

"Caddie. Next time we talk, if you don't have *ten* good reasons why not, or not yet, you *are* taking this job."

"Mike—" But the line cuts off before she can say more.

He wouldn't let her speak. There's good reason Number One.

Of course, if she can't handle interviews any better than she did today, she's of no use here, and she might as well go to New York. Half the time that she's in the field, she's caught up in the futile act of taking mental photographs for Marcus. And maybe she wouldn't hear his voice so often if she were in a new place.

She goes to her bedroom, stands in front of the bed a minute, then reaches down and pulls out Marcus's journal. Balancing it in her hands, she's overcome again by that mixture of desire and aversion. For three days, she has restrained herself from looking at his pictures or reading his words. It's getting more difficult.

If she looks at it, she's decided, it will be section by section, exactly as he put it together. She will follow the unwritten rules that came—implicitly—with the journal. And this is Rule Number One: Take it in order, page by page.

Rule Number Two: Look at it only when alone, and don't talk to anyone about what you find there. This is between you and Marcus.

And Rule Number Three: No rushing, no skimming. Study each picture long enough to understand what he'd been thinking, to see the path of his mind.

She settles herself in bed, leaning against the pillows with the journal on her lap, a muggy breeze blown in by the Jerusalem night. She takes a deep breath and turns to the second page.

The colors strike her straight away. Marcus clipped and pasted from photographs to create a mosaic that spells out three large letters: RED. The letters are black, white or red only. The different shades and shapes of red, though, surprise her: daring red, injured red, innocent red, in drops and splatters and waves.

At first the effect is merely interesting, but the more Caddie looks at each letter, the more awed she is by what he did. The pieces of photographs are cut largely from scenes of attacks and fighting that he'd covered. She recognizes a number of them—she'd been there, too. A leg blown off in a bus stop bombing. A pregnant woman, wounded and hemorrhaging from her distended belly. A little boy holding his sliced-open cheek with spread fingers in a desperate effort to keep blood and flesh in place.

The only exceptions to the violence-linked scenes are the faces of leaders. Marcus apparently took those during one speech or another. In each tiny black-and-white headshot, their mouths are contorted, caught in midexclamation. These are the very shots that would be rejected by mainstream newspapers and magazines for unfairly making a head-of-state look ridiculous, but Marcus found a use for them. He selected and cut and positioned each photo next to its neighbors. So carefully, in fact, that it almost seems predestined, as perfect and unlikely as the pyramids. She closes her eyes and imagines him composing this collage. She can picture his concentration, the hair falling over his forehead. That habit he had of lightly biting his bottom lip. She can almost hear his music in the background, Coltrane or Elvis Costello.

That page is followed by six others covered with photographs enlarged far too much for professional use, blown up like hyperbole, a storm of graininess. Real scenes made unreal. Those shots are from the worst of it. A woman lying dead on her side, a watermelon cradled in her arms. A girl in school uniform slumped against a brick wall, head tilted, mouth ajar and an open book on her lap, as though she were sleeping in class instead of slain in crossfire. A boy, five, shot through his right eye. The Red Crescent worker who'd been trying to reach that boy when he took a bullet himself, photographed sprawled on his back beneath the front wheel of his ambulance, so recently dead he still looks surprised.

Most of these events, Caddie remembers witnessing. But on second glance she realizes these aren't the same snaps he'd published to such acclaim on front pages or magazine covers. Each photo has a journalist in the frame—a fellow photographer or reporter from print, radio, TV. And that's what he chose to bring into sharp focus: the faces of journalists. How had he managed, during the crunch of a breaking story, to remember to take these shots too, these shots that had to be for personal use only?

Pete is in one shot, clearly evaluating the scene, his fingers on his right hand making indents in his cheek, his eyes taut. Marcus captured the Pete she knows, always watching, always analyzing. Another photo shows Sandra, the one who'd ended up dead in Sierra Leone, crouched as though to protect herself, one hand holding the camera to her eye, the other held out like a traffic cop stopping an oncoming vehicle. Her body is shadowed by the neighboring building as though she is half-in, half-out of this world. Eerily prescient.

No one shows fear, Caddie notices. A couple of the journalists even appear blasé, as if they were strolling down the Champs Elysees. Caddie had never paid attention to any of this in the field, never thought to turn her eye on *us* instead of *them.*

She is the subject in two of the shots. In one, her eyes are slightly closed—perhaps in reaction to the sound of a gunshot or an explosion? She can only guess.

In the other, a boy lies on the street in front of her, wounded or dead, out of focus. Herself, she barely recognizes.

Her hair is pulled back, her stance erect. What interests her most is her expression—determined and defiant, yet tinged with exhilaration. There seems to be, in her face, an actual hunger for moments of violence. Had Marcus seen that in her? Is it what she'd really felt? She rubs her forehead, wishing she could remember with clarity.

"You're Victorian," Marcus had told her once.

They'd been lying together on the rumpled sheets of her bed. It was late at night; they'd covered a difficult story that day, five dead. She doesn't remember the details of the sex they'd shared but she remembers that they hadn't talked at all, not about work, not about anything. Those were the first words she remembered him saying to her that day. And she'd found them insulting, and rolled away.

"Not about sex," he'd said, reaching to trace her shoulder bone with one finger. "Not that. But about the rest of it. You're buttoned-up and voyeuristic at the same time, like the Victorians were."

She'd gotten up, gone into the bathroom. She'd stayed there for half an hour, until he'd fallen asleep. She didn't know how to explain to him, she didn't want to try to explain, if he didn't know himself. *Voyeurism*, as he called it—focusing on getting in close, nabbing the quote, catching the color—was a way to dehumanize death. To keep it nameless and remote and rob it of its power. And that was necessary if she was going to be able to cover it. If she was going to be able to live through it.

After the photographs is a yellow page that seems intended

to serve only as a divider marking the end of a section. On it is a bit of writing in Marcus's hand:

We used to be as one. Now I'm odd man out. I've stolen a piece of these lives, these deaths. Someday I'll pay them back for the theft.

That first part is more cryptic than the photos by far. What could he have meant? Marcus was at the center of any gathering he joined. Charming, funny. Everybody liked him.

The idea of stolen lives has a more familiar ring. He'd mentioned it once or twice. A late night two months ago, for instance. They'd been in Syndrome, a Jerusalem jazz-and-blues bar. Earlier in the day they'd covered a house demolition with all that jarring pathos. A Palestinian family clung to one another outside, the teenaged son accused of being a "terrorist" the one absent relative. The family watched a roaring bulldozer slam into their home. Then it climbed over the rubble to swipe its shovel at a lemon tree in what had, only moments before, been their backyard. Two birds flew from the branches a second before the shovel hit, uprooting the plant. Marcus managed to get it all in one terrific shot—escaping birds, weeping family, bulldozer, tree. A front-pager for sure. Maybe even a magazine cover.

They'd been with a group of colleagues that night, but now it was only the two of them, and his earlier excitement over the day's photograph had vanished. He began to talk in a quiet voice, his words like islands surrounded by silences. He said he'd spent years making his reputation and money off anguish or death and then escaping it whenever he wanted. The people whose images he'd greedily taken were always left behind. He felt he owed them.

For a rant, it was brief. But she was more accustomed to laughter than darkness from him—more comfortable with it, too. She had no easy response. "Your pictures make a difference," she said at last. It took too long to say it, though, and sounded lame, even to her. He studied her. "Shall we have another drink or head home?" she asked, searching for a way to break the tension.

Then, abruptly, he did it for her. He cracked a joke, something about how when he won the Pulitzer, he would demand that they engrave on a plaque the names of everyone he'd ever photographed, dead or alive. She laughed, relieved. She's not sure, now, whether or not he laughed too.

She wishes she could return to that moment, argue further. She'd be more articulate second time around. Yes, she'd tell Marcus, photographers and reporters do suck up images and details at the worst moments in people's lives, becoming briefly as intimate as lovers before vanishing. But it's not immoral. Recording people in moments of anguish, documenting it and then moving on, serves a purpose. It yanks the privileged from their complacency, sometimes. And sometimes, someone comes to help. At the very least, the horrors don't go altogether unnoticed.

She can think of only one way to get what she needs. It's for Marcus, she tells herself. For Marcus as much as for her. She reaches for the telephone, cradles it in her hands for a second, then dials Goronsky's number.

Eight

DOWNPOUR ALL DAY that ended only at sunset, leaving the heavens washed clean. Now the clouds have drained from the sky, and a full moon helps her track the car's direction: east, then south, then east again. The radio is on low, a woman's voice singing. They pull off the main road, still the engine, quench the lights. Three of the men are smoking; a pack of Marlboros sits on the dashboard, and the car upholstery stinks of stale tobacco. The man on her right pushes the button to roll down his window. The first burst of moist air refreshes, but it quickly turns heavy like a hand over her mouth. The walkie-talkie in the front hisses, and out of it issues a male voice, command-like words indistinguishable to Caddie. She wants to ask why they are waiting, when they will go again. But when she clears her throat, the men on either side of her grow rigid. Words will not be welcome, evidently. Questions are not permitted. Observation only.

Five silent men, faces like closed curtains. She knows only one—the driver, Avraham. *Know*—that's too strong a word. She met him an hour ago at the entrance to the settlement. He nodded and smiled when she introduced herself. She couldn't see his expression: the reflection from his wire-rimmed glasses hid his eyes, leaving only a thin nose, narrow lips, side curls. His bookworm build, wispy beard and soft-looking skin made him seem not much beyond boyhood. She was surprised when he said he was a father, and even more when he pulled pictures of "my children" from his wallet: five of them, all age four or under, no twins among them. Caddie was trying to figure the math when he explained: Palestinians killed his wife's sister, pregnant at the time, in a drive-by shooting. She left behind two children. The husband fell apart, fled to the States and ensconced himself in a conservative *yeshiva*. So Avraham and his wife took the kids—what else, he asked Caddie rhetorically, could they do? They are raising the two to remember their dead mother, and every night they refer to her in their prayers. "I expected better than this," Avraham admitted at one point, and it sounded like something he said often. "Better than this," he repeated softly.

He turned away, then, to shove four M-16s into the trunk of his Subaru, though it was easier to imagine him reading the Torah by candlelight than toting rifles. He cleared his throat and kicked at the ground. "What excuse did Adam give to his children for why he was expelled from Eden?" he asked.

"You're asking me a *riddle?*" she said.

"He told them, 'Your mother ate us out of the garden,'" Avraham answered with a smile. "My oldest loves that one."

And Caddie had laughed, not at the joke but at the incongruity of the moment and the pleased expression on Avraham's face.

She hasn't told any of her colleagues she's being allowed to go along on this nighttime mission. She knows they'd be stunned to hear she'd managed it, particularly now, with tensions high and getting higher. She still can't figure how Goronsky worked it, how he even knows Avraham. Nor does she know what he told Avraham about her. Whatever it was, Avraham seems cautiously trusting. "Sasha speaks well of you," he'd said. She had to search through her memory before she recalled that Sasha was the diminutive for Alexander. "And I trust Sasha, so his word is good for me. But the others . . . well, it's best to stay quiet in the car. We can talk afterward, if you want."

After a dozen minutes another car pulls up. The driver—big, much taller and wider than Avraham—squeezes out. He wears a yarmulke, as do all the men in her car. His shirt is short-sleeved. The dark hair that coats his arms moves in the night air and makes Caddie think of the legs of a thousand overturned spiders. He grins at Avraham, then reaches across to grasp the hand of the man in the front passenger seat. He sees her in the back and glances at Avraham with a clear query in his eyes. Avraham apparently answers with an expression. The man shrugs with his eyebrows, then returns to his vehicle without speaking. The other car's windows are fogged and impenetrable, so she cannot count how many people are inside. Avraham pulls back onto the road, followed by the second vehicle.

She tightens her scarf around her head and rubs her right hand along the leg of her jeans. They drive for about eight minutes before reaching a small hillside village, maybe four dozen houses and a mosque. "The Village of the Condemned." That's what Avraham called it when she'd asked where they were going. He'd said it simply, without inflection, as though she would know what he was talking about, as though it would answer questions instead of raising them. The Village of the Condemned.

A man's voice comes again through the crackling of Avraham's walkie-talkie and he turns off the car radio. He mumbles into the walkie-talkie, something Caddie can't make out. They park in front of a home next to the mosque. A cat freezes in their headlights, then darts away. On a clothesline atop the flat roof, two small pairs of a young boy's pants flap in the breeze. A flowering vine reaches over the top of the walled courtyard, which is covered with the graffiti of spray-painted political slogans, the letters as large as a toddler. An orange plastic ball rests in front, along with a child's miniature dump truck carrying a load of dirt.

Avraham pops the trunk. The men next to her swing out and move to the back to collect their M-16s. She knows M-16s. She knows them as weapons of revenge, not simply destruction. The bullets that come from them do not bore through bodies, but somersault. They leave desperate, ragged holes in torsos and limbs. Once she saw a Palestinian doctor kick a chair in fury at the damage a single slug had caused in the chest of an eight-year-old boy.

She slides over to the door to follow the men from the car, but Avraham stops her. "Stay here." The first spoken words since this trip began and she briefly considers ignoring them. But she still needs this man. She wants, in fact, to make a contact with him directly so she can use him again without Goronsky's involvement.

So she'll do as he says. As long as she can keep an eye on the men through the car window, she'll stay put.

Nine of them move in a throng into the courtyard and toward the door of the house. Their steps are jerky; their arms swing oddly. Two glance quickly over their shoulders. One moves around the side of the house, disappearing into dark-green shadows. Another takes the butt of his rifle and raps it against the door. Caddie leans forward. She sees no life signs, no glow of light or shift of curtain. The settler bangs on the door more urgently. Still no response.

But this does not appear to frustrate her group. In fact it is, it seems, not unexpected. After a few minutes they back up to the cars in what appears to be a coordinated movement, though there's been no discussion. One yells in Arabic. "Your sons are dogs, the offspring of bitches and whores. Keep them lashed up, or we will." Three settlers fire shots over the top of the house—rapid-fire, one boom eclipsing the other like a fireworks finale—as the rest surge back to the vehicles.

The two men who'd been sitting next to her yank open the doors and shove in, panting, suddenly expanded, straining for space within the confines of the backseat. The shooters turn to come back, and Avraham starts up the engine.

"Shall we do the mosque?" one of the men in the backseat asks, and his eagerness is audible.

Avraham shakes his head. "Not this time." As soon as everyone is in, he pulls away. But he does so deliberately and without rush, as though he has every right to be here and he wants to make that clear to anyone who might be peeking from behind a curtain. He keeps his window down, his elbow hanging lazily out. He's going two, maybe three, miles an hour, followed by the other vehicle.

"Who was the greatest financier in the Torah?" he says over his shoulder to Caddie in an offhand voice. She stares at him, wordless. He goes on, "Noah, because he was floating his stock while everyone else was in liquidation." He laughs softly. Caddie manages a smile. No one else responds.

Do they consider this foray successful? To Caddie's eyes, it's as though they've spent the day in preparations for a party that has now been canceled. The man to her right is urgently stroking his trigger with one finger. She shifts in her seat, hoping his safety is on. "That's it? We leave now?" she asks, but no one answers.

When they reach the village's edge, Avraham's walkie-talkie grumbles. He pulls to a halt near two parked cars, one sky-blue, the other white. Avraham and the man sitting next to him slide out, joined by two from the other settler vehicle. The small troupe advances. The parked cars are empty, as far as Caddie can see, but the men pace around hungrily, as if they were playing hide-and-seek and searching for someone within, or underneath, or behind.

Then, without warning, Avraham draws back the butt of

his rifle and thrusts it against the blue car's windshield. It shatters with a sharp crack. Caddie flinches at the noise.

She straightens to watch Avraham batter the windshield again. Tiny sections of glass hang, then fall. She sees in his eyes that he is alone—he and his gun and the car. His face is taut; his movements are unexpectedly fluid and fierce. His scrawny arms seem to have grown longer, more muscular. He wipes his upper lip on his sleeve. In two long strides, he moves on to the other car, the other windshield. This time, Caddie watches steadily as he shatters it.

"No," Caddie murmurs aloud.

Another man pulls out a knife. He squats and slashes the tires. They deflate with such a loud *whoosh* that she can hear it through the closed car window, so fast that it seems like part of a slapstick comedy. In under a minute, shredded black rubber hangs limp.

Yes. An involuntary thought.

The other two men break side windows, reach in to yank open doors and then slice through the upholstery with long and furious swipes of their arms. There is no mistaking the hot frenzy in their faces.

Yes. For the sake of Avraham's dead sister-in-law. For her unborn baby.

Both cars, heavily wounded now, list to one side. Upholstery stuffing bleeds out of them. Still, there is more to do. One man jerks a strand of wooden beads off a rearview mirror, hurls it to the ground and grinds it under his heel. Then he twists off the mirror itself.

For the tears of Avraham's wife.

Another man grabs a paperback book from the backseat of the white car, rips it apart with his hands. His mouth is open, his teeth unexpectedly pink in the moonlight. He hurls the pages and picks up a rock, which he uses to shatter the headlights.

For the two children who are already forgetting their mother's face.

Avraham rams the door of one car with the butt of his rifle. The man with the knife, his face lit by the headlights, kicks the side of the other vehicle, kicks it over and over, batters it uncontrollably with his booted foot. Shuddering blows that continue beyond the point of purpose.

That, that is for Marcus.

Her own right leg, she realizes, is trembling as if with exertion. Her hands are gripped, her nails digging into palms, her cheeks chilled. She breathes with such effort that the men sitting next to her surely have noticed. She glances to one side, then the other. They both stare straight ahead, unmoving, lips taut. She holds her breath and tries to still herself. To restore the distance.

Out the rear window, she sees the village behind them, silent, lifeless, though surely the villagers hear the ruckus. Inside their homes, certainly, they are huddled against the darkness of this night. Now frightened by the fury, they will later plan their own vengeance, retribution carried out against Israelis who are unstained by this crime, exactly as the owners of these cars are innocent of the crime against Avraham and his sister-in-law, against Marcus and her.

She sinks back as the havoc hushes. The four settlers abandon the vanquished cars. The one who was sitting in the front passenger seat pushes in, followed on the other side by Avraham, who leans into the back to speak to his companions. Avraham's face is blotchy, blood stains his lower lip where he has bitten it, his shirt is wrinkled. "We'll wipe them out," he says in his soft, throaty voice, the same tone she's sure he uses to recite evening prayers with the five children. "We'll hunt them down and destroy them, little by little."

Little by little. My enemy is fled into the bush, Caddie thinks. *For now, yours will have to do.*

BACK AT THE SETTLEMENT, all except Avraham collect their weapons and disperse quickly.

Avraham looks at her as though his eyes are feet testing a bog for solid ground. That look of open tentativeness surprises her, and reminds her of her first boyfriend, the one from the cornfields. "You did good," he says. "You stayed quiet. Now what will you do?" He kicks at the dirt, not angrily but casually, like a schoolboy. "Will you write about a bunch of insane settlers? A gang of Israeli cowboys?"

"Of course not."

Still studying her, still cautious and appraising, he nods. "Good," he says. "Sasha said you wouldn't, but I didn't know, for sure, if you could resist—if any reporter could. He said you understood. The way he tells it, you have a right to be angry, too. You've had your own trouble."

My own trouble. Goronsky knows about Lebanon then, somehow. Her stomach feels hollow. But she'd suspected as much, she reminds herself. Besides, she cannot consider it now. "That's right," she says.

"So you know it's not simple," he says. "We have no common language with these terrorists *except* violence."

"I understand," Caddie says.

He clears his throat. "So. What are you going to do with what you saw?"

"I'm not going to do anything with it," she says steadily.

Avraham's eyes narrow. "Nothing?"

"Not yet."

Avraham shifts his weight. "Why not?" he says after a moment.

"I want to see more."

"More what?"

She hunts for a neutral word to describe what she has seen. "More of these patrols."

"Why more?"

"Seeing takes time," she says.

Avraham looks off into the night and his eyes grow vague. "I didn't plan for this, you know," he says. "Life takes unexpected turns. It disappoints. Then you either sink—or you act."

Caddie holds her pen over her notepad. "How can I get in touch with you?"

"Revenge is ancient," Avraham goes on, his tone insistent. "It defines the limits for the other side."

She drops her arms and raises her chin so he can see her face square-on. "I know, Avraham," she says.

Still he hesitates.

"A phone number?" she asks again.

He looks down at the car's tire, kicks it once, but casually, his previous fury fully spent.

He wants to be understood. They all want to be understood.

He rattles off a number. She repeats it as she writes it down and thanks him one last time.

SHE DRIVES HOME with the radio tuned to music—American-emigrant-turned-Israeli-rock-star Rami Kleinstein, whom she normally doesn't like, but now she turns the volume way up and hums along, willing herself not to think about the night, the shattered cars, the silent village, the expression on Avraham's face, her own quickened pulse.

Mr. Gruizin is at the entrance to the building when she gets there a few minutes after midnight. He seems to be pacing. "Up howling at the moon, are you?" she asks with a smile.

"You expecting anyone?" His voice is low, protective.

Oh God, oh yes, she thinks. She didn't want to hope that he'd be here, but she was hoping.

"Someone is at your door."

"It's fine," she says. "I'm sure it's fine. I think I had an appointment."

"At this hour?" Mr. Gruizin shakes his head. "Not likely." He offers her his arm. "I'll walk you up."

"Really, no need—"

"I've seen this fellow hanging around before," Mr. Gruizin goes on. "I don't like his looks." Then he actually seems to blush, though it's hard to tell in the poorly lit hallway. He lowers his head. "What a thing to say. I'm sorry. In these times, though, we must be cautious."

"Kind of you, Mr. Gruizin. But you don't—"

He's already taken her hand and settled it on his arm, covering it firmly with his own. He's on a mission and not to be stopped now.

"Hope you had a pleasant evening, my dear?" Mr. Gruizin says in a loud voice as they climb the steps. "Enjoyed yourself, did you?" He is talking simply to be heard and she doesn't answer. They reach the landing that leads to her apartment, and there he is. He stands straight. His face looks pale in the dim light, his eyes are black obsidians.

"Hello, Goronsky," Caddie says. "Mr. Gruizin, this is Alexander Goronsky. He helped me on a story I was covering tonight."

"Oh yes? Well, but business can be discussed tomorrow. Surely you should rest now, my dear?"

"Hello," Goronsky says. He takes Caddie's hand as though to hold it. She shakes hands with him, turning it into a formal gesture.

Mr. Gruizin looks back and forth between them, chuckles and shakes his head. "Forgive me. I've become a meddlesome worrier in my old age." He pats her arm. "Good night, my dear."

Mr. Gruizin walks back down the stairs, his footsteps resounding in the night's quiet. Caddie quickly opens her door and Goronsky follows her inside. "So? You were with them?"

She doesn't want talk. She has jumped from a high dive, is tumbling through air and needs something to break the fall. She begins to unbutton his shirt.

"You saw how they work?" Goronsky asks.

She touches his chin with her fingertips, kisses it, then peels his shirt back from his shoulders, inhaling him, but he is still talking.

"What did you think? Avraham, he's committed, yes?"

She doesn't understand what he's getting at, and it's difficult to concentrate on his words. She mainly notices his animated tone.

He takes her arms, making her stop and look at him. "Avraham acts," he says. "He doesn't crumble. He responds."

She swallows and straightens. "You want to *talk?*" She rubs her forehead. "Avraham responds, yes. But is responding necessarily good?"

"Always. As long as it is measured. You have to respond when you are hurt. Otherwise, you lose yourself. I saw it in my mother." He studies her a moment. "And you. Did you find what you needed?"

What you needed. A neutral question, one a reporter might ask a colleague about a story, but from Goronsky, it seems broader, more encompassing. She doesn't normally talk about what she needs. For years, she's told herself she doesn't have the same requirements as other people.

Now, unexpectedly, her cravings have turned intense, consuming and *wrong*. They make her feel soiled.

And he knows it. Somehow, Goronsky knows it.

She goes to the kitchen for a glass of water, and he follows. She turns to him. "What did you tell Avraham about me?"

"That you were an excellent reporter. That you had a lot of experience. That you could be trusted."

"What else?"

"That's it."

Damn, he's a good liar. She could almost believe him now, if she didn't know better. She returns to the living room, to the window. "Avraham said you told him something about an experience I'd had. One that would make me sympathetic to their cause." She keeps her back to him. She'd like to hear his voice without seeing him.

He is standing right behind her, not touching her. "You mean what happened in Lebanon to you and the photographer. Your friend."

"More than a *friend*." Caddie faces him then, aware of a wash of emotions. Anger, because he had no right to tell Avraham. Shame, because she's just used her relationship to Marcus for effect, and she's never done that before. And desire, strong, to see how Goronsky will react.

"More than a friend," he repeats coolly.

"How did you find out?"

"It is not a secret."

"You asked somebody?"

"It came up."

"With whom?"

"I can't remember."

She recognizes that her voice sounds taut and shrill, while his is reasonable, and suddenly this seems an inane conversation—after all, he could have heard about Lebanon *anywhere;* as he says, it's not classified information. She throws herself on the couch. "I don't care how you found out. The question is, where do you get off telling Avraham about it?"

"Those men are suspicious of reporters. You know that."

She waves her hand. "So what?"

"You have something that sets you apart. You've been through this."

"What makes you think—"

"That changes your perspective."

She wants him to explain *himself*, not her. "Listen. You gave me the entrée to Avraham. I'm grateful. But I don't *owe* you, you understand?"

"Of course you don't owe. You wanted to see this. I wanted to help you by setting it up. I thought we both . . ." He breaks off. "I had this idea," he says, almost as if speaking to himself, "that you would understand, eventually, what I knew from the start."

"I don't even know what you're talking about."

He sits on the arm of the couch. "The way I told it to Avraham, and the way I see it, is that your experience makes it easier for you to understand the views of these men, to realize that their position is ethical. They believe accepting so-called fate is more immoral than their vengeance. They think to do nothing would be like leaving your lover's body out to rot. Don't you think the same thing?"

"I don't know, Goronsky."

He grabs her hand. "We'll go to Lebanon together."

She pulls away.

"It makes sense," he says. "And you need it."

Stop. Stop talking, please, now.

"Once burned by milk, one will blow even on cold water," he says.

Caddie puts her hand to his mouth. She doesn't want any more words, any more thoughts, any more talk of Avraham or Lebanon. It's been an evening, another one, punctuated by an irretrievable turning point. Already—although she will not think of it—she's committed violations on half a dozen levels. And the night isn't over yet.

She feels Goronsky's hand near her neck. She tugs off the scarf that she'd worn over her head, that has since slipped to her shoulders, and touches his chin. And then his chest. And then his shoulders, and his arms as she roughly removes his watch. His thighs as she reveals his legs and pulls him toward the couch.

She looks everywhere except his eyes, because she wants neither to measure his expression, nor to consider her own. No more weighing, no more admissions. No more milk and water and blood. Let him think what he will about her motivations, her emotions. All she wants right now is to wave her arms and dance beneath the eye of some ignorant God until He finally pays attention, and then, with Him watching, all she wants is to vanish defiantly, nakedly, between the holy pews with Goronsky and be consumed, consumed by the prayer of oblivion and silence, internal, thick and suffocating; the oblivion she will receive like Communion if only she reaches out to touch him in the right way and keeps her eyes averted; the inner silence that will come—it *will*—with her body slammed senselessly against his, world without end, amen.

"Go," SHE INSISTS blindly an hour later as his fingers touch her lips, then waver on her shut eyelids. Her eyes are damp, but her mind has been emptied. Now she doesn't want to see him. After all, she doesn't know him, this Goronsky. She doesn't trust him.

She does not trust herself.

"Go?" he asks.

She doesn't answer.

"Open your eyes." His voice rises. "Look at me."

With her eyes sealed, the strains in his tone become salient, as distinct as teeth on a comb. Exasperation. Frustration. A plea.

"Look at my face."

But this gift of oblivion, she senses, will last only if combined with the blindness.

"Go."

"Tell it to me with your eyes open."

She'll keep her eyes shuttered. She'll wait for him to comply.

He takes both her shoulders. Shakes them gently. "Caddie." She doesn't answer, and he finally lets her go. She hears him rise, turn away from her. A moment's hesitation. She senses him watching her. She can feel his gaze, hot, as if she were standing next to a fire. Then she feels a rush of movement and hears him shove the coffee table. She hears it fall onto its side, dumping books to the floor.

Still she doesn't open her eyes.

She imagines her lids stitched together and she tries not to breathe, not to acknowledge in any way her participation in this life. There is another pause before she hears him begin to dress. She listens to him pull on his shirt and pants. She does not flinch when he brusquely touches her cheek with the back of his hand.

When she hears the squeak of the front door's hinge, she looks—looks too late, because she sees nothing except a blur: the door is already closing. She finds herself up, one hand against its warm wood, the other on its cold knob. Thinking of calling him back, but unable to act.

SHE WAKES ON THE COUCH at four in the morning to an ache in her arms and pulsing in her forehead: *They didn't actually hurt anyone. There's that.*

And then this: *I won't go again. Won't ask to go. Won't ever get that close to the line.*

And then this, which makes her roll onto her side and stand: *Damn him. Damn him for making this happen.*

She isn't sure which him she means. She shakes her head as though to free it from thought, goes to the kitchen, pours herself some juice. She doesn't want to think what might have been Marcus's reaction to tonight. To her. Maybe she does need out. Maybe Mike is right.

Goronsky's scent, their scent together, lingers in the living room. She cracks open the window, then goes to her bedroom to pull out Marcus's journal from under her bed. She supports it carefully, as though it were a sacred book that could redeem her. She wipes off the already assembling dust.

She grabs a blanket, returns to the couch and opens the journal to the next section. It is a series of rapid shots Marcus took with the motor drive running. He'd printed them in a yellow wash, so what would normally be black is the color of mustard and what would be white is pale like champagne. The snaps are all taken from the waist up, of a man hurling a stone. The first shows the stone balanced in both his hands. Then, incrementally in each frame, like those old-style flipbooks, the man cocks back his arm so the stone is directly behind and above his right ear, and he finally sends it forward. The series of photographs locates Caddie so fully in the moment that she can hear the stone sing. In the final one the man's arm is extended, one finger pointing.

Caddie finds herself focused less on the action of the man's arm than on his expression. In the first shot he looks calm if watchful, but by the final shot, which had to have been taken only a couple seconds later, his mouth is twisted, his face full of fury and pride. Caddie immediately recognizes the transformation. Despite its familiarity, or maybe because of it, she's fascinated. The way Marcus captured it. The way she can take it in piece by piece.

The more she stares at that final shot, when this nameless man has already heaved his stone and is looking with his changed face to wherever it has landed, the more she feels in her bones what she is certain this stranger must have felt at that moment. The exhilaration. *I did it. I got them, those bastards.* She tries to adopt his satisfaction, imagine it as her own, the way she shared in Avraham's. But she cannot. A still life, apparently, is not adequate. Too pure, too isolated.

At first she doesn't think Marcus jotted anything on these pages, but she examines each one carefully to make sure, and then she finds the words, painstakingly small, surrounding the outside of a photograph, one sentence inscribed on each side like a frame.

A disease. I got to get out.

For an insane moment, those words—the second sentence, specifically—buoy her. He would recognize the feelings within her. *God, I can't wait to talk to you.*

Then, of course, she remembers. The moments for talking to Marcus are gone.

She goes to the kitchen, pours a glass of milk and warms it in the microwave. Sipping it, she returns to the couch to look at his words again, to touch his handwriting on the page, to imagine his hand moving to make each letter.

Rule Number Three. Look at each section long enough to understand what he'd been thinking.

He'd been worn down. Yes. He wanted a break. Of course. But as she stares at his scrawl and drinks the warm milk and wills comprehension, she's forced to acknowledge: he'd been considering ditching the whole damn story. No—no, more than considering, because once a journalist writes words like this, he's moved beyond contemplation. Maybe Marcus even had another job lined up, dear God. But either way, there's no doubt. He'd been on the cusp of leaving: the Middle East, the hopeless politics, the bloodshed.

And her. Their imprecise, laugh-a-minute, cautious but central, apparently not-so-dependable relationship.

When the hell had he intended to tell her?

Nine

AGAIN SHE'S THERE, in front of the blue car. Only this time she carries a Remington slung over her shoulder like a purse. She takes the rifle into her hands and inhales. Then she uses the butt end, as Avraham did. She's battering the windshield now, hammering until it cracks. Afterward, she sees there aren't only two cars this time, but car after car, parked, waiting. She's going on to the next, pitching her whole body into the destruction, drops of sweat tumbling from her temples, her chest expanding with satisfaction. And then to the next. Pounding. And again.

It's the pounding that finally wakes her.

She's in Jerusalem. In her apartment. She must have fallen asleep over Marcus's journal.

But what is this hammering? It goes on as though war has broken out. And then she realizes it is her own door.

Someone is knocking, urgently.

"Just a second," she manages. She struggles to sit up on her couch, rubs her eyes. "All right," she calls more loudly, more clearly. This isn't Ya'el, who would use her spare key, and even if she'd lost it, would never pound on Caddie's door. In fact, none of her neighbors would do this. Goronsky. Damn Goronsky. Damn him for coming here so early and being so loud. Damn him, most of all, because she wants him, even now. She tugs on her jeans and yanks open the door.

A form stands in the dim hallway, smaller than Goronsky.

"Hell," says a male voice, "you look awful. Let's go to lunch."

"Rob!" She steps back, dizzy suddenly. "Rob," she says as she moves away and reaches to straighten her shirt.

"Yeah, your clothes *are* a bit off-center." He looks past her into the apartment. "What are you, throwing raucous parties, then sleeping on the couch? You've kicked yourself out of your own bedroom? That's extreme, Caddie, whatever nastiness you've done."

She's too tired, too just-awakened and surprised, for repartee. "No, I—I was working last night late so I—" She waves her hand vaguely. "What are *you* doing here, anyway?" It's Lebanon, she remembers. That's why he's here. He'll want them to go together. Which makes so much more sense than going with Goronsky.

"I called." He walks past her into the apartment. "You didn't get my message?"

He sounds like sandpaper. What has happened to his smooth radio voice?

Then she remembers the coffee table is still on its side in

the living room, and Marcus's journal is on the floor. "Message?" she asks as she moves to the couch and scoops the journal into her arms, giving up subtlety for expediency. "What message?" He is watching her with a quizzical half-smile. "Oh yeah, there was something, but only a couple words and then it broke off."

"Hey, maybe *you* should do heavy coffee intake while *I* have lunch."

She shrugs and hustles down the hall to shove Marcus's journal under her bed. Then she returns and slumps into the couch. He's still standing, watching her.

"I was up late," she says. "Working."

He glances at his wristwatch. "It's *eleven*."

She smiles. "Well, let me at least splash some water on my face." But she doesn't move. Now that she's starting to wake up, she notices he doesn't look too good. The burlap bag that holds his radio equipment is smeared with something the color of absinthe that seems to have texture. His shirt looks like he wadded it up and stuck it under a rock for a week. His shoulders are pointy, as though he's lost weight. His face is gray. "You here to work?"

He shakes his head. "Passing through. I'm headed to New York for a break. I'll be out of here by tonight. So let's go. Up, up, up. Don't have all week." He tries to gesture her to her feet.

She laughs. "Oh yeah. I remember you. You're a cup of boiled impatience."

"I'm hungry," he says. "Couldn't stand that crap the airlines call food."

"Give me a sec. You woke me out of a dead sleep, you know." The blood rushes to her cheeks at her choice of words. She looks at her knees as she rises. "Okay, we'll go. Okay."

Mia Café is a block away. It's open air with a few Formica tables and some folding chairs. Caddie orders a croissant and coffee, Rob a *shwarma* and a Maccabi. She feels more alert with the first sip of caffeine. He keeps studying his palms and dusting them off on his jeans as though they're dirty. She wonders when he's going to mention going back to Lebanon.

"So what are you on to these days?" Rob asks.

He's pallid and his eyes are unfocused. Well, he's changing time zones. And he's probably downed a miniature on the flight in this morning. At least one. Maybe already smoked a joint in a bathroom somewhere, too.

But it's more than that. He reeks of chaos.

"I'm not supposed to be covering the spot stuff now." She shrugs.

"So what are you doing?" he repeats.

"Violence. I'm trying to do a feature about the effects of violence." Her voice sounds tentative, untruthful. But Rob doesn't seem to notice.

"That fits," he says in an oddly satisfied tone that leaves her uncomfortable.

She doesn't want to ask what he means. "And you? Where you been lately?"

"Hell. Otherwise known as Chechnya."

"Oh yeah, I heard. I keep thinking that war is already over."

"It was. Now it's not. Now it makes the head bashing in *this* part of the world look like a playground tussle." He sounds taunting. He takes a slug of his beer, starts to wipe his mouth on his sleeve, but picks up his napkin and looks away.

"How long you been in?"

He scowls. "Went there right after."

"That's tough," she says.

He doesn't respond for a minute, his attention seemingly centered on his food. Then he looks up. "Want to hear about it?" He doesn't wait for her answer. "The incessant barking, that's the first thing you notice. Wild dogs everywhere—the sign of people dead or fled. It's all over my tapes. That and the wind shooting through abandoned farmhouses." He takes a slug of beer. "But I did find villagers, too. Starving, freezing and saving every cent to try to pay off the Russian soldiers so they won't be bombed. How's that for *corruptzia?*"

He pushes back his plate, picks up the salt, shakes a little into his right hand and tosses it over his shoulder. He seems unaware of his gesture.

"The Russkies try to make everything sound benign," he says. "When they question a Chechen, they use what they call 'children's mittens.' Cute name, huh? You know the string that slips through coat sleeves to hold two mittens together so kids won't lose them? In this case, they attach live wire to their victims' fingers, both hands, and connect them with another wire slung across the back. Then they flip on the current." He takes another slug of beer and smiles. "Does a good job of encouraging the tongue."

If he's pushing for some response, she's determined to disappoint him. Caddie feels certain—though she couldn't say exactly why—that it's important to show no emotion. "And you?" she asks. "You got what you wanted there?"

He shrugs. "Great material. No doubt about that." He studies the palm of his right hand as though he is reading it like a fortune-teller, then stares at her. "You remember how Marcus looked afterward?" he asks. "Vacuous eyes and a neat hole in the back? That's heaven compared to the way these guys in Chechnya are going." He drinks again, a big gulp like a long-distance runner. "Think rare meat loaf," he says.

She puts down her croissant. She takes two drawn-out breaths, trying to think of a response. "Hey," she says, finally, "you ever think about doing something to balance that out?"

"What out?"

"What happened to Marcus."

"What do you mean?"

Why is he being so obtuse? "Maybe you know someone from Chechnya," she says. "Someone who, for some money, would go into Beirut and . . ." She lets her voice trail off.

"What are you talking about, girl?" Rob says. "That's a place you don't even want to go." He leans back in his chair and stares at her. She sits up straight. If she has to endure this inspection, if she has to be the only one who sees the importance of responding to what happened, then okay. After a minute, a drawn-out grin contorts Rob's face. "Nothing matches the shock of seeing one of your own go down, does it?" he says. "Guess that's why we're doing what we're doing now, the three of us."

His way of catching up is starting to make Sven's remote telephone manners seem charming.

"Look at *me*," Rob says. "I used to cover the diplomatic scene, remember? Analysis pieces. Now all I want is *bang-bang*. A moth to the flame. Sound familiar?"

"No," she says. "You—" She hesitates. She and Rob were never close. But, what the hell, she'll ask anyway. "You using?"

"And you would too, filing from there," he answers.

She looks out the window. That's not true. She's never been much interested in drink or drugs, although Rob doesn't know her well enough to realize that.

"Why don't you stop, then?" Caddie asks after a minute.

"And do what? Go to London and become some bored old fat fuck covering cricket matches, like Sven? I'll pass. Hang around this less-than-Holy Land like you because I can't bear to leave the scene of the crime? No thank you."

"That's not me," Caddie says. She keeps her voice cool.

"Yeah?"

"This is a perennial good story," she says. "Great action, great quotes, front-page stuff. That's why I'm here."

"It's Jews and Arabs fighting and plenty of random slaughter," he says. "You get your bloodletting on a regular basis. There's the key."

"Hey, listen," she says. "Did Marcus ever, by chance, say anything to you about wanting to leave?" The question comes out bitterly, and she flushes even as she asks it. Damn, she's revealing her ignorance, and to *Rob*. But she's after a change of subject.

"No, but I can believe it," Rob says. "Anybody who's sane has got to decide it's enough after a while. And that's everybody except you and me, right?" His smile is distasteful. "I'll bet you're out there every day, taking the risks. Making sure you've still got the devil's luck. Am I right?"

"Oh yeah," she says with heavy sarcasm. "That's it."

"C'mon, admit it, Caddie. To me at least." He starts talking machine-gun fast. "It's intoxicating. Russian roulette. Whose name is written on the bullet? Someone you've passed on the street, shared a joint with, or maybe a bed? In this game, there's no thrill like survival."

He takes another hit of beer. He's wired, and the beer isn't mellowing him out.

"You're no healthier than I am," he says. "I wanted to see, and I have. Those moments on that Lebanese road are going to brand us for the rest of our fucking lives. Nothing will ever be the way it would have been if Marcus hadn't bit it. There will always be shadows at the edges of our internal screens. And we're always going to be trying to punish ourselves."

"C'mon, Rob."

"That's right. Punish—and maybe you especially."

She makes a scoffing sound. "Me? For what?"

He laughs, low and mirthless. "For starters, for not doing anything about that guy talking on the walkie-talkie at that checkpoint."

"What guy?" she asks. "*What* walkie-talkie?"

"A bunch of armed militants not known for mental dexterity got pissed at Marcus," he says, "and used that walkie-talkie to set up the hit. I see it now. I think I even suspected it at the time. But I brushed it off. I mean, I spent weeks arranging that damn interview. I didn't want *anything* to interfere." He makes a sound a lot like snorting. "And then I never *did* get to Yaladi. A big zero."

"I don't remember any walkie-talkie," she says. "But even so, Rob, what could we have done?"

He spreads his hands, open-palmed, as if to signal the inanity of the question. "Go another way. Make the driver change his route."

"The driver, yes." Caddie feels a rush of interest despite her distrust of Rob. "The driver. I always thought he was somehow connected."

Robs stares at her a moment, then nods. "Makes sense, you thinking that," he says. "Another reason for you to feel guilty."

"*Guilty?*"

Rob wipes his mouth with a napkin. "After all, you chose him," he says.

"What?" she says. "*You* chose him."

Rob laughs.

"You were in place in Beirut before us, you and Sven," Caddie says. "You—not we—knew these people. You—not we—chose the driver. I was worried about him from the start."

"You don't remember that I brought you two guys and you picked that one? You called him the lesser evil."

What the hell is he talking about? She's aware of an inner din, a chewing noise like broken gears. "I don't know why—" she says. "But—"

"Most of all, though, I'd suspect," Rob interrupts, "you feel guilty for pushing Marcus into Lebanon."

"What?"

"Because he should have been, of course, in New York."

She feels the blood rush to her cheeks, her stomach tighten.

"Maybe you're not aware of it," Rob says. "You always had a gift for denial. I admire you for that. Wish I did. But watch out, Caddie girl. You're as done in by the past as the rest of us."

"That's a load of crap."

"You aren't moving on. And if you keep the pause button pressed long enough, eventually you'll run out of that luck of yours. You'll end up buried here, smack between some furious Jew and a mad Shiite."

"What the hell are you talking about?"

"Get close enough to violence," he says, "and you'll get burned in the end. That's the lesson of Marcus. Burned." He spits the word out, then takes a breath. "But of course, you know that by now. It's not really about survival anymore, is it?" He's talking slowly, as though to make each word count. "It's about self-destruction. About hating yourself enough to want to do yourself in."

She's having trouble finding air. "You're full of shit," she manages.

Rob shrugs. "A little too much honesty for your taste, Caddie girl?"

"You're drunk, worn down, stoned, I don't know what."

He takes another gulp of beer. Then he grins. He has the nerve to grin, and somehow that, coupled with him calling her "Caddie girl," gives her strength.

She stands. Concentrating on keeping her hand from shaking, she pulls too large a bill from her pocket, drops it on the table and turns to go.

"Thanks for the illuminating talk," he calls after her as she leaves the café. "We'll call it even, by the way. One lost story for one lunch."

CADDIE TAKES LONG STRIDES, putting distance fast between herself and Mia Café, trying for deep breaths to mask the echo of Rob's voice. She hasn't forgotten, no. Rob is totally screwed up. Caddie is the one who remembers.

He chose that guy, that surly wild driver who took them down that dirt road past the woman and her child. *Did* one of the men have a walkie-talkie? She doesn't think so. But no denying that her fucking memory has become clumsy. There *were*—she recalls it now—two possible drivers. She remembers Rob trying to decide which one to take. She didn't have any role in that. Did she?

Even if she had, what was he implying?

Nothing worth thinking about. He's gone off. Too many shattered nights, too much of whatever he's using. Under normal circumstances she wouldn't let him rattle her.

But is he right?

Slumber parties. That's what Caddie thinks of now, a mainstay of her adolescence. At every sleepover, predictable as nightfall, they launched into horror tales in the dark, the way girls must do everywhere. They sat in tight circles in their button-up pajamas, as one with their tiny inhalations and nervous laughter. Everyone took a turn, the only rule—unspoken—being that each subsequent narrative had to ratchet up the stakes. Each one had to be more realistic, more directly threatening. So they began, Caddie and her friends, with strange wispy creatures in British graveyards, and moved to murders in America and ended with crazy men who held their daughters prisoner in cellars on the very street where they were huddled.

Caddie had fallen asleep for nights afterward recounting the stories in her head. They added excitement to her bland, one-dimensional days. A harmless thrill, too, because she knew she was personally immune from danger. That conviction held both in Grandma Jos's house—no matter what had befallen her parents—and in the Middle East—no matter how often she saw wounded crumple to the ground like wadded-up paper.

Since Marcus, though, she *has* imagined it. Her body sprawled, one leg bent awkwardly, blood seeping from above her right ear. Boys dragging her by her arms over the bumpy pavement, and then, recognizing it is too late, ditching her behind a barrel until the day's shooting is over. Pete cursing her privately, then praising her in public. Some newspaper executive searching fruitlessly for living relatives. Colleagues, maybe, designing a memorial web page for her. Just like they did for Marcus.

And her insides twist, her neck muscles pinch, her hands turn slippery with sweat.

She stops walking. She's been flying along without any awareness of destination. Now she takes stock. She's in the middle of a busy sidewalk, near a newsstand and the place she and Goronsky had dinner one night. She notices an ache in her chest, a soreness in her legs. What a lousy night's sleep. What a lousy morning. She's wiped.

Even so, she's not ready to go back to her apartment. She is, she realizes, only two blocks from Bank Leumi. Ya'el.

INSIDE THE UNDERVENTILATED, overly fluorescent bank, she takes the stairs to the second floor, where Ya'el and four other employees sit at desks in a large open room. Ya'el is peering down at a small stack of papers and doesn't glance up until Caddie sits in the chair next to her desk.

"Hi." Ya'el looks surprised to see Caddie but sounds comfortingly normal.

"I'm not crazy, am I?"

Ya'el laughs. "Maybe we better come up with a good working definition before I answer."

"It's Rob," Caddie says. "I mean, I had no idea. You should have seen him."

Ya'el leans forward. "Who?"

"Physically he looks awful. Verbally he ripped into me."

Ya'el, serious now, touches Caddie's hand. "Let me get you some water."

"Going to Chechnya may have pushed him over. I mean, I had nothing to do with choosing that driver."

"What driver?"

Caddie shakes her head. "What am I saying? You don't even know who Rob *is*, do you?"

"That's okay," Ya'el says.

"He was with Marcus and me. In the Land Rover. Hot in here, isn't it?" Caddie takes an envelope from Ya'el's desk and begins fanning herself. "He never got in touch with me, not once afterward. And now he shows up," she takes a deep breath, "out of the blue. I don't even know what he's accusing me of, exactly."

"Wait." Ya'el goes to the cooler and brings Caddie a paper cup of water.

Caddie waves the water away. "Do you think I should go? Back to Lebanon? He didn't even bring it up. I thought he would."

"Absolutely not." Ya'el shakes her head, fast. "I *know* the impulse, Caddie. I *know* the anger. But it's a bad, bad idea."

Caddie wishes she could clear her head. She takes a sip of water. Ya'el is, of course, absolutely the wrong person to ask about Lebanon. Ya'el would prefer it if Caddie never went near the West Bank. "Did you realize that Marcus was thinking of quitting?" Caddie asks. "Leaving here?"

Ya'el studies her a moment without speaking, then shakes her head slowly.

Caddie slumps back in the chair. "Of course not." Marcus and Ya'el weren't close. Caddie is acting deranged. She realizes, then, that this is the first time she's spoken to Ya'el since they went to the mechanic's shop. "I shouldn't have barged in here like this. You're working."

"No, I'm glad you did." Ya'el takes her hand. "I want to help, Caddie. I really do. This is not something you get over. It's something you finally incorporate."

"Ya'el? I'm sorry for the other day."

"It's okay."

Caddie rubs the back of her neck with one hand. "But I've got to go now."

"Stay. I get a break in ten minutes. We can get a cup of coffee."

Caddie shakes her head, rises, then sits again, and speaks fast, before she can change her mind. She has to say it aloud. "Do you know he wanted to be in New York that week?" she asks. "I'm the one. Oh God. I talked him into postponing it, into going to Lebanon with me."

Ya'el squeezes Caddie's fingers.

"If not for me, he would have been in New York. Do you know that?"

"Caddie, we all feel like traitors for surviving."

Caddie is surprised to feel her eyes filling. She can't attribute this to dust, damnit. "Sorry," she says.

"Don't apologize."

"No, really, coming in here like this. I've got to go."

"No, you don't."

"I absolutely do," she says, standing, "I do," rushing down the stairs, ignoring Ya'el's voice behind her, Ya'el calling her name.

AFTER BANK LEUMI, Caddie walks more slowly, as though her legs were stone. She lets her hand run over a rocky wall bordering the sidewalk as she pulls herself along. The very first time Jerusalem's ancient dust settled on her tongue and between her teeth, she knew this city was for her. A stewpot of frenzy and serenity. A contradictory mix of passion for life and ardor for afterlife. A center for needle-sharp moods that reverse within seconds: tender one moment, defiant the next. It appealed to her—no, more appropriately, filled her—as if Jerusalem were the missing marrow to her own bones.

Not far from home, she stops in front of a newsstand and stares at the selections. *Ha'aretz, Yediot, Jerusalem Report.* The newspapers and magazines merge and separate. The day's timing has been thrown off: it feels like it should be darker outside than it is. Colder, too.

She hears humming behind her, off-key and a bit shrill, but lovely in an odd, elusive way. It's Anya. She wears sandals instead of being barefoot, and she looks serene. Her eyes are focused. Good signs, all. This is a day when Anya seems clear enough to listen, and to talk. This is a chance, then; the one Caddie didn't realize she was waiting for but suddenly doesn't want to miss. Yes, Anya is crazy, full of elusive words. But her craziness may hold an eyelash of truth indistinguishable to most.

If Caddie rushes Anya, though, she knows from experience that Anya will be frightened and flee. The conversation will end before it begins. So she waits for Anya to approach, to look at her and smile, to raise an arm in greeting. Caddie sees words written in black ink on the inside of one of Anya's loose long sleeves. "Peace," Anya says.

"Anya, can we talk a moment?"

Anya smiles and takes Caddie's arm. Anya's right hand feels rough and warm, like a cat's tongue. She smells strongly of dusty gardenia. She doesn't seem to notice as Caddie turns her hand to read some of the writing on the inside of her clothes. "Lord, Who Watches Over Us . . ."

Does Anya recall Caddie's name? Can she even pull up her dead husband's name anymore? Caddie has no idea.

"Looking out my window a few days ago," Caddie begins, "I saw you on the street. Do you remember?" Anya's smile deepens; that is her only answer, if it *is* an answer. Caddie presses. "You seemed to be trying to tell me something."

Anya stops, tilts her head. "What could it have been?" After a moment she snaps her fingers, an odd gesture coming from her. "Oh yes. About your friend."

Caddie's breath turns shallow. "What about him?"

"The one I've seen you with."

Caddie moves closer. "Who always wore cameras around his neck?"

Anya begins picking at the skin on her throat. "We should not overanalyze, overplan," she says, her voice growing shriller.

"I *knew* you wanted to tell me something about him," Caddie says.

"Lenin was afraid of spontaneity. Believed it was dangerous." Anya speaks rapidly and her hand begins moving over her own chest, her fingers pinching.

"Tell me what you were going to say. Please."

Anya's face is chalky now, except for a red blotch on each cheek. "I see these things." Her voice is anguished. She backs away.

Caddie tentatively gathers Anya's hands into her own. "It's all right. What things?"

"Terrible, terrible things." Anya pulls away. "The colors, that's worst of all. The red."

Caddie holds her breath, afraid of what Anya will say next, needing her to continue. Anya glances skyward, murmuring to herself in an agitated way, pulling at her dress with her right hand. She drops her head and falls silent for a few moments, then looks up, her voice sharp, urgent. "Are you spontaneous?"

Caddie strokes Anya's arm. "Anya," she says. "What about my friend?"

"You should be." Anya claps her hands twice. "Lenin was wrong."

Caddie looks down the street, empty except for a soldier at the corner reading a newspaper. Maybe if she plays along, Anya will grow calmer and they will eventually get to whatever she saw or felt about Marcus. "Spontaneous," Caddie says. "Maybe. But I like to make plans."

Anya shakes her head, serious as if they are disagreeing over a momentous issue. "Don't be afraid," she says. "Spontaneity is in the family of wonder. And you know what Sir Thomas Browne said about wonder."

Caddie takes both of Anya's hands in hers again. "Can you tell me what you wanted to say about my friend?"

"Your friend." Anya's face is growing ashen again, her expression frightened. She begins to breathe quickly, and points down the street toward the soldier. "Him," she says. "Oh God, I am sorry. You will never see him alive again."

The soldier looks up as if he senses he is being spoken about. He smiles slightly, a little vainly, at the two women watching him.

Anya groans, drops to her haunches. "Only the greedy man. Should desire to live. When all the world. Is at an end," she says in a chant, her body rocking slightly.

Caddie suddenly sees herself as if from afar, bent over this poor crazy woman, imploring her for answers. She reaches down and gently pulls Anya to her feet. "It's okay. Never mind, it's okay."

Anya blinks as if she's suddenly stepped into sunlight. "Thank you." Her smile is weak. She holds a finger to her lips, requesting silence. "Sir Thomas Browne," she says. "'We carry within us the wonders and love we seek without.'"

Her color is coming back. Her voice is taking on a preacher's ardency. "O Jerusalem, Jerusalem, you who kill the prophets

and stone those sent to you. How often have I longed to collect your children together, as a hen gathers her chicks." She
shakes her head sorrowfully and makes a quarter-turn, melo-
dramatically, as though on a stage, her arms held slightly apart
from her body.

The line between intuition and insanity is narrow, so narrow. Like the difference between a reporter's best instincts and
her blind arrogance. " 'Bye, Anya." Caddie speaks so softly that
she thinks at first she is not heard.

Anya waves slightly. "But you were not willing," she says as
she steps away. "And now your house is left desolate."

Ten

"IT'S ME."

She leans against the wall, telephone pressed to her ear, weakened a little by the intimacy of this shorthand between them. Her desire is sharp and immediate, triggered only by hearing those words. But she reminds herself that she doesn't actually know who the hell "me" is. A professor? Or a right-wing extremist?

He gives up waiting through the phone's dead air. "I need to see you. Okay?"

God, she loves the way his voice sounds, how it mirrors her own neediness. She takes a deep breath.

"Now?" he asks.

"I was on my way out," she says. *I can stay in*, she wants to say.

"This afternoon, then?"

"Yes."

"I'll come to your apartment?" he says.

No. Because if he comes here, she'll reach for him, she'll fall into him, she'll forget that she has to ask him something. She has to ask, straight out, about his association with Avraham. She has a vision that keeps intruding. Not one of him with her. One of him breaking a windshield. Him pointing a rifle.

"I'll meet you on Ammunition Hill," she says.

"A *battlefield?*"

She laughs at his tone. "The weather is great. So is the view. No one's there except the tourists, and they're preoccupied by trenches." She takes a deep breath. "Two o'clock," she says, and hangs up.

HE COMES BEARING CHEESE and crackers and sparkling water, his eyes soft and eager. Her stomach tightens when she sees him. Butterflies? She wishes they were butterflies; that would tickle. Instead, the sensation feels more like something chewing her insides out. She wishes now that they were alone, somewhere private.

They walk past a bench and sit beneath a pine tree. He spreads out a handkerchief and places everything down precisely, as though it could determine his future. Caddie can't stop herself from touching his hand. He looks up, his expression vulnerable.

"What?" she asks.

"I forgot the glasses."

"Glasses, on a picnic?"

"Each picnic should have its own character," he says.

"Some require *glasses?*"

"And others fine china. And others only black olives and bread."

She can't prevent a smile. He is watching her, waiting. "So?" she says after a minute.

"I want to clarify some matters."

"Sometimes you speak so formally," Caddie says. "Is it only in English? Or in Russian, too?"

"First, about Lebanon. I apologize for telling Avraham."

Caddie waves her hand, looks away.

"I should have apologized from the start," he says. "But morning is wiser than evening."

"It's forgotten."

"I don't want to forget. I want to know about it. From you."

She looks at him closely; she can tell he does want to know. But she shakes her head.

Goronsky picks up a pine needle, uses it to prick his palm gently, then lets it fall. "I got angry the other night."

She glances away, pretends an interest in a guide loudly conducting a tour in German twenty feet away. The guide, flanked by about two dozen tourists, carries a canary-yellow flag.

"It's because my mother used to refuse to look at me, too," Goronsky says. "My strongest childhood memory is of knowing I was invisible to her. Nonexistent."

But at least, Caddie considers saying, *at least you knew why*. As a child once, Caddie asked Grandma Jos why her mother didn't live with them. Grandma Jos, grating hard chocolate for a pudding, stared into middle distance and grimaced as if the question pained her. "She doesn't like staying," she said after a moment. "That's it. Now leave it alone." Then she popped a sliver of bitter chocolate into Caddie's mouth, ending the discussion forever.

Caddie says nothing to Goronsky. Why does speaking seem more frightening than covering the clashes? She watches the guide point in broad, looping gestures as the tourists rotate their bodies to follow her motions.

"Some days my mother became so depressed she couldn't see anything," Goronsky says after a moment. "She would forget to shop for bread or milk. We could have put our teeth on a shelf, we had so little to eat." He leans forward and she finally looks at him directly. His face is composed, his eyes dark. He seems to be gauging her.

"Then she had other days," he says. "Remember the first time we went out together to that café? You told me about covering a tornado. When you described it, I knew that was the word I'd been looking for. My mother would become a tornado. Everything she touched, she would hurl. Shattered dishes, dented lampshades. Books with splintered spines."

Caddie wants him to slow down. She doesn't want to miss any part of his story. The air rushing past the Jerusalem slopes has turned raw and she rubs her arms against the chill.

"She talked to herself during it all," Goronsky says. "I could never fully make out the words. Sometimes I would grab her waist, her arms. No more, no more, I would say. But I wasn't strong enough, I wasn't—"

His tone, the expression in his eyes, make it impossible for Caddie to stop herself from reaching out to touch his cheek. He takes her hand, holds it.

"It's funny, but those were our best times in some ways." His fingers entwine with hers. "Afterward, when she was spent, she would hold me. Cling to me, even. Sometimes tell me she was sorry." He falls silent for a moment. "She smelled like damp tea leaves and cinnamon."

A few feet away, the guide is speaking in a somber, indistinguishable murmur. Describing, probably, the predawn battle here in 1967, a huge concrete bunker exploding into chunks small enough for a child to cradle in his hand. Hand-to-hand combat that took thirty-six lives by sunrise. Body parts tossed like salad. All that day, a thick smoke hung over this hill as if to hide something shameful.

The tourists knot themselves around their guide. And Caddie, in a single flash, feels Marcus leaning into her. She senses the heat and weight of his body, hears the grinding noise as the Land Rover swerves sharply. "They popped up out of nowhere," she says, almost against her will. "It was another interview, that's all. We had no way of knowing. No way." She takes a breath, her eyes on the hills. "But I keep thinking I should have known. That, in fact, I *did* know, only I didn't pay close enough attention. The day felt off from the very start. So what was I doing, letting myself be distracted?"

As lost as she is in those moments, she's still aware of Goronsky sliding closer. "By the time I was together enough to write," she says, "it was already written. Old news. So I couldn't even turn it into a story. You know, Marcus thought we should connect to the people in our stories, and I didn't. And now I don't know what's right—what to close myself off to and what to let in. All I know is—" She takes a deep breath, catches herself. "I don't think they should live if Marcus . . ."

She tries to focus on a cumulus cloud overhead. Goronsky is stroking her right palm with his callused fingers now. She imagines him digging a hole in garden dirt with his hands, planting something.

"How about if we go back?" he says after a minute.

"Already?" It's not the response she expected. She's a little disappointed, but she doesn't want to show it. "Okay, sure." She pulls away, starts to get up.

He puts a hand on her leg to stop her. "No, I don't—I mean Lebanon."

Her chest tightens. "This again?" She keeps her voice light.

"Don't say no," he says. "You have things to do there, Caddie. A balance to restore."

Balance. The same word she used with Rob. How is it that Goronsky so often sounds like her echo?

"Just moving on is not a virtue when people we care about are destroyed," he says. "Integrity requires something more." He hesitates. "Let's take a trip together. Don't plan. See what happens. Sometimes the appetite comes during the meal." He leans forward. "Besides," he says slowly, "Ludmilla Federova, my supervisor, sent a fax. I have to finish here, Caddie. They want me back in Moscow. I'd like those last few days with you."

So there's an end. Another one. "We're still going with this professor fairy tale?" Caddie asks, more bitterly than she intended.

"Let's talk about Moscow later," he says. "First Beirut. Four or five days. This is the time."

She knows so little about his Moscow life. Where he lives, where he goes for picnics, with whom. She turns away from him. The guide has finished her spiel and the German tourists are staring through their sunglasses down into the winding trenches with such intensity that Caddie would think, if she didn't know better, that the ditches themselves held a vital secret. This is their few minutes to wander. But they aren't wandering. They practically cling to one another, immobilized not by the awful history of bloody Ammunition Hill, but by their inability to truly imagine it. Not only is it a remote and odd tourist stop, but there aren't any souvenirs, not even postcards. It's just something that happened once, and that is over now.

Goronsky clears his throat to reclaim her attention. "I could set up a meeting with Yaladi, if you want."

She is startled to hear him say that name aloud. "Yaladi? What's he to do with you?"

"He funds extremists."

"But why would he talk with you?"

"I have links," Goronsky says.

Caddie remembers a particular photograph of Yaladi, widely published. She remembers his thin face and wide eyes, his apparent sincerity as he leaned forward into the camera. All things to all people, a good-looking man's man. "Have you ever spoken to him?"

Goronsky shakes his head. "I could find a way."

As strange as it sounds, almost presumptuous, she believes him.

She remembers Yaladi quoted as saying at a rare news conference in Beirut that he "loved" journalists, that through them he stood the best chance of being understood. She never expected to be able to ask Yaladi directly how a journalist on the way to a prearranged interview with him could have ended up dead. She tries to imagine what his expression would be as he faced that question. She feels certain he knows who did it, if not why, and wonders if he would tell her. Maybe he would even help set up a hit—no, it would have to be someone else. But there are always seedy characters hanging around Beirut hotels. She could find the right person, even without help from Rob or Sven. A thousand bucks would be plenty to arrange a killing in that country.

"You're not going to die there," Goronsky says abruptly.

She hadn't been thinking of that, but the conviction with which he speaks makes her sit back.

"You'll be fine," he says. "Pushing, questioning, writing it all down—you'll be doing it for a long time."

A rush of something close to rage shoots through her. "We *all* feel that way. We *all* see ourselves as going on, even as being crucial in a small way. We can't imagine our *little burning flame,*" she says the words sarcastically, "being extinguished. And it's only a comment on the weakness of our imaginations." She stands. "Marcus felt invincible, too," she says. "He felt invincible that very day. And he had plans. Lots of them."

Goronsky leans back against the tree. "When I was study-ing psychology, my classmates sat around dreaming of an in-triguing psychotic patient who would, one day, walk into their offices and elevate their status. Like Luria's famous S. All *I* wanted, for years, was to understand my mother's mind."

"This is to do with Lebanon?" she asks.

He looks out over the city. "The first thing I did when I got here was to go up along the coast. To where my parents were attacked. To smell the ocean, touch stones, walk the beach. See if I felt anything." His face is composed. "I didn't. A sense of waste, yes. But no greater understanding of my mother. No finality. Not even a rush of self-pity, though I ex-pected *that*."

The wind is picking up. She leans closer to catch his words.

"Afterward, though," he says, "I did see what I had to do next. That's why I'm suggesting it for you."

She wants to return to Lebanon, that's a given. She wants to return even though this unspoken pact she'd imagined among her and Sven and Rob—to come up with a plan, to go together, to set things right—doesn't exist.

His hand on her arm feels unnaturally warm, almost hot. "I've got to get back to work," she says.

"Shall I book the flight to Lebanon, then? We'll go through Cyprus?"

She glances toward the tour guide, who is waving her flag and leading the group away. "I'll think about it."

"Good," he says. Nodding. "Good." He takes her shoul-ders, kisses her.

Dizzy, she digs her heels into the ground for a moment. Then she turns and walks down from the old front line.

SHABBAT AFTERNOON. Caddie slouches in an easy chair, bare feet propped on the windowsill to catch the breeze with her toes. Ya'el is on the couch, escaping her kids for a few moments. Despite her presence, the air is heavy with silence. The machinery of the apartment building buzzes as though to comfort. Two cars, maybe three, murmur on the street below, traveling far slower than the speed limit. Children speak at some distance, behind perhaps a half-dozen closed doors, their soft-hued tones holding a sense of gravity. This is the hush born of a holy day, a day meant for introspection.

The relentless, horrid hush. The one she's been avoiding.

The quiet of Caddie's childhood was a painful, enforced restriction. Now that she can choose, she shuns, out of conviction, all those stuffy places where No Noise is required: churches, libraries, lecture halls. She and days of mandatory silence are as compatible as a Jewish prayer shawl and a Palestinian *keffiyeh*.

"I can hear my grandmother," Caddie says. "She would warn me that it's a sin to dislike God's days for any reason—let alone because they're too damn quiet. But I can't help it."

"Not me. I'll perform any ritual in the book for ten minutes' peace. Now hush." Ya'el closes her eyes.

Caddie stands, circles the border of her living room. What does someone who's trying to avoid thinking do with a day of compulsory introspection? If she found herself in a dark hall-way, she wouldn't waste time considering. She'd step forward and strike a match.

"Caddie," Ya'el says, eyes still closed. "Sit down. Please."

Caddie positions herself in the easy chair again. All right, then. Goronsky's proposal: one issue she's been avoiding.

She could keep it as simple as a pilgrimage, this trip to Lebanon. A return to that place where the bush began to move, then morphed into a man, then fired a gun. She fears certain details may soon escape her: the sharp cerulean of the sky, the way the dust lay on her cheeks, how the birds cried out skittishly as Caddie and the others shot along that naked track in the Land Rover. In an effort to preserve at least the place, she could take a camera, a tape recorder, perhaps a bag-gie to fill with dirt. It's sentimental, but no one would ever have to know. And maybe she'd have a chance to identify those bastards. Look them directly in the eyes.

Even though she doesn't know who's responsible for killing Marcus, the "street" surely does. She can't find a killer-for-hire online, and no colleague is going to come up with a recom-mendation. But she could find one herself. She'd make some calls, say she is working on a story. How much would it take? A thousand dollars would surely cover it. She'd have to ask for proof of a job done. She wouldn't want a photograph—too graphic, too tangible. Maybe a small, vague article in a Beirut newspaper confirming the death? Then she'd have a single face-to-face meeting, shove the cash into waiting hands and leave. Leave Beirut for good. She wouldn't tell Goronsky, but even if he guessed something, he'd soon vanish back to Moscow. That would be the end of it.

She'd love to look that driver in the face again. That bastard. She remembers the heavy way he stared at her when she insisted he stop for the woman. There's the off-chance, of course, that he wasn't in on the ambush. Maybe she'd see only an impoverished, struggling Beruiti, a fundamentalist but still just a man, bumbling along, doing the best he can. It's possible, she guesses.

And if she saw the other, that's where her thousand dollars would go. No regrets.

The timing is ideal. Jon returns to Cairo at the end of next week, and she returns to the daily grind. If she makes the trip soon, she needn't tell the newspaper anything. Slip there, slip back. Nobody's business. And then, she imagines, she'll have cleaner emotions. Maybe an eagerness for something fresh. New York might even seem a viable opportunity.

But to make the trip with Goronsky? That's more insane than the rest of it. Not only her attraction to him, which scares her, which seems stubborn. There's another issue, the crucial one she forgot to raise on Ammunition Hill. Exactly how does Goronsky know Avraham?

Ya'el stands, stretches. "I have to get upstairs to the girls." At the door, she turns to take a searching look at Caddie and nods as though seeing something definable. "The day has its purpose. Use it."

Caddie pours herself an orange juice and rolls her neck, listening to it crack. Avraham. Another topic she hasn't wanted to think about.

Yes, yes, she'd decided absolutely not to approach him again. She'd wadded up the phone number he gave her and tossed it on her dresser, intending to throw it away.

One more time, though, might give her exactly what she needs. With the right anecdote, the right quote, her story will pop up like a shadow puppet illuminated against a wall. She'll have something to show for all this. Combine it with a trip to Lebanon, and she may finally be able to move forward.

But what if the settlers attack the cars again? For a second, she relives the thrust of the men's arms, the fireworks of shattered glass. She feels again the shuddering of the Land Rover as it sped forward. She thinks of the swagger, the mayhem, the power of that moment when one becomes predator instead of prey. The tight flame that runs between men when the sun is down.

Her breathing becomes faster. Something heaves within her chest like the movement of a boulder.

She rises, paces once around the room, picks up her notepad, tosses it down. The room feels stuffy. The phone, when it rings, is a relief. "Hey." Pete's voice is warm. "A bunch of us are at the American Colony. Come join us."

She holds the phone against her ear with her shoulder and hesitates only a beat. "Be there in half an hour."

THEY SIT IN THE COURTYARD, two tables pulled together near the Turkish-style fountain, and right away Caddie feels guilty. Guilty that she's dressed in her tight jeans, that she put on dangly earrings, that she orders a glass of Domaine de Latroun wine from the nearby Trappist monastery, as she always did with Marcus. Guilty that it's all still going on, a group lounging around drinking and laughing and sharing anecdotes from the field.

It's more difficult than she expected, to talk, to smile. But she feels her colleagues watching her, so she leans back in her chair and sips the wine, even though she doesn't really want it, doesn't really trust herself with it. She asks for water, too, and then a refill, and another, and she keeps drinking the water, drinking and drinking to give her something to do with her mouth besides the forced smile.

There are visiting journalists, some she barely knows, because a U.S. envoy named McCormick is in town talking peace. They are speculating about whether top Israeli leaders will come to a session with the Palestinians, hosted by McCormick, if it is held in east Jerusalem.

"Hey, can't we talk war?" Pete says. "That's where the photos are. I can't wait until McCormick goes home."

"I want to talk about his chances of pulling off this meeting," says a woman journalist whose name Caddie can't recall. She's mock indignant. She pulls back her long dark hair with one hand, then lets it fall again. "Peace is more important than war to my copy right now," she says. "We're leaving town Friday. You can talk about whatever you want after we're gone."

"Amen," says Pete, drawing laughter.

"Yeah, everybody always leaves town," Caddie says into a lull. "You're all so fickle. Even my grandmother skipped out on me eventually, though I guess it's churlish of me to count death as a betrayal." She laughs, but no one responds.

She takes another drink of water, embarrassed, and then escapes to the bathroom, slipping down the stairs to the darker lower level, one hand gliding along the cool stone wall. As she's standing at the sink, the visiting journalist comes in. Slightly dropping her chin, she looks at Caddie over the shiny brass fixtures and squeezes her hand. What the hell is her name? Caddie hates this artificial intimacy. "I heard what happened," the woman says. "I'm so sorry." She keeps squeezing and leans forward, her hair falling partly over her face.

Caddie tries to smile. "Well, thanks," she says, lying. "Thanks for mentioning it." Then she flees from the bathroom. *I will not be famously known as the reporter who was with Marcus when he died.*

She takes the long way back to the table—still no peace, the hotel is crowded as usual. Then, sitting around that table watching the Palestinian waiters and the other customers, she loses track of what exactly they are all speaking about. She keeps smiling and nodding as long as she can.

"I've got to get going," she says finally, after what seems an acceptable length of time. Pete insists on walking her out.

"You know, I think you're almost back to normal," he says in an upbeat voice as they leave the courtyard.

"Normal?" She barely stifles a groan. Is this how it goes, then? Is this truly how one returns to normal? Maybe next time she won't feel bad about the earrings, the wine?

But she doubts it. It's hard to imagine she'll ever want to return to the American Colony again. Maybe, in fact—and here's the worst thought—maybe she'll never be restored to even an acceptable facsimile of what she was before.

"You were," Pete is saying, "a little too reckless for a while there."

By the side of her car now, Caddie shoves her fingers in her pocket to grab her keys. "Like you aren't?"

"I'm careful."

"Shit, Pete. You've been hit by rubber bullets, what? Three times?"

"Four. And if any one of them had been live . . . But hey, I'm fifty-three. This is what I'm doing with my life. I'm not going to get married ever again. I don't have kids." He opens the car door for her. "You still have—other possibilities."

"I don't want other possibilities."

"Caddie. You don't know that."

She's starting to hate his tone. She gets in the car. "You think that," she says, "because I'm a woman. You assume a man makes this kind of choice deliberately, but a woman must secretly want to be a wife and a mother."

"No, Caddie."

"Yes, Caddie."

"Look." Pete leans down to her window. "I don't want to have this argument. It's been hell for you, I know that. I know you and Marcus were tight."

She inserts her key into the ignition, then turns back to Pete. "Hey, did Marcus ever say anything to you about wanting to leave Jerusalem. To quit?"

Pete hesitates. "Not specifically. But I knew he was getting tired of it."

"Howdja know that?" She keeps her voice light.

"Little things. He was morose sometimes, which wasn't like him. Other times, he was too cocky. I take risks, sure, but it's calculated. With him—well, sometimes even in the field, his head was somewhere else. Then, when the action was slow, he'd ask about other stories I'd covered, good places to live in the States. He was considering his options."

Hell. Casual colleagues had known more than she did.

Perhaps her face gives something away; perhaps there's only so long one can go on disguising one's feelings. "Hey," Pete says, "he was probably going to tell you." He shifts and straightens. "He was, I'm sure. I bet he was waiting for the right time."

Pete knows shit. Shit about her, or about Marcus and her. And the last thing she wants is his pity.

So she lies again. "Thanks. Thanks for giving me a call." And she gives a half-wave and pulls out of that parking lot, away from the shade trees and the wrought-iron tables and the jasmine scent and the detached, laughing journalists, as fast as she can.

AT HOME SHE PULLS her tan duffel bag out of the closet. Generally she packs light and quick, cramming her clothes and papers and toothbrush into the bag fifteen minutes before leaving on a trip. But she unzips it now, and throws in a shirt and two pairs of underwear. A symbolic act. She hasn't made up her mind, no. This is like a promise to herself, though. She didn't die in Lebanon. She's not buried yet. She hates that expression Pete used, *move on*. She has things to do first, before she considers what will be next and where it will be.

Then she lifts the journal out from under the bed. She's still pissed at Marcus for planning to blow off the story and her with it, and for never letting on. Maybe if she'd known— whatever. Bottom line: she's in no mood to linger over the journal's last photographs, search for its final words. She doesn't know when she ever will be. But it's been an unpleasant evening. She wants the comfort of *some* presence. So she shoves it under her pillow. It's all she has, fuck it: a dead man's diary.

Eleven

GORONSKY IS LEAVING a phone message as she opens the door to her apartment, returning from the *makolet* with cheese and grapes and thoughts of picnics. " . . . got our tickets," he says. "Two more days. Call me, Caddie. Call as soon as you can."

He sounds like someone desperate to hear her voice, and it makes her shiver. She's never had that before—or, more accurately, never allowed herself to have it. He's as hooked as she is—could he be? She thinks of calling him right back, catching him with his hand still on the receiver. But she wants to think before she feels. She listens one more time to his words, turning up the volume so the sound from the tiny speaker fills the room.

She reaches for the erase button, then stops, halted by a sense of having forgotten something crucial. She walks around the apartment, hoping to jog her memory. She hasn't missed an interview. She isn't expected anywhere. "What?" she asks aloud, and stands in the middle of the living room, listening as though the building's creaks could answer her.

In the bedroom she sits cross-legged in front of two weeks' worth of clean laundry on the floor. She folds carefully, trying to concentrate on flattening the wrinkles with her palm, clearing her mind.

Someone should be told. That must be what's nagging at her, what feels forgotten. Someone, a colleague, should be clued in about Lebanon. Just in case. Street Journalism 101: don't take off without letting another warm, safely based body know where you're going.

It's got to be Jon—who else? So far he hasn't spilled any secrets to New York. He hasn't gone neurotically superprotective on her, like Pete. And he'd surely cover for her if Mike found out about the trip and blasted her for leaving without informing the newspaper. *Jon knew.*

She'll tell him it's for her feature story. Gathering material. And though Jon will know she's lying, he won't give her a hard time. That's not in his makeup.

Decided, she ditches the unfolded clothes. Before leaving, she dials Goronsky's hotel room. He's not there, so she leaves her own message. She's not as brave as he is, though. She controls her tone so it doesn't fully reveal her need.

"YOU DON'T HAVE TO KNOCK," says Jon, looking up from the computer as she taps lightly at the office's open door. "Unless this means you're angling to become a visitor here instead of resident correspondent?"

"Looks like you've got the place pretty well cleaned up for me," she says.

"And you better appreciate it. It wasn't easy. There were times when I couldn't see over the stack of newspapers and used Styrofoam cups."

"Four more days," she says. "Going to miss it?"

"Oh, Cairo's all right."

"Yeah, but it doesn't have your old haunt, Balfour Street."

"You remember that?" He laughs. "My first time. But I don't go back there."

"No?"

"That might make it feel like more of a loss than it really was."

She smiles at his wistful tone.

"Actually," he says, "I'm ready for a little break from Jerusalem. It's a pretty draining assignment. *You've* done it for almost five years. Time for a change, Caddie?"

She studies him, then shakes her head. "Mike told you, did he?"

Jon laughs. "But it *is* a good offer."

She gestures to take in the office. "What, give up all this for New York City?"

"It's a promotion, kiddo. A pay raise. A great mix—some time in the field, some time in the big city. Hey, it might even lead to something besides all this endless, hopeless bloodletting."

"You say that like it's a bad thing."

"You know, a sane job."

"What *is* a sane job, anyway?" she asks.

"Me? I was always into archaeology," Jon says. "That's what got me to Egypt in the first place." He picks up a paper clip and taps it on the desktop, his voice growing ardent. "Not archaeology as politics, the way it's done here—not searching for signs of who peed on this land first, in order to win a point in the debate over who gets to pee here now. But as layers of the past, brought back to life." He pauses, and offers an abashed grin. "Mike *did* tell me to work on you, but the fact is, I can sincerely say I think it's perfect for you. A good opportunity."

Caddie doesn't reply.

"No one doubts that you're tough, Caddie. You've kept going, haven't missed a beat. It's almost inhuman."

"Gee, thanks."

Jon begins unbending the paper clip. "Maybe I'm pushing you to take this offer because of where *I'm* coming from. Lately I've been thinking."

"That's always dangerous," Caddie says. She picks up an old *Herald Trib* from the desk, spreads it on her lap, runs a finger blindly over the front-page headline.

Jon falls silent. He opens the desk drawer, pulls out small needle-nosed pliers and uses them to finish straightening the paper clip.

Shit. Did I do this to Marcus? Push him away when he wanted to open up?

Marcus, here in this office. It was a Wednesday, the day of

the regular foreign ministry briefing, four days before Beirut. That would make it, what? Six days before the ambush. Both of them leaning against the edge of the desk.

"I need out, Caddie." That's what he'd told her, his voice grave. "I truly—"

She'd cut him off. "I know, I know. You need breaks. One every three months—that's your credo," she said.

"But that's not what I mean. This time—"

She waved her hands to stop him. "So fine, take off. Only Lebanon first. Please."

He stood, ran a hand through his hair in clear frustration. "What's the big deal?"

Caddie shrugged. "Sven e-mailed me. He and Rob are going. He wouldn't say exactly what they had cooking, but he said it would be good."

"Caddie. In the Middle East, there are a million good stories today, and another million waiting to happen tomorrow." He hesitated. "Is it that you want me to stay?"

"It's that I want you to go to Lebanon with me. Your work, Marcus, is unmatchable."

He groaned and looked away. "My damned photographs." But then he dropped it, putting on the light touch she needed. "All right. Anything for you, m'dear."

Now she lets the newspaper fall to the floor. "Sorry, Jon. Thinking what?"

Jon tips his head in a way that makes him look even more boyish than usual. "My mom used to say if she imagined something bad, like her kids being kidnapped or hit by a car, it wouldn't happen. As though the thought itself was a vaccine against tragedy. Or at least that *particular* tragedy." He focuses on a growing pile of bent and straightened paper clips while he talks. "Growing up, I made fun of her," he says, braiding two paper clips together. "But I ended up just as superstitious. I had an idea, deep down, that if I could hang on to this *distance,* watching other people's lives flipped inside out, I'd be immune. Like being a reporter kept me safe or something. Which is an insane idea, of course." He lowers his paper clips to look directly at her. "Go to New York, Caddie," he says.

"Jeez, Jon. They'd have to torture me to get me to talk as earnestly as you do." Then she winces. She's doing it again.

"What you, what Marcus—" Jon stumbles, and returns to working with the pliers. "It got me thinking. Trying to figure out why *I* do what I do—instead of, say, archaeology."

She takes a deep breath. "And so, why?"

He hesitates, looking at a corner of the ceiling. "I don't know," he says at last.

She leans toward him across the desk. "For Christ's sake, *I'll* tell you why. Because we get a front-row seat to all this *passion*. We get to write about it, make it ours. Because the life-and-death drama of this story raises our adrenalin and clarifies our minds and keeps us so busy we *can't* get bogged down in the bullshit minutiae of normal life—the mortgages, the Sunday barbecues, the PTA meetings. All that stuff is—goddamnit, face it—boring. What do you want, to spend the rest of your years as a *dead white male?*"

Then she stops, silenced by the phrase. Its coldness. Its literal meaning.

Jon, however, merely looks amused. "I don't think you'd be bored in New York," he says.

"We're recording people at their most profound moments," she says. "This is a critical conflict. Maybe *the* critical conflict. We're trying to understand, and then explain. Isn't that a noble goal?" She hesitates before going on. "And besides, maybe being here, reporting on it, is the best answer to the violence. To the deaths." She leans back in her chair, suddenly weary, and wondering how much she believes of what she just said.

Jon seems to be concentrating on his paper clips. "Think of the people we know who've been at this a long time," he says mildly. "They're all single, or divorced, or with grown kids they see once every three years."

"Your point?"

He smiles at her arch tone. "This is an unhealthy addiction. There's only so much one can take before pulling out—or going nuts."

"*If* it is an addiction," she says, "it's one that makes us more alive."

"All addicts think that, don't they?" Jon clears his throat, and she sees a blush creep up his neck. "I'm not trying to say anything about *you,* by the way," he adds.

She looks at her hands. "Right-o."

"Probably I'm burned out right now," Jon says. "Temporarily."

The silence, then, is self-conscious. After a moment he holds up the paper clips for her inspection. Amazingly, he has fashioned them into a tiny, intricately chorded bridge that arches as though over water.

"Where'd you learn to do that?" she asks.

He shrugs. "I was a kid. I played with paper clips. It beat sitting around doing nothing but listen to my parents argue on Sunday afternoons." He offers it to her.

She takes it, oddly touched and embarrassed at once. This confessional session hasn't ended badly, but she still prefers the way interviews usually finish: a handshake and a thank-you. A hell of a lot less awkward.

"What brought you by, anyway?" Jon asks after a moment.

She rises. "Nothing in particular." Enough confidences for one day; she doesn't have the energy to mention Lebanon now. "Just getting air."

WITH SPEED, but aimlessly, Caddie walks the Jerusalem streets.

She shoots past the open-air cafés with their scent of *falafel* and *baba ghanouj*, the taxi drivers yelling greetings to one another out their open windows.

Past the dawdling tourists floating bewildered in a sea of fast-moving foot traffic, like leaves above a current.

Past a stand of money changers, an Armenian ceramic shop, a Steimatsky bookstore.

Why did I prevent him from speaking?

She finds herself on the edge of Mea She'arim. One of the

city's extremes. She didn't plan it, not consciously, but it suits her perfectly. She covers her hair with the scarf she always carries in her backpack and parks herself on the steps in front of the main square. It's still lunchtime, so children are outside playing: girls with long braids, boys with their *peyot*. Women wearing wigs beneath their scarves and men in layers of black pass her quickly, most without a glance in her direction. The children, not quite so well trained yet, even in this strict ultra-Orthodox ghetto, peek at her sideways for several minutes before becoming bored, more interested in their own diversions. A group of kneeling girls plays *kugelach*. A half-dozen boys with a ball argue in Yiddish.

On the walls around Caddie, posters warn against television and mixed-gender swimming. The children don't think to question the message—don't, in fact, even notice these placards of admonition. They're simply part of the daily landscape. *What comfort, when one is without doubts.* Every child must experience this phase, however briefly, though as far as Caddie can remember, she was always skeptical.

One girl disengages herself from the *kugelach* players and skips toward Caddie. "Hello," she says in English. "You don't remember me?"

Caddie studies her face, then recognizes something in her smile. "Of course," she says. Not by name. But this is one of Moshe and Sarah's daughters. The one who came into the kitchen and recited part of her mother's doughnut poem. "How are you? What are you doing here?"

A darkness passes over the girl's face so briefly Caddie almost misses it, then she smiles again. "Visiting. Ema is here also. She will want to see you."

"Oh, well," Caddie begins. She doubts that is true. But before she can devise a way to object politely, the girl takes her hand and pulls her into a narrow alleyway. Here the houses are stacked and huddled together in tight rows. Frail balconies reaching from both sides of the street meet above their heads. The sound of male voices reading the Torah pours from a *yeshiva*.

The girl presses against a door on a ground floor, pushing it open with her shoulder. "Ema?" she calls.

"Here, Ruthie." Sarah appears from an inner room followed by another woman. She is carrying a dish rag. She wears a blue-and-white loose dress that reaches to her ankles and, again, a brightly colored scarf. Her eyes widen. *"Shalom,"* she says.

"Look who I found," says Ruthie proudly, and she pushes Caddie in the direction of her mother.

"A surprise," Sarah says.

"I was taking a walk when your daughter spotted me and . . ." Caddie breaks off. "You're visiting friends?"

Sarah nods. "Come in." She is gracious, but Caddie hears the caution in her tone.

"I don't want to intrude," Caddie says. "I was only—"

"Ruthie, the *bureka*s are almost ready," Sarah says. "We eat in half an hour." She turns toward Caddie. "But come in now. Please."

"I can only stay a minute."

The girl waves to her mother and heads out the door, back

to her game. The other woman slips away, too, deeper into the house, closing a door behind her.

Caddie and Sarah sit next to one another on a worn plaid couch. The living room, with small windows and a low ceiling, is cave-like, lit by a single lamp. It smells of sour milk and dust. Caddie hears the clatter of dishes being stacked in the kitchen. "A vacation?" she asks.

"Of sorts, I guess." Sarah, straight-backed, spreads the dishrag on her lap, folds it. "Until tomorrow."

"Is Moshe with you, then?"

Sarah shakes her head. "He has work."

Caddie looks at her questioningly, but says nothing.

Sarah's chest moves as though she is silently sighing. "It's the children."

"They're okay?"

"Samuel is doing poorly at school and the girls worked themselves into a fit of tears last week. Moshe and I agreed we needed to get them away for a few days." She smoothes the rag on her lap. "We don't allow television or radio, of course. But somehow they hear about every ambush, every explosion—"

"Hard to escape it," Caddie says.

"I try to explain," Sarah says. "It will be all right, once our leaders stop restraining the army. Right now, however, the Arabs are so bold against us."

"So the settlers are taking steps of their own?" Caddie asks, probing lightly.

Sarah looks at her hands. "The Arabs were never alone in

Judea and Samaria, you know. Before us, it was the Jordanians, and before them, the British, and before them, the Turks. But we love this land more than all of them put together. And that makes them hate us."

It's all Caddie can do not to wave her hand, to wipe away fake generalities like this. "Don't you ever think about moving?" she asks. "Taking your children somewhere where daily life would be easier?"

Without hesitation, Sarah shakes her head. "Two kinds of people find their way to this place. Those who leave, and those who stay."

As simple as that. Caddie imagines Sarah pigeonholing people into two neat groups: those who *move* on versus those who *hang* on. She knows, now, on which side of that line Marcus fell. As for herself, that paragraph is still unwritten.

"You're so sure about things, aren't you?"

"Yes, I am."

"I envy you that." Caddie leans forward to pick up the only item sitting on the scuffed coffee table: a plain-looking periodical called *Consistency, a Journal of Ultra-Orthodox Thought.* "What would you do, though, if, despite all this certainty, you found that you *had* made a mistake?"

She is thinking of her and of Marcus, but as soon as the words are out of her mouth, she feels a flush spread on her cheeks. She flips through the periodical, trying to look casual. How crazy must she sound? To invent such a question, to ask it in her mind, is fine. But, dear God, not aloud, not aloud.

Sarah, though, acts as if her words were entirely natural.

"Teshuva," she says. "It means you recognize what you did wrong, you're sincerely sorry for it and won't do it anymore."

"And that's all it takes?" Caddie gives a small smile.

"Of course, you need to set things right if you can. But perhaps the restitution lies in changing yourself."

Caddie closes the periodical, replaces it on the coffee table. Sarah's advice seems, at once, too easy and too difficult.

"Well, I'd better go back and help with the cooking." Sarah rises and Caddie follows her to the door. There, Sarah stops. "By the way," she says, "I *have* made mistakes."

Caddie hesitates. "Any you want to share?"

She is surprised that Sarah returns her smile, and even more surprised when she reaches to squeeze Caddie's hand. "Maybe," she says. "Next time."

CADDIE BREWS A CUP OF CHAMOMILE TEA, slips on an oversized sweatshirt, lights a candle and sets it on the windowsill in the living room. Then she pulls out Marcus's journal and settles on the couch, leaning against the pillows, a blanket over her knees.

She rests the journal on her hands, battling her own reluctance to open it. She's not angry with him anymore, not that. It's that she knows when she's finished, when she's examined all the pictures and read all the words, it'll be over. He'll be dead. Again.

She moves her hands over the cover, opens it and looks at that first picture, the one of her among the men and the weapons. Then she lets the journal fall open to the final section.

The first photographs of this part show Palestinian men in a small West Bank facility for the insane. She remembers doing that story with him. Victims of fighting who'd gone nuts, many now chained to their beds. One thought he was Cleopatra's husband. Another snapped at her like a mad dog. Young, most of them. Men who, after gazing with clear vision at the rest of their lives and realizing what they could expect, became irretrievably distant from this world. And who could blame them?

Marcus chose two shots for his journal. One shows a man lying stretched on his bed, grinning, his head cocked as though gazing at the heavens. Caddie would not guess he was crazed if she didn't look closely at his vacant eyes. The other shot is of a man in the opposite physical position: curled into a ball, his arms wrapped around his head, one open eye visible. Different ways of being crazy? Is that what Marcus intended to show? Or maybe nothing that specific. Maybe he was simply being loose. That was the advice he always gave her when she groaned in front of her computer, fighting with a story. "Write loose," he'd say. "Sometimes some zigzagging is necessary in order to reach the center."

The next photographs, then, are wholly unexpected after all the other shots in the journal, the pictures of bloodshed and journalists covering it.

One snap shows a dining room table laid out with food. By a *keffiyeh* in the corner, Caddie sees it is a Palestinian home. A second photo is of a girl holding a doll. The picture doesn't show the girl's face or body, only her slender arm, her hand and the doll.

Then a shot of three Moslems standing in a row, hands clasped in front as they pray in a small room somewhere. Except for the photograph's mood of tranquillity, this is closer to trademark Marcus. An overdone subject, actually; a cliché in another's hands. But not with what Marcus managed to capture in those three faces—stubbornness in the fully devout old man in the middle, rebellion mixed with piety in the younger two on either side of him.

How did he manage it, eliciting these plays of feature, then trapping them with a push of the button? Had he acted invisible? Not in her presence. She'd seen him chat with his subjects between pictures—sometimes even during. Engaging them, often charming them. Yet he managed to catch them as if they were totally alone. Nothing artificial in their demeanors, nothing held back. That's why he'd won the awards.

The next: a close-up of some gray, dusty shrub in clear, bright focus. Absolutely unremarkable. Prescient, though, in a way that startles her.

Then a thumbprint-sized photo that shows only the outline of a face, the features themselves darkened. Caddie recognizes it as herself. Staring at it, a wild hair of an idea comes. *This is it. Proof that he intended to ask me to go with him.* Looking at that ID-sized snapshot, she's convinced momentarily. Then she realizes, it's just a picture.

And besides, would I? Would I have left the story for him?

She quickly drains her teacup in an effort to stop the stinging of her eyes.

The final photo is of him. The only one in the journal. He

took it with a timer, she guesses. He turned his back to the camera, bent over with his blond hair hanging, stared at the lens from between his legs. And he smiled. A childish, carefree pose. Caddie can almost hear his laughter. She'd loved that laugh, for all it promised her. She'd depended on it. And he knew it. So he kept giving it to her. Even, apparently, when he had to pretend.

This smile, though, is genuine. He's not feigning here. The photo is worth the whole journal to her.

She almost wishes that was it, the final thought. But a last bit of writing follows.

"War strips us naked. I'm horrified by what I find in me."

Nothing more.

Horrified by what I find in me. It means he would have forgiven her. Forgiven her erratic reactions over the last few weeks: leaping close, dashing away, teetering on a sheer edge of too much or too little. Pardoned, even, her refusal to listen when he tried to tell her—more than once, she's sure—that he didn't want to keep taking pictures filled with black and white and red. Didn't want to aim his lens at more wounded, more dead, another survivor or aggressor. Didn't want, goddamnit, to catch a flight to Lebanon to hunt for more.

Her selective deafness. Her rigid boundaries.

She flings her cup across the room. It hits the wall with a thud but refuses to break. She presses her forehead against the joyful, captured image of Marcus, and stays there, frozen, as though waiting for an answer.

Twelve

AVRAHAM IS IN THE DRIVER'S SEAT again and she's sandwiched in the back and they've just drawn away from this evening's "Village of the Condemned"—a different village but a catchall name, Caddie has learned. Avraham's car is in front, with the companion vehicle from the other settlement behind them. This trip has been, until now, what Caddie figures must be the usual: screaming of vulgar threats, releasing of random shots into the dark. Somewhere in the middle of it, Avraham called back to her a Torah riddle: "What kind of man was Boaz before he got married? Ruth-less." And he laughed, like a man cheered by an evening out.

The settlers seem marginally more comfortable in her presence. Though they still are vigilant about not touching her, they hold their bodies less stiffly and have met her glance once or twice. She'll wheedle some quotes tonight somehow, and she'll write this story, though she can't quite see its shape yet.

She has time to find the words, though, because tomorrow is Lebanon. She'll fly via Cyprus and land in Beirut and walk into the Intercon and avoid the bar and the third floor where she stayed last time, and it will be okay, it will be fine. She'll do other things there, not writing, but what exactly, she isn't sure yet. She's been trying not to think too much about that.

To block it out now—the future, the past, the checkpoint and the driver, the woman and the child—she leans forward to study the darkness. That's when she notices, to her left, an eerie radiance. A small glow seeping from a cave-like area in the rocks to their right.

Her confusion is brief, followed by certainty. Ambushers. Ambushers hiding in the fissure, warming their hands by a tiny fire, waiting for the revenge she knew was coming.

Another surprise attack. To tell the truth, she's been expecting it.

But how many are there? Is it a shallow cave that hides one or two, or a deep tunnel that harbors ten? And how well armed?

She sees herself as if from the sky. Crammed in the backseat between two men, again. No one else noticing, again. Blood pulses at her temples. Avraham's Subaru isn't as open as a Land Rover, but at this close proximity, she and the others are easy targets.

"Wait." Again, her voice is soft, damnit, so quiet that Avraham doesn't hear. "Wait," she repeats more loudly.

Avraham slows the car, glances back. She gestures toward the cave.

He sees it, then. Proof that she's not inventing phantoms in the night. They all see, and all lean forward in the car. Avraham murmurs into his walkie-talkie, brakes and kills the headlights. He nods and the man sitting next to him gets out, joined by someone from the second car. Their abrupt, wind-up-toy strides tempt Caddie to inappropriate laughter.

Through the open window, she hears one of the settlers yell in Hebrew, "Who's in there?"

No reply. The rocks look slimy in the moonlight. Her breathing quickens.

This time, it'll turn out differently. This time, none of hers will get killed.

"Get out," the other settler says harshly in loud Arabic. "Now."

Still no response. The two Israeli settlers exchange words. By the way they bend their knees, Caddie knows they're preparing to charge. She tightens her body, waiting.

Before they can storm the mouth of the cavern, though, three men shoot out from behind the boulders. Caddie ducks, fingernails digging into her palms, but there is no immediate ping of gunshots. So she peeks up to see each body flinging itself in a different direction. Three sets of stick-arms and narrow legs rotate wildly. Half a dozen scuttling feet scatter pebbles.

One settler fires a shot. The other pursues the fleeing forms. *Get them, get them.*

The man on her right swings out of their car. The one on her left is breathing hard as he follows. Only she and Avraham are left behind. A settler from Avraham's car—*her car*—catches one, jerks him by a scrawny arm to the cave. Hauls him with that tight knot of anger that does not shock Caddie, that in fact has become as familiar as the inside of her own arms. Avraham switches on his headlights, and the two of them, Israeli and Arab, are lit up in a way that seems garish, unreal. The villager wears a white T-shirt bearing the word "Marlboro" in red letters. He is hollow-chested, about twenty-five. His face is hairless, rigid. His mouth: a flat horizon. His eyes: holes.

The expression of one who would kill.

In a quick, fluid movement, the settler pushes the Palestinian's head to the ground. His forehead hits first, a split second before his palms can break the fall. "What were you doing in there, you fucking baby-killer? Making bombs?" The settler shoves his M-16 into the back of the man's neck.

She turns to peer out the car's rear window. No one is pursuing the other two who fled from behind the boulders. Those two are vanished in the dark, huddled somewhere or still running, out of reach. They've escaped. But this time it's not so hard to accept, because this time, one is in their hands.

And now at last she can see how it turns out when one is caught. How it might have turned out that day in Lebanon.

Five Israeli settlers surround the lone villager. She scoots to the door, intending to join them. She presses down the handle.

A breath of hesitation. And then time stretches.

Tan boots, scuffed and square-toed. Gray lace-ups, army issue. She sees them as if they were huge, as if they were all that could fit on the screen of her vision. She tries to look away, but cannot. Legs cocked. Feet released with force. Grunting.

Stomping. Boots inclined again. Thick black soles caked with dried mud. Milliseconds that last beyond the Second Coming. Then released again.

The man's face is turning pulpy. Caddie suddenly needs more air.

She looks away, and then back again, and finds that instead of his face, she notices the movement of his body, and it startles her, the way it crumples and closes in on itself and then arches and curls again. Jerkily, like an uncoordinated dancer trying to follow the beat.

Only it isn't dancing.

She is outside the car now, but halted, as, abruptly, a settler grabs the Palestinian's right hand and flattens it to the ground, holding it there until another steps on his arm. A third shoves his boot against the man's back so he's lying flat. A fourth lifts his boot and brings it down, hard, his long side curls bouncing. Crushing the Palestinian's fingers. Three times.

The air vibrates. Out the car window, the men blur. Images flash in Caddie's head—Marcus, Kevin Carter, Goronsky—and she is hit with the rush of half-a-dozen competing emotions, but there's no time to sort them out.

The settler with the gun grips the Palestinian's mangled, bloody digits and snaps back his wrist. It makes a cracking sound. The man cries out, turning his mouth into the ground as if suckling his mother. "There," says the settler. "It'll be a little harder for you to attack us now, you son of a whore."

Caddie stands suspended between the Palestinian and the idling car.

Avraham is yelling out the window. "*Maspeak*. Enough, I said. Let's go."

The settler who caught this runaway in the first place steps back, reluctance vivid on his face. One settler gives the Palestinian a final booting.

And then the prone man—a boy, really, Caddie sees—is alone.

He is facing her direction. His cheeks are bloody, unrecognizable. She cannot see his eyes, only the shadows where they once were. He is bent improbably at the waist.

He isn't moving, not even the up-and-down of breath.

Oh God.

"Shouldn't we—?" Her words feel thick and unwieldy in her mouth.

Avraham looks at her. "Get in," he says. Then he turns toward the men. "C'mon." The engine growls. There's a long moment of superawareness: Caddie tastes smoke from the cave's fire and exhaust from Avraham's car. She hears, amplified, the sound of the settlers' footsteps on the dirt and her own thin breathing.

Then, incredibly, the beaten boy manages to speak. Somehow he musters the strength. *"Airi fe sabahak,"* he says. Caddie knows the curse. My dick on your forehead.

One of the settlers stops, turns toward the boy. "What did you say?" he says in Arabic, his voice like the cold steel of a gun barrel.

The settler is close to her; she knows even as he hoists his M-16 that she can tell him to stop; she can reach out to grab his arm. She starts to raise her hand. The settler points his rifle three feet above the boy's body. If he fires now, it will be a warning. Harmless.

Behind her, she hears Avraham's sharp intake of breath. She wants to twist around to look at him, to verify that he—this joking, wispy father of five—will prevent anything more from happening. But she can't turn away from the boy, who has shifted his head so that she can now see his eyes, calm, appraising. Watching her, not the settler with the gun.

From the car behind her, she hears the sound of cloth sliding along car upholstery. Someone is going to break this moment. She's sure of it.

And then everything slips into fast-forward, like she's a balled-up child, hurtling down a hill, dizzy with speed. The settler lowers his gun; with one arm slack at his side, he fires, almost casually, as if it were an afterthought. The Palestinian boy blinks as darkness spurts from just below his neck. Caddie stumbles back, finds herself in the car, finds the car pulling away, the black of the night draining air from her, the boy's eyes still on her long after they've left.

In the car, none of them speak. None of them touch. She is reduced to one eye, one pursed mouth, no body and no mind at all.

At the settlement the men in the backseat push themselves from the car, trying to purge themselves of her as they would spit out a bad taste. Only Avraham hesitates, leaving the driver's door open to give them a little light.

"I want to tell you something. About Efraim. The one who was—" He hesitates, his face holding a glare. "Kicking the Arab," he says.

She doesn't correct him.

"Efraim and his brother were close. Best friends, you might say. They grew up together, studied together, fought in the same army unit. They got married on the same day, a combined wedding." Avraham looks at the ground, then up again. "One afternoon last year, the brother was driving to Ofra when he saw a pregnant woman standing beside a parked car at the side of the road, waving. She was an Arab, but he stopped anyway. It was a setup. A man appeared from behind a tree and shot him in the head."

Caddie remembers this killing. She even wrote about it—a paragraph in a roundup of the day's violence. She takes a deep breath.

"At that very second," Avraham says, "Efraim was calling his brother on his mobile phone. The Arab answered and said, 'He's dead.' He said it over and over. Laughing." Avraham shakes his head. "He dropped the phone when another Israeli motorist approached. Then he got into the car with the pregnant woman and they sped away." Avraham turns partly away from her. His shoulders slump slightly and he looks for a moment like he might spit, but he doesn't. He straightens. "When you think of tonight," he says, "think of that."

When she thinks of tonight, whenever she can think of it, she knows it won't be of Efraim or his brother.

"You know how rare it is for someone like you to be permitted to go with us?" Avraham asks. "An outsider, a woman. Sasha said you were *with* us. He said you sympathized."

"I—" She clears her throat. She needs to speak, but words feel awkward. "I sympathize with everyone here," she says.

He shakes his head. "That's not how it works. Not even for a reporter, not if she's allowed this close. Either someone's your enemy, or they're not."

And was he their enemy, that Palestinian? *Her* enemy?

"Remember what you said before?" Caddie asks. "How our lives don't turn out like we expected? How *we* don't turn out . . ." She trails off, swallows. "I can write that."

"You can't write about this," Avraham says. Not insistently, the way Moshe would. Just decisively, coolly. Maybe a little sadly. "You print it, in any way, and we'll deny it. Totally and fully. We all will."

They stand there leaning against Avraham's car, the two of them. The moon, halfway up in the sky, is badly formed, like a smeared thumbprint. The night has turned breezy. "Avraham." She hesitates, shivering, chilled by the perspiration that has gathered at her temples and the base of her neck. "Tell me about Goronsky."

"Sasha?" Avraham stares at her.

"About what he does for you."

"I thought you were friends."

"Does he ever go with you?"

Avraham shrugs. "The key part he provides is information."

"Information?"

"About terrorists."

She swallows a laugh. "Terrorists? Like the boy tonight?"

"Their names, where they live, where they work," Avraham says, ignoring her. "He knows things, he knows how to find out. Our own Shin Bet refuses to give us those details, unfortunately. Our leaders live in their homes in Jerusalem, a long way from here. Sasha understands the nature of our struggle. He understands from his own past."

"He told you about his past?" Something he said only the two of them shared?

"Terrorists killing his wife and child? From the beginning."

"Wife? Child? No. He was—" Caddie stops herself. Avraham has it wrong. Or *she* does—and if she does, she has it very wrong. She tries to speak slowly. "So he tells you who to go after."

She feels Avraham's stare. He swings shut the door to his Subaru, locks it. "I'll walk you," he says, gesturing to her car parked on the other side of the road.

"Avraham? Is that what he does?"

"Ask him yourself." He crosses the street, then turns and faces her. "I'm done," he says.

Something in the way he says those words triggers a wave of nausea. She looks away and waits for it to subside before speaking. "So that's how it will be?"

"This isn't my *story*," he says. "It's my life."

. . .

HER CAR FIRES straight down the settlers' West Bank highway in the dark of night. Her hands on the steering wheel look ghostly; her veins stand out. Her mouth feels full of sour saliva. She needs to stand beneath a shower.

She tries to summon forth the image of Marcus, the weight of his body leaning against hers. She tries to reawaken her righteous anger. All she sees is the Palestinian's eyes, his ruined body.

She feels dampness on her cheeks. "Fuck this," she says aloud. "That's so beside the point: you crying."

She had, she knows, a moment in which she could have changed everything. And now she owns that moment. It belongs to her, as much as it does to the Palestinian and to the settler who pulled the trigger. Maybe more.

She remembers, suddenly, a promise she made to herself a year and a half ago in Ramallah, when Marcus was still alive, when they still kissed and made love and had arguments about how involved a journalist should be, where the line was drawn. Caddie was standing in the street after a clash—three dead, six wounded—when she saw a group of men stumble around a corner, maneuvering as awkwardly as a party of drunks, except instead of arms flung around shoulders, they clutched a plank of splintery scrap wood. On it lay a small girl, about two years old. The men were yelling for an ambulance, their urgent voices colliding. Caddie stared at the child. Apart from a bit of cherry-colored blood around the corner of her mouth like sloppily applied lipstick, she looked asleep. But by the limp way her body bounced and the bleached-bone shade of her skin, Caddie knew her for dead.

The men were blind to it, though. They kept screaming for help until an unearthly wail rose above their voices. It came from a grandmother who followed them, recognizing what they had not.

They stopped, looking in confusion from each other to the child and back again. Gently they set the plank on the ground. Then backed off a few steps as the grandmother, eyes of glass, took the toddler's head in her lap, stroked her cheek and rocked.

She began to hum then, that grandmother. And it was her lullaby, fragmented by gasps for air, that cut through Caddie's body as sharply as any bullet could. Aware of Marcus taking pictures of the child, she turned away to interview others. But she couldn't stop looking over her shoulder. After Marcus finished, Caddie approached the grandmother and knelt, notepad in hand. The old woman gazed at her. Openly, with plain brokenness. Without seeing Caddie at all. Any question Caddie asked, it was clear—even the woman's name—would be unanswerable.

"C'mon, Caddie. Let's move," Marcus called, patting his pockets to make sure he had all his film.

And so Caddie left. And that night—really, right away, but by that night for sure—she knew she'd made a mistake. She should have gone to the mourning house and eaten the hummus and eggplants and watched the neighbors visit and stayed too long and asked too many questions and then been too silent and waited until it was not just another death, but a particular death, a particular girl and her grandmother. A story that she could write that would become real, and maybe take a sliver of the thorn out of the old woman's chest and put it in someone else's. She didn't talk to Marcus about it, she was temporarily incapable of bantering and she didn't want to hear his I-told-you-so, so she just made a private promise. Next time, she'd stay. Next time, she'd write the story.

Only she forgot.

Tomorrow, there would be a mourning house in the Village of the Condemned.

But tomorrow, she'd be on a flight to Lebanon.

A blaring horn interrupts her. She's left behind the West Bank and entered Jerusalem's limits without noticing. Finding herself halted at a traffic light that has long since turned green, she hits the gas too quickly, scorching rubber as she speeds on.

Thirteen

CADDIE HESITATES outside the door to Goronsky's second-floor hotel room. The fluorescent lights in the hallway hurt her eyes. She's achy, in need of a deep sleep that has eluded her but will come, she is sure, after Lebanon. After whatever Lebanon will be.

When she knocks, he answers instantly, as if he'd been hovering, waiting. A damp towel rests on his shoulders and the room is slightly steamy. Except for shoes, though, he's fully dressed. Black socks, slacks, a blue shirt. No tie.

He reaches to her waist and pulls her into the room. "Good, you're here. The flight to Cyprus has been delayed an hour and a half. I called."

"Goronsky—"

He waves his hand, cutting her off. "Give me just a minute." He steps into the bathroom.

She glances around his room. Fleetingly his. About to be

abandoned. One suitcase stands upright near the door. Another is open on the bed, partially packed, with a pile of papers arranged on top. In the trashbin lies a disposable razor. Atop the television sits a glass. Everything appears intentionally placed and orderly, except newspapers that are scattered on the edge of the couch, and the city of Jerusalem that insinuates itself through the expansive window.

She sits on the couch and begins scanning the top newspaper. She hasn't kept up with the daily news, and that will have to change once she's back from this trip. The paper is folded open to a story of a Palestinian woman and her daughter shot dead in their home. The article says the grandmother had been forced outside, but looked through a window to see her daughter-in-law kneeling to shield the child. The grandmother heard a shot then, and fled. The article says four of the brothers are in Israeli jails, accused of being involved in terror attacks, and that local Palestinians blamed Israeli settlers for killing the mother and child. It ends with that standard line: the incident is under investigation.

She tosses the story aside, glances at the next newspaper and notices it is opened to an article on the very same incident. In fact, she sees as she flips through the stack quickly, there are four different papers in all, each one folded open to that story, the slaying of Randa and Salwa Silwadi.

In a flash, she remembers. His body leaning forward, drawing out her words. His long fingers touching hers so briefly for the first time. His shrug in the direction of the café owner. Silwadi Café. Randa and Salwa Silwadi: these are the killings

Halima's uncle was talking about, the ones on his poster. She hadn't linked them to Goronsky until just now.

Her vision blurs. Her head feels thick. She lifts it to see Goronsky a few steps away, watching her. "I think I've got everything packed," he says, gesturing around the room.

She looks down at the newspaper in her hands, and back up at him.

He straightens.

She opens her mouth, but her throat clamps, preventing speech.

He steps closer, then seems to read the resistance in her expression and moves back. "I gave Avraham information," he says. "I only did for him what I did for you. Like the list of supplies the hospital needed."

She shakes her head and lifts the newspaper slightly in her hand. "It wasn't the same."

He sits on the arm of the couch, lifts his shoulders, then drops them. "When someone you love is killed and you do nothing, that's wrong."

"I don't want to discuss that."

"But that's the crucial point."

"The mother. The child," she says. "Silwadi Café."

He looks up at the ceiling. "I never touched anyone myself. That's a line I never crossed."

The way he says that cuts through her. Me neither, she wants to say. But those words are so deceptive. "What kind of person are you?" she asks instead.

He looks down at his hands. "An enabler," he says.

"Enabler." Something tightens in her gut, then springs loose. "You persuade other people to do your work. People like me."

"Please, Caddie."

"This story you *never told anyone before*. Your personal tragedy. Which was it, Goronsky? Was it actually your wife and child? Is that why you wanted to hurt someone else's wife and child?"

He turns his face to one side as though she's slapped him, but then he straightens and meets her gaze. "It was my father and my sister," he says. "I told you the truth about that. I don't blame you for not believing. But it was true."

"And to Avraham, you lied?"

"I wanted him to trust me. I wanted him to know some part of it, but not all. So I changed it a little. With you, it was different. Right away, I *knew*. The way you carried yourself. The way you protected yourself. And then, our childhoods." He's leaning forward, toward her. "I wanted closeness. You understand?"

She doesn't answer. She won't be pulled in, won't be made an accomplice. Father, or wife? Neither? Maybe it was the most important thing between them once, but it's not anymore, not even close.

"You came here," she asks, "planning from the beginning to find an Avraham?"

"Nothing that clear." He paces the room. "I wasn't sure what I wanted. I tried to make contacts. The Palestinians were easier than the settlers. At least until I met Avraham. I liked him right away. I mentioned some of the Palestinians I knew, gave him some details. He asked for more. That's how it started."

"You knew how they used your information?"

He hesitates for a second, long enough for her to shudder at the hopefulness built into her question.

"It would be easy to lie to you, Caddie," he says. "That's the opposite of what I want now."

She sits on the couch next to the open suitcase. "Did it help? Did it feel like payback, giving Avraham your information?" *Or letting Efraim shoot the villager?*

Goronsky stands and walks to the window, his back to her.

"Because of you, a child is dead," she says, looking at her own hands.

He doesn't turn when he answers. "I was a child, too."

She rises, touches her neck. She is intensely conscious of her arms, her legs, her chest. She doesn't recognize them.

When he finally faces her, she expects to be repulsed. Instead, it's as though she can fully identify, at last, the quality that draws her to him, that connects them more profoundly than she's ever been connected to anything. The same something within her, something corruptible. The trait she kept hidden, even from herself.

She knows what she wants, then, and it surprises her. She wants it slowly, with her eyes open this time. She steps closer to him. She moves her hands to his neck, his shoulders. Then she stops, suddenly awkward in an unfamiliar way. Stingingly self-conscious, and aware that she's grown so far from the relative purity of that girl in the cornfields.

He takes her hands and shifts her chin so she has to look at him directly. She would rather twist away, but she knows the moment requires full clarity.

He puts his head to one side and with this gesture, she sees Marcus. Marcus: in Goronsky's posture. Marcus: in the breeziness of his expression as he observes her.

It sucks away her breath.

They are standing in a wash of pale sunlight that pierces the window, and Goronsky reaches to lace his fingers through her hair—exactly like Marcus. She begins searching him rapidly then. Touching his cheeks, his chest. In answer to her urgency, he is measured. Unhurriedly, he presses the warmth of his palm against first one part of her, then another, as if memorizing the diagram of her body. Each hollow, every muscle, the solidity of each bone. This surprises her. This is not Marcus. In fact, she's never been so traversed.

Maybe his deliberateness is what does it, what finally stills the racket within her. That internal hurtling noise that has, for weeks, surfaced and submerged and surfaced again. The turbulence of some gigantic machine careening forward at reckless, pointless speed. It's been there constantly, though she's pretended not to hear it. Now it dies down, and then out. Spent.

At last, she can hear everything else. The gathering of his breath. The percussion of her heart. The humming of his flesh against hers.

She turns her attention to his forehead, his shoulders and chest: the solid bits that conceal the fragments within. He bends to her, cups her breast. His gesture holds sorrow, as though they were mourning together.

Above them, she hears the deep reverberation of a fighter